A Helping Hand

"You called me here," the vis

"I . . . I called you here?"

The apparition smiled, revealing a small gap between her two front teeth and a dimple in her left cheek. *"You asked for a tutor."*

Sabrina blinked a few times in nervous succession. *A tutor?*

The specter patted daintily at the ringlets curling against her temple. *"I'm the spirit who's come to help you, luv."*

Praise for
A Ghost of a Chance

"Delightful, enchanting, and whimsical, full of wonderful characters . . . Ms. Claybourne has a sense of humor, which comes through on every page, in sparkling dialogue, amusing situations, and a unique plot." —*Rendezvous*

"Casey Claybourne succeeds with this fun-to-read tale and in the process, shows she has the talent and ingenuity of a superstar." —*Affaire de Coeur*

Turn to the back of this book
for a special sneak preview of
Heavenly Bliss
the next Haunting Hearts romance!

Titles in the Haunting Hearts series

STARDUST OF YESTERDAY
SPRING ENCHANTMENT
A GHOST OF A CHANCE
HEAVEN ABOVE
ETERNAL VOWS
WHISPERS ON THE WIND
A SPIRITED SEDUCTION

Titles by Casey Claybourne

A SPIRITED SEDUCTION
A GHOST OF A CHANCE
THE DEVIL'S DARLING
MY LUCKY LADY

A SPIRITED SEDUCTION

CASEY CLAYBOURNE

JOVE BOOKS, NEW YORK

A SPIRITED SEDUCTION

A Jove Book/published by arrangement with
the author

PRINTING HISTORY
Jove edition/May 1997

The Putnam Berkley World Wide Web site address is
http://www.berkley.com

ISBN: 0-515-12066-9

A JOVE BOOK®
Jove Books are published by The Berkley Publishing Group,
200 Madison Avenue, New York, New York 10016.
JOVE and the "J" design are trademarks
belonging to Jove Publications, Inc.

PRINTED IN THE UNITED STATES OF AMERICA

10 9 8 7 6 5 4 3 2 1

*With thanks to Susan Krinard
and her unfailing genius and to Callie Goble,
research goddess extraordinaire*

*This book is dedicated to readers.
To each and every one of you who share
my love of a good story.*

Casey Claybourne
P.O. Box 601706
Sacramento, CA 95860

Chapter One

"We could kill him! We could poison him with something truly awful and then bury his body where no one could ever find it. Maybe behind the dovecote where all the ivy—"

"Theodore!"

Sabrina silenced her brother with a look that doused the murderous spark in his eyes. He pushed out his lower lip and she shook her head firmly. Eight-year-olds were a frightfully bloodthirsty lot.

"What have you been reading, Teddy, to put such ideas in your head?" Sabrina asked. "One simply cannot go around murdering viscounts."

"No, it's not at all the thing," Andrew put in, his youthful countenance as grave as any undertaker's.

Although only thirteen, Andrew was very mature for his

age, a serious and thoughtful boy. The rapscallion Teddy, however . . .

"But Papa—"

"Papa might have been a bit daring, Teddy, but he would have most certainly drawn the line at murder. Even in a time of crisis," Sabrina asserted. "I know that you miss him—we all do—but we cannot lose our heads."

Even as she spoke, Sabrina wished she might temporarily be rid of hers. Her skull pounded with a severe case of the megrims that made it hurt even to blink.

"I can take care of this. I can. I only wish that you two had never learned of this nasty business. If it weren't for a certain someone listening at keyholes . . ." She frowned at Teddy who squirmed in his chair like a long-legged puppy.

"Now see here, Rina, you must allow me to help," Andrew insisted. "You should have told me when the banker arrived. I am the man of the family now and I will not leave you to get us out of this muddle alone."

Sabrina leaned forward and affectionately nudged Andrew's spectacles from the tip of his nose to a more secure position.

"I have had plenty of experience with muddles, Andy. Never fear. I'll keep the wolves from our door. Especially that one very odious wolf, the Viscount Colbridge."

Teddy snorted and crossed his arms across his thin chest. "Well, I say the bloke is bloody cheeky trying to steal Simmons House right out from under our noses."

"And *I* say"—Sabrina shot him an arch look—"that you ought to watch your tongue, Theodore Simmons, or I'm going to triple your time at Latin exercises."

That threat served to quiet young Teddy for a few seconds, long enough for Sabrina's gaze to linger on the frayed fabric at his jacket's elbows. Not only was the coat sadly threadbare but it was also two sizes too small.

She bit at the inside of her lip. *Well, he'll simply have to make do with one of Andrew's hand-me-downs.* It would undoubtedly be too large for him, but what else could be done? With the bank threatening to call in their mortgage, she could not squander their pennies on luxuries like new clothing.

Her head pounded more fiercely and she glanced to the window where the rain pelted the glass in angry bursts. Lightning lit the sky in a flash of white, accompanied by the crackling roar of thunder. It was a dreadful night that followed a dreadful day.

Sabrina rose from the divan and felt the chill of the room sneak beneath her skirts.

"Run along to bed, boys, it's growing late. Ask Hattie if she'll tuck you in, for I need to do some reading tonight."

Teddy grumbled but dutifully clambered from his chair. He cast a dubious glance at the shelves of books lining the library walls.

"How can you enjoy all that horrid reading, Sabrina? It bores me stiff, it does."

Sabrina ruffled his mop of pale yellow curls. Her youngest brother was not the scholar of the Simmons family.

"One can learn a great deal from books, Teddy. All types of things. In fact, there is virtually nothing that can't be learned by reading history or literature.

"For instance . . ."—her tone turned teasing—"these books could tell me which Shropshire native plants are most toxic to unscrupulous viscounts."

"They can?" he asked, his eyes suddenly aglow.

Sabrina bit back a smile. "You *are* a scamp. Come on now, off to bed with you."

Teddy threw his arms around her waist and gave her a brief yet sturdy hug before he bolted out the library door—no doubt intent on making one last piece of mischief before the day was done.

As his footsteps clattered down the uncarpeted hallway, Sabrina turned to Andrew. Her smile faded. "Please don't look so glum, Andy. We aren't going to lose our home, I promise you."

Andy's quiet gaze touched upon bare spots along the wall where once fine landscapes had hung. "We've already lost so much."

Sabrina knew he wasn't referring to the paintings. They'd lost Papa this year. Mother, the year before. Times had been hard at Simmons House.

And it looked as if they were getting harder.

"Perhaps if I spoke to this Viscount Colbridge and explained our situation, he'd be reasonable about it," Andrew said.

Sabrina allowed herself only a stiff nod. *Reasonable indeed.* 'Twas a relief that Teddy hadn't eavesdropped upon her entire conversation with their banker, Mr. Bardwell.

"Yet . . ." Andrew scratched at his chin with its dusting of blond fuzz. "If the viscount is anything like his late uncle, we might have some difficulty in making him see reason, wouldn't you say?"

Sabrina merely nodded again.

From what she'd learned this afternoon, Lord Colbridge had not one whit in common with his deceased relative, Lord Calhoun. "Calhoun the Old Prune," as Teddy had dubbed him, had been an irascible old fellow who'd lived a monk-like existence the seventy years he'd been neighbor to Simmons House. He'd never married, never entertained nor paid calls. He'd rarely been seen outside his home and when he had been, he'd not once been seen to smile.

His nephew, however—if one were to believe the gossipy banker Bardwell—was London's answer to a modern-day Lothario.

At first, Sabrina had not been certain why Mr. Bardwell

was sharing so much personal information with her about the stranger who wanted to purchase Simmons House. "A rake of historical proportions," the banker had called him.

Interesting, yes, but so? What could it matter to her if Lord Colbridge had recently dismissed his French paramour? Why should she care if the viscount was known to be "extremely generous with his ladyloves"?

It had necessitated a broad wink of Bardwell's rheumy eye for Sabrina to finally grasp the banker's innuendo. Granted, it had taken her aback for a moment. Even two. But she was far too pragmatic to dismiss the idea out of hand. Desperate times called for desperate measures, she had said to herself. And the more Mr. Bardwell had expounded on their financial situation, the more desperate matters had begun to appear.

"Why does he want Simmons House anyway?" Andrew asked, cutting into her thoughts. "What is wrong with Lord Calhoun's home?"

Sabrina stepped over to the hearth where the fire was dwindling to embers. A shiver raced through her as thunder again split the night with a mighty roar.

"Supposedly Lord Colbridge thinks Leyton Hall too small," she answered, bending down to toss a modest scoop of coal onto the fire.

"Calhoun's place isn't exactly a Simmons House, is it?"

The pride in Andrew's voice was both understandable and a little sad. This house, their home, was all that was left of Andrew's birthright. Over the years the stables had been thinned out, the hunting lodge sold, the family jewels pawned. As the debts had continued to mount, Papa's investments had continued to go sour until eventually nothing had remained. Nothing but Simmons House.

"I really think I should speak to the viscount," Andrew insisted. "If he's any kind of gentleman, he'll hear me out."

"But he's *not* any kind of gentleman," Sabrina mumbled under her breath. "At least, not according to Mr. Bardwell."

She turned away from the fire and her heart contracted a notch to see her brother standing there with his slim shoulders squared and his fuzzy chin raised. And his spectacles once again teetering at the tip of his nose.

"Andrew, I think you're right. We should meet with the viscount and discuss our situation. However, I believe that I should be the one to speak with him."

"You, Sabrina?"

She hastened to soothe his adolescent pride. "You are very wise for your age, Andy—truly you are—but it might be better if I were to address this matter with Lord Colbridge."

Andrew thought for a minute, then gave a sober nod. "Yes, I suppose that would be the sensible way to go about it."

Dear Andy. Always so sensible. So much like herself.

"Agreed, then," she said. "Now, would you be a dear and hunt down Teddy and drag him off to bed for me? I'm sure he's driving Hattie 'round the bend."

Andrew turned as if to leave, then hesitated, his expression as easy to read as one of Teddy's old primers.

"Don't fret, Andy. I give you my solemn vow. I will do whatever necessary to make certain we don't lose Simmons House."

He gave her a weak smile, his lips a bit wobbly. "I know you will, Rina. . . . And that's what worries me."

As he closed the door behind him, Sabrina wondered if it had been only overnight that her brother had gone from child to young man.

She pulled her shawl close about her, ignoring the insistent pounding in her temple. Out of habit, she walked over to the immaculately kept bookshelves and began scanning the titles, seeking counsel from her faithful mentors: Plato, David Hume, and, of course, Mary Wollstonecraft.

Always, when faced with difficult questions, Sabrina had sought answers between the pages of a book. All her life, she had relied on the only people she could truly count on—history's great scholars and writers. When there had been no one else to depend on, no one else to burden with her concerns, she had always had her books.

Her fingers hovered over the well-worn binding of *Vindication of the Rights of Woman*. From memory, she quoted, "'Love is . . . an arbitrary passion . . . without deigning to reason.'"

She knew it was no coincidence that that particular quotation had risen to her mind.

As it was for Sabrina, reason had been everything to Wollstonecraft. Although the theorist's essays had praised "deep feeling," Wollstonecraft had argued that sensual love—passion—did not benefit women, but only served to enslave them to men.

Long ago Sabrina had decided that she would never be enslaved by such a "pernicious" emotion as Wollstonecraft described. She was too logical, too reasonable to be weakened by something as ephemeral as passion. Sabrina Simmons made her decisions from a wholly educated perspective.

And this night she was poised to make one of the most far-reaching decisions of her life. One she had given careful and deliberate consideration. One she did not believe Mary Wollstonecraft would approve.

The only decision left to her.

Sabrina's hand fell away from the book. It felt like madness. But how could it be mad when it was based on cool deliberation?

Her heart clamored a denial: the viscount might be unattractive or mean-spirited. Repulsive, even. Yet hadn't Bardwell said he was young and comely?

She took a deep breath, and the smell of leather and aged

paper was like a balm to her nerves. There was no other sensible alternative.

For even if she could dissuade Lord Colbridge from purchasing their home, what then? They still wouldn't have the monies to pay their mortgage and the bank's patience would not hold forever.

The words "extremely generous" echoed in her thoughts as she stared blindly at the titles before her.

What, after all, would she be losing? Her chastity was of little value without a dowry to accompany it.

On occasion, poverty might be forgiven if a young woman possessed exceptional beauty, but such was not her case. She was too thin, too tall, too ordinary.

And although she might have preferred to bestow her virtue on a man she cared for, she certainly entertained no notion of ever "falling in love."

The only risk, therefore, lay in her ability to succeed.

Slowly Sabrina ran her fingers over the contours of her face. Could she do it? Could she with this pointed chin and these sharp cheekbones seduce the Viscount Colbridge? Make him desire her enough to take her as his mistress?

Resolve sent her into action.

With feverish movements, she began to snatch books from the shelves. She had told Teddy only earlier this night that one could learn anything from history and literature.

Surely she could learn to become a great seductress.

Tomes piled high to her chin, Sabrina dropped onto the sofa and spilled her books beside her. She grabbed the first that lay atop the heap.

Homer's *Iliad*.

Helen of Troy.

Sabrina thumbed through the pages until a passage caught her attention. She loosely translated, "Watching Helen as she climbed the stair, the old leaders said to one another: It is no wonder that men . . . have borne the pains of war for one like this. Unearthliness. The woman is a goddess to look upon."

She slammed the book shut. "A goddess, hmmph."

Helen had an obvious advantage over Sabrina. Unearthliness.

"No, I need a seductress with more commonplace appeal," she muttered as she picked up the next book.

"Ah, perfect. Theodora, Empress of Byzantine." Now here was a young woman who'd made the most of her assets. She'd parlayed her skills as a prostitute right onto the throne.

Sabrina settled the book onto her lap and read until her fingers began to cramp with cold. She looked up to see that the fire had died down while the thunderstorm continued to rage. The wind was howling outside the window like Cerberus at his hellish post.

She set aside the history of Theodora to add another ration of coal to the fire. Crouching down on the hearth, she rubbed her hands back and forth in front of the flames, trying to coax a degree of warmth back into her icy fingers.

As she stared into the dancing flames and contemplated the task she'd set for herself, doubt entered her thoughts.

"None of that," she chided herself in a stern voice. "I'm quite sure that Cleopatra didn't waste any time on self-pity when she had to save Egypt by giving herself to Julius Caesar. She did what had to be done."

Just as *she* would do what had to be done.

Nevertheless, as she returned to her reading, Sabrina was haunted by the feeling that she was not up to this assignment. Her experience with the opposite sex was confined to boys; she knew nothing of men.

Hours later, after finishing with Theodora and then Nell Gwynn, she dropped her head back onto the sofa with a sigh. Faith, but she was tired and yet she'd barely begun her research. She did not feel at all confident that she could carry this off.

From the corner of her eye, she surveyed the pile of books still to be read.

The problem was that nowhere in literature did it explain *how* these women had seduced their men. What clothes had Nell worn, what fragrance had she used to so captivate Charles II? How had Cleopatra lured the world's most powerful men into her bed?

These questions played through Sabrina's mind as she half-drowsed, tucked into the corner of the divan.

"Lord, but I need help," she mumbled sleepily. "I need a tutor to instruct me how to go about a proper seduction."

A draft suddenly swept through the room, colder than any that had gone before it that night. Clinging to her soporific state, Sabrina shivered and curled more tightly into the sofa. In the back of her mind arose the crazy notion that she smelled . . . frangipani.

"Coooo-ee!"

Sabrina's eyes snapped open and she found herself staring at the ceiling.

"Gor, what a trip that was. I'd wager me hair is mussed something awful."

Sabrina whipped her head around in the direction of the strange feminine voice. What she saw caused the air to *whoosh* from her lungs.

It was an apparition. A hallucination. A . . .

"Ah . . . ah." Her throat closed. Words were stuck somewhere between her brain and her mouth. She must be dreaming. She rubbed furiously at her eyes.

"Oh now, don't be doin' that, luv. You'll give yourself wrinkles, you will."

Sabrina's fists froze in midair. This . . . this *delusion* was talking to her about wrinkles?

A giggle pushed its way past her clogged throat and emerged as a sound Sabrina would never have recognized as coming from herself. It was a frightened sound. It was a slightly hysterical sound.

"I've given you a start, haven't I?" The apparition clucked its tongue like a mother hen.

"The strain has got to me," Sabrina whispered. "I had thought I was managing, getting along well enough, but to suffer this manner of nightmare—"

"But I'm not your nightmare, Sabrina luv—"

"You know my name?"

Sabrina fairly choked on the question. Naturally, her own delusion would know her name. That would make sense, wouldn't it? But what *had* her tortured brain been thinking to construct such a wildly improbable hallucination?

Hair bleached nearly the color of Teddy's was curled closely to the apparition's head and topped by a bonnet that must have been some milliner's idea of a prank. It had feathers, it had ribands, it had pearls, it had lace. It had everything but a live parakeet.

The smiling face beneath the hideous headpiece could have been called pretty, if not refined. A coquettishly placed beauty mark enhanced both a Cupid's-bow mouth and a roundish button nose. From tiny, shell-shaped ears swung the gaudiest earbobs conceivable, fair to blinding with all their multicolored glass.

Sabrina had not known her imagination capable of such invention.

"Of course I know your name," the vision said. *"That's me job."*

Sabrina winced. Perhaps if she closed her eyes and went back to sleep, this thing would go away.

She was about to do just that when the specter's shawl slipped from one shoulder. Sabrina's eyebrows shot up.

"Immodest" was a paltry term to describe this particular décolletage. And if paltry characterized the neckline, only superfluous could describe the flesh beneath it. Good gracious, but she'd never seen the like . . .

Sabrina shook herself. But she wasn't *seeing* the like. She was only imagining it. She was only imagining the garish furbelows encircling the skirt of that scandalously sheer gown. . . . A frisson of fear raced up Sabrina's spine.

Everything about this apparition was sheer. Why, she could see straight through her!

"Oh, dear. Oh, dear." She squeezed her eyes shut. "There must be a logical explanation for this. There must be."

"But there is."

Reluctantly Sabrina opened her eyes to find that the delusion had come nearer. She pressed herself back against the sofa.

"You called me here," the vision said. *"Don't you remember?"*

"I . . . I called you here?"

The apparition smiled, revealing a small gap between her two front teeth and a dimple in her left cheek. *"You asked for a tutor."*

Sabrina blinked a few times in nervous succession. *A tutor?*

The specter patted daintily at the ringlets curling against her temple. *"I'm the spirit who's come to help you, luv."*

Sabrina felt suddenly light-headed. "Sp-spirit? As in ghost?"

The apparition laughed, a rich, feminine sound that jiggled her feminine attributes. *"Fancy that, I've plum forgot to introduce myself."* She held out a transparent hand. *"Nell deNuit, at your service. Or should I say . . . the ghost of Nell deNuit?"*

Chapter
Two

Blimey, but I haven't been given much to work with.

Nell mentally shook her head as she looked Sabrina over with a critical eye.

Too thin. The girl had no bosom to speak of. And a bit on the tall side. But she had good bones, and her hair might do all right. Maybe a snip or two of the scissors—

"No!"

Nell stopped short in her cataloguing of Sabrina's assets.

"No what, luv?"

"No, I cannot believe it. Ghosts simply do not exist." Sabrina crossed her arms over the baggy front of her dress. "Without empirical evidence to the contrary, I am sorry but I cannot accept such a notion."

Gawd, she's got learning! Nell winced. Brains without bubbies, what a rotten piece of luck . . .

" *'Um-peerical?'* " Nell asked.

Sabrina hesitated, giving Nell a dubious look that questioned whether or not she should be conversing with something she didn't believe in.

"Empirical," she primly corrected. "Relying upon practical experience or observation."

Pursing her lips, Nell thought for a moment. *"So, you're sayin' that you've got to have proof? See it for yerself before you can believe it?"*

"Precisely."

Nell beamed and spread her arms wide. *"Well, take an eyeful then. You can plainly see that I'm here. Here's your proof, your practice-able experience."*

A tiny frown crept across Sabrina's brow.

"You say you cannot believe without proof; what more proof can there be? You are *seeing me with yer own eyes. I'm as 'peerical' as they come."*

Nell held her outstretched pose, waiting. It was dreadful important that Sabrina believe in her or how else could she carry out her mission? She couldn't help the lass if the girl couldn't believe in her. She had to convince her; she just had to.

Slowly Sabrina pushed away from the cushions and rose to her feet. She was standing only an arm's length away now and Nell could see that the girl had very fine eyes. A clear blue-green that could be played up real nice.

At the moment, those eyes were narrowed with uncertainty and misgiving. Sabrina took a trembling breath and Nell could almost see the struggle the girl was waging.

"I . . ." Sabrina said, her voice shaking. "I am supposed to believe that you have been sent from . . ."

"From Heaven," Nell supplied. *"Though I haven't yet seen it since I've been bidin' my time in Purgatory, you understand."*

Sabrina nodded in a vague way, which said she didn't understand at all.

"You see, dearie, I've not yet earned my berth upstairs since my time on earth wasn't . . . well, it wasn't all it should have been, let's say. At least, as far as the powers that be are concerned." She winked at Sabrina, who blinked back. *"Not that I was a bad person, mind you, 'tis only that I guess I didn't quite measure up. What with my business and all."*

Sabrina's harried gaze ran up and down her in a flash. "Your business?"

Nell rolled her shoulders and settled the shawl about her, not meeting the girl's eyes. *" 'Tis nothin' to be ashamed of, although some ghosts might try to tell you different. 'Tis a service, that's all. One that's as old as time and not to be done without."*

Sabrina's light gasp forced Nell's gaze back to her. "You're a . . , a woman of easy virtue?"

Nell grinned in spite of herself. Glory be, but the girl was an innocent.

"Close on, Sabrina, but not quite. Abbess, aunt, bawd. There be plenty of names for women like me, but I've always kinda fancied 'madam.' Sounds so Frenchy, don't you think? The Madam Madame Nell deNuit, patroness of London's famed Academy of Aphrodisia."

She curtsied with theatrical flourish. When she rose, she saw that Sabrina looked like someone had shoved a poker up her slim back.

"The heavens have sent me a procuress?"

Now, 'twas fortunate that she was an agreeable ghost, or else Nell might have been feeling a bit put out by Sabrina's tone. Not all that friendly, if the truth be told.

She stifled a sigh. *" 'Twas either me or Lucretia Borgia, and I don't think you would have got on with that sly-boots*

Eye-talian piece. That one's full of 'erself, she is; been stuck in Purgatory ever so long."

Sabrina reached blindly for the arm of the sofa. "Lucretia Borgia?" she choked out.

"Know her, do ye? Well, I'd say you and me are better suited for the task you've set for yerself. After all," she added smugly, *"seducin' gents is me specialty."*

Sabrina sank back onto the divan, her blue-green eyes wide and wild-looking. "But what of Cleopatra or Madame deMaintenon? Why couldn't I have been sent someone like that?"

"Oh, luv, they've long gone on to their greater reward. It's us that's still in Purgatory who's got to prove ourselves."

Sabrina gazed up at her and, for the first time, Nell saw a glimmer of acceptance in the young woman's face. "My word, it's true, isn't it? You *are* a ghost."

"As sure as old George's dicked in the nob," she cheerfully pledged.

"O-o-oh my." Sabrina pressed an unsteady hand to her forehead. "Plato was right."

"What's that ye say?"

"Plato. He claimed that the soul was immortal and imperishable."

Nell wasn't sure what imperishable might mean, but she certainly understood immortal. *"Well,"* she confirmed with a wide smile. *"Your friend Play-toe told you true, luv. 'Cause here I am."*

"My frien—"

Sabrina stared at her. And stared at her hard.

"You know . . . you don't seem very old for someone who is supposed to be dead. I mean, you couldn't be more than what? Thirty?"

"Oh, go on. I was fair on to thirty-four when I snuffed

out." Nell touched a ghostly cheek that once had been as smooth as the finest Chinese silk.

"Thirty-four?" Sabrina echoed. "It wasn't—you didn't expire of . . . ?"

"No, no. 'Twasn't the pox," Nell assured her with a throaty laugh. *"The devil's consumption did me in."*

"Oh." Sabrina frowned again and slowly sidestepped her way over to the hearth. As if she were afraid to turn her back on a ghost.

Nell merely fingered a dangly earbob.

Sabrina was having a rough time of it, all right—accepting the fact that an honest-to-goodness spook had popped into her library. But then, considering what she had seen so far of the girl, 'twasn't all that surprising.

She was a funny little miss, this Sabrina. A genuine bluestocking if Nell had ever seen one. Imagine looking in books, instead of a mirror, to figure out how to catch a man! Why 'twas plain as day that the girl didn't have a whit of vanity. With her dowdy black gown and her face screwed up sober as a judge, Sabrina could have been a bleedin' nun. And odds were she was as innocent as one.

Nell flicked at her earring again. She was going to have to break Sabrina in easy. Show her the ropes bit by bit.

At least it helped that the girl had pluck. She'd have to be for the course she'd set for herself. Nell had seen it far too many times: a gently bred girl pushed by circumstances into the petticoat market. Most got on all right. . . . After a while.

Nell sashayed over to the sofa and plopped herself down.

"What say we settle down to business, Sabrina dear? You want me to teach you to seduce a man, right? Who's our mark? Or does it matter?"

Sabrina blinked and folded her hands in front of her. The fire's glow silhouetted her slender frame.

"I am sorry, Madame deNuit, but I fear there's been a terrible misunderstanding. Please, I don't mean to give offense; however, you're not at all the sort of ghost—that is to say, I do apologize, but I am going to have to refuse your generous offer of tutelage."

Fustian. Little Miss Prim-and-Proper still wasn't convinced.

"I am sorry for the inconvenience," Sabrina went on, "however, I must ask that you return from whence you came. This is a very difficult time for me. I wish I could be more hospitable, but I just can't. If you would be good enough to go back to . . . wherever, I'd thank you for your consideration."

"Go back?" Nell fluttered her hand to her chest.

"Yes. Go back," Sabrina repeated more firmly.

This was it, the moment of truth. Nell took a breath and mustered a look that she hoped looked credibly chagrined. *"I am sorry, luv, but I can't go back. 'Tisn't possible. You're stuck with me, Sabrina, whether you like it or not."*

Sabrina didn't like it. She didn't like it at all. She would have quite preferred to believe that this was nothing more than a nightmare brought on by one too many servings of Hattie's egg cream.

"Not go back?" Goose bumps rippled up her arms. "Of course you can! You can return the way you came."

Nell shook her head, setting into motion the ridiculous bonnet's ribands and pearls and feathers. *"No, luv, 'tain't possible. Not yet, at least. Not 'til the next full moon."*

Sabrina's gaze shot to the window. The storm had finally squalled itself out and a small patch of sky, where the clouds had pulled away, revealed a perfectly round ivory sphere.

"But it is full."

"Yes. And 'twas at the stroke of midnight that I arrived."

Sabrina felt her heart rate accelerate beneath her bombazine gown. "Are you saying that you cannot return for another month? Midnight at the next full moon?"

Nell smiled broadly. *"Aye, you're a sharp one. That's just what I'm sayin'."*

Sabrina closed her eyes and opened them again. This couldn't be happening. It couldn't.

And yet it was. The ghostly madam's argument regarding empirical evidence had been surprisingly sound, how could she dispute the truth of what was right before her eyes?

Don't lose your wits, Sabrina, she admonished herself. As extraordinary as the situation was, it wouldn't do to get all missish and scatterbrained about it. *Think, girl. Use your head.*

Fact one: She had been sent a ghost.

There. She'd admitted it. She accepted that an unearthly being was, at this moment, removing its gloves in her library.

Fact two: She was saddled with this specter for thirty days.

Very well. She could endure thirty days. Sabrina lifted her chin, although it slipped a notch when Nell casually raised her skirts and proceeded to adjust her scarlet—yes, scarlet!—silk stockings.

"Madame deNuit!"

The ghost dropped her skirts and looked up at her with that strangely captivating, gap-toothed smile. *"Yes, Sabrina, luv?"*

"Madame deNuit, I must protest—"

"Oh, call me Nell, won't you? After all, we're goin' to be downright chummy 'fore this is done."

Chummy? With the spirit of a bawd?

"Nell . . ." Sabrina cleared her throat and assumed her no-nonsense voice. "Are you certain there is no other way that you can return prior to the next full moon?"

"Ooh, quite. Fact is that come midnight next month, I'll be whisked away without no say in it at all."

"I see." Sabrina hid her disappointment behind a thoughtful frown.

"But don't you worry none, girl, 'cause if anyone can teach you how to seduce a bloke in a month's time, it'd be me."

Sabrina flashed a glance to Nell's overfilled bodice. "Hmm," she murmured noncommittally.

Nell must have read her skepticism, because she rose from the divan with a worried pout on her painted lips. *"You are goin' to let me help you, aren't ye, Sabrina?"*

Sabrina pursed her own unadorned lips. "I honestly don't know what I'm going to do with you, Madame deNuit."

"Nell."

"Nell," she reluctantly conceded.

The ghost had picked up one of the books from the sofa and Sabrina reflected on how odd the book's solidness appeared in Nell's translucent fingers. Evidently, the ghost could manipulate material objects. What other powers might she possess?

Just then a purely awful thought sprung into Sabrina's head. What if . . . what if everyone could see her ghost? Dear heavens—her horrified gaze flew back to that brimming bodice—what if Teddy and Andrew could see *this*?

"Nell, am I the only one that can . . . can see you?"

"Just you, luv."

Relief flooded her, but for only a second.

"And, 'course," Nell went on, *"sometimes the li'l ones can see us. They 'ave the power to believe, you see."*

"Oh dear."

Nell glanced to her sharply. *"You 'aven't got wee ones 'ere, do you? I've never got on with the urchins, loud li'l beggars always haring about."*

"I do," Sabrina assured, taking hope that Nell might not stay if she knew about her brothers. "Loud, rowdy. You probably won't care for them at all."

Nell frowned, then smoothed the wrinkles from her brow with a forefinger. *"May'aps they won't be able to see me."*

Sabrina thought of Teddy with his incredibly vivid imagination. "I doubt that. My littlest brother is only eight and a most inventive child."

"Hmmph." Nell shrugged a ghostly white shoulder and dropped the book back onto the sofa. *"I'll 'ave to try to stay out of 'is way, then."*

Sabrina sagged against the wall, a bookshelf jabbing her square in the middle of her back. Her headache was returning, and her limbs were growing heavy with fatigue.

"Nell, I am sorry, but I am simply too tired to think. After a night's rest, I can resolve what's to be done with you. But first I must get some sleep."

Reproachful eyes met hers and Sabrina felt exactly as she did when she sent Teddy to his room without supper.

"Don't say you're not goin' to let me help you, Sabrina. 'Tis the whole reason I've come to earth."

Sabrina bit her tongue and glanced heavenward. This must be some celestial jest.

"Nell, I-I just don't know. I have never much believed in anything like angels or ghosts and now I am supposed to let *you*, a brothel owner who's been dead—"

"Six years."

"Who's been dead six years," Sabrina continued, "teach me in the ways of men?"

She swung toward the bookshelf and, by chance, the title staring her in the face was *Vindication of the Rights of*

Woman. She thought that Mary Wollstonecraft must be looking down at her right now and shaking her head in dismay. But looking down from . . . where?

Sabrina turned around. "Nell," she asked hesitantly, "where you come from—what is it like?"

A stillness passed over the ghost's translucent features, and she averted her eyes. *"It's borin'. The most bloody borin' place ye could ever imagine. And it's empty and cold. It's just a cold, flat . . . nothin'ness."*

An empathetic shiver scurried up Sabrina's spine and she wished she hadn't asked. "And what about tonight? Do you sleep?"

"Sleep? I don't think so. But, don't worry 'bout me none, luv. I'll just wait for you here. Waitin's somethin' I've got real good at."

"You won't go anywhere, will you? You'll stay here in the library?" She was concerned about Andrew and Teddy, of course.

"If that's what you want, Sabrina, that's what I'll do. Nell deNuit aims to please."

"Aims to please," Sabrina mumbled. Then why couldn't she find a way to return to where she belonged?

Sabrina's temples throbbed unhappily, reminding her of how very tired she was. She had to get to bed.

Casting a worried glance at the voluptuous, diaphanous figure sprawled across the divan, she said, "You promise me that you won't go wandering about the house?"

"God's oath," Nell vowed, and trailed a finger over her generous bosom.

Something between a smile and a wince curved Sabrina's lips. "Very well. I will see you in the morning, then. And we can work on resolving this—ah . . . this problem."

After such an emotionally turbulent day, Sabrina was convinced that she would sleep like the dead, so to speak.

But she did not. Her dreams of cherubic angels were chased by nightmares of chain-rattling ghosts so that when the dawn finally arrived, it came too early.

She awoke in the cool gray of morning, feeling as she'd done when she'd snuck into Papa's cherry brandy. Shoving away the coverlet, she sat at the edge of the bed, her night rail twisted around her knees from her restless movements during the night.

She took a deep breath and her lungs filled with the lingering scent of frangipani.

"Oh, no-o-o-o."

There could be no mistake. It hadn't been a dream; it hadn't been a delusion. Last night, Sabrina Simmons had met a spirit.

Panic, as unfamiliar to her as ghosts, shot through her in a pulse-quickening rush. Sabrina never panicked. She was too levelheaded for that. Nonetheless, she knew that she had to get out of the house. She needed to think before she faced Madame deNuit again.

Not bothering to wash her face, she threw on her moth-abused riding habit with little care to the correct matching of buttons and buttonholes. Instead of arranging her hair, she stuffed the braid she'd worn to bed under her hat, then pulled the hat down almost to her ears to hold the mass in place.

As noiselessly as a shadow, she crept downstairs, taking especial care to be quiet as she passed by the library. Although curiosity tempted her to peek in—to confirm what she knew in her heart must be true—she first had to put her thoughts aright. Sabrina always liked to have her thoughts in order and last night's events had certainly scrambled them.

As she made her way to the stables, the morning cold

formed white puffy clouds of her breath, reminding her yet again of Nell. The ghost who would not go home.

After saddling up Licorice, a foul-tempered beast, Sabrina set off across the park in the direction of the river.

It was an uncommonly beautiful Shropshire morning. Fog skirted the valleys, filling the green glens like thick clotted cream. The unique scent of dawn carried on the wind as sunrise married pink and gray in its dusky light.

The cobwebs started to clear from her head as she rode over the dew-kissed fields, and Sabrina set out organizing her mental chaos. One concern that had plagued her sleep last night was the matter of Nell's predicament. She had been too tired to think it through earlier but the ghost's sorrowful description of Purgatory had lingered with Sabrina in a most unsettling way.

Last evening, Nell had more or less intimated that the reason she'd been caught in Purgatory was because of her occupation. One that was far from respectable, to be sure.

The obvious question that followed—and one Sabrina had failed to consider until now—was: If Nell had not been admitted into heaven because she'd been a madam, would Sabrina also be barred if she became the Viscount Colbridge's mistress?

Truthfully, she had never given much thought to the afterlife; she'd never really asked herself if she believed in heaven and the like. She'd lived an honorable life and had concluded that she would be dealt with honorably upon her death.

However, if a brothel owner was refused a celestial resting place, how would a fallen woman fare? Would she, once she'd seduced the viscount, be doomed to an eternity in Purgatory as Nell had been?

Sabrina's agitation pushed Licorice into a brisker pace. But Nell hadn't really been sentenced to Purgatory forever, had she? She was here on earth, if only for a visit. The ghost had said she was "biding her time" until she could move on to her greater reward, so evidently Nell harbored some hope of advancing to heaven. Her fate was not set.

More to the point, however, Sabrina had to ask herself whether the prospect of an eternity spent in Purgatory would sway her from her course. Would she be willing to make that sacrifice? Would she risk such a penance in order to save Simmons House for Andrew and Teddy?

Her uncertainty faded in an instant. She would do anything for her brothers. Anything.

Nothing was more important than protecting those boys. From the beginning, she had shielded them as best she could, hiding from them the truth about their mother's illness. The boys had known that "Mama was not well," but Sabrina had refused to let them be burdened by the knowledge that she shared. That their mother yearned for death. That upstairs, concealed in the farthest corner of the west wing, hid a woman too frightened of living to live. Ultimately, Emily Simmons had willed herself to death.

If Sabrina had guarded her brothers from their mother's irrational fear, she'd also shielded them from their father's wildness. With a passion and an abandon that bordered on reckless, he had lived every minute as if it were his last. His death, only a few months after their mother's, had left the Simmons children penniless and alone.

Sabrina's heart constricted.

They were everything to her. The romantic love of which poets wrote was—as Wollstonecraft argued—nothing but a deceptive passion, a fleeting thing that could not stand the test of time. What bound Sabrina to her brothers was "love."

So how could she stand by and see them lose their home? To others, Simmons House might only be four very

nice walls and a roof. But for her brothers, who had lost
everything, their home was the last anchor, their last tie to
security and stability. She vowed she would save it for
them even if it cost her her soul.

Which brought her full circle back to her dilemma. The
seduction of Lord Colbridge . . . and her spectral tutor.

Undeniably, if she'd had any say in it, Sabrina would
never have requested a madam to instruct her in seduction.
And certainly she would not have chosen someone like
Nell, with her cockney accent, her suggestive mannerisms,
and her garish attire. But to be fair (and Sabrina liked to
think of herself as fair), the bawdy Nell did have a certain
earthly—or was it unearthly?—allure.

And who was she, Sabrina Simmons, Leychurch's resident bluestocking, to say what men found attractive? Why,
she hadn't the foggiest idea what a man liked in a woman.

Especially when it came to one particular man.

What would a hedonistic, empty-headed womanizer like
the Viscount Colbridge find desirable?

Sabrina's lips pursed with disdain, as she wondered what
type of man the viscount could be. A man so poor in intellect that he could only find pleasure in the flesh, and not in
the mind? He'd have to be very pleased with himself, she
surmised. A self-important rake accustomed to women
swooning at his feet. He'd be a proper dandy in tight pan-
taloons and fussy cravats. Why, she could almost picture
him: beautifully classic features with blond curls falling
about his brow in affected artlessness. Cinnamon-brown
eyes that could entice with a single look but that lacked a
spark of intelligence.

"Mindless fribble," she judged. A being that was as for-
eign to her as the man in the moon. Of course, she hadn't
any notion of what would appeal to a man like that.

But Nell would.

Realizing that she'd been unconsciously spurring Licorice on faster and faster, Sabrina eased up on the reins, slowing to a walk. The horse's flanks shuddered as Licorice labored for breath.

The sun was now up and toiling to burn away the mist that hovered over the dew-damp earth. Sabrina shivered and turned her face eastward, seeking out the meager warmth of the early morning sunshine.

A sense of fatalism settled over her, oddly calming.

She would accept Nell's tutelage. She would learn to be a seductress. She would be Lord Colbridge's mistress.

And with that decision, Sabrina took another step toward her fall from grace.

It was Licorice's gleeful neigh that alerted her. She turned her attention to the horse and saw, with a start, that she was on a collision course with a massive tree branch.

Intent on getting a drink from the river, Licorice was headed down the embankment, oblivious to the fact that his rider would be clobbered by the oak limb hanging above the water. Or perhaps not so oblivious.

Sabrina pulled on the reins, but the rebellious Licorice would have none of it. Onward he plodded.

The limb loomed closer.

Sabrina yanked mightily, but the old animal had a mouth of iron.

"Stop, you beastly creature! Stop, I say!"

Licorice must have been feeling vengeful after the paces Sabrina had put him through, for he surged forward and ducked his head under the branch. Sabrina was left with a choice: either get swacked in the face by the oak limb or jump.

Into the icy waters of the Severn River she leaped.

Chapter Three

"*The perfect woman?* Blast it, Francis, must you be so naive? The words 'perfect' and 'woman' suit each other as well as abstinence suits Prinny."

Sarcasm made his tone sharp, but Richard Kerry didn't really give a damn. For all that Francis was an entertaining fellow—and his oldest and closest friend—sometimes his ingenuousness was more than Richard could stomach.

"But isn't that what you've been seeking?" Francis argued. "A paragon?"

Richard slanted a glance to the Earl Merrick who was bobbing along awkwardly on a fine-footed bay.

"I'd be a sorry fool," Richard scoffed, "to waste my time looking for perfection in a woman."

"B-but what of Miss Wetherby?" Francis sputtered. "She's gentle, refined—the loveliest woman the *ton* has seen in years! Surely you'd allow that the lady you plan to marry is deserving of the term."

Perfect? Charlotte? A woman whose idea of scintillating conversation was the newest shade of Scotia silk?

"Who says I plan to marry Miss Wetherby?" Richard countered, just for the sake of being perverse.

"Come now, Richard, you needn't play your games with me. All London knows you're going to ask for her. Your families share a history; she's incredibly lovely; and, you *must* marry."

"Yes, I must, mustn't I?" he muttered with a notable lack of enthusiasm.

Removing his hat, Francis ran an agitated hand through his blond hair. "Good God, man, we're talking about a diamond of the first water! You could hardly ask for more in a lady."

"Yes, but 'tis one thing to bed them, Francis, old boy, quite another to wed them."

His friend made a sort of choking sound. "You might be a rake, Richard, but there are times when I'd swear you don't even like women!"

"What's not to like? A warm mouth, pillowy breasts . . ."

Francis's lips tightened and he shot a look at Richard's lame leg. One Richard wasn't meant to see.

"You're an ass, Colbridge."

He shrugged indifferently. "So I've been told."

Francis held silent for a moment, then picked up his argument where he had left off.

"I had thought the entire reason we came to Shropshire was so that you could prepare your uncle's house for your new bride. If you aren't going to offer for Miss Wetherby, I don't know what we are doing out here in the middle of nowhere."

Richard flicked his gaze to the valley beneath them

where pockets of color staged spring's arrival. The Severn River snaked its way through the green fields, darting in and out of gnarled stands of oaks, its waters glistening like a polished mirror-glass.

Richard would not have described Shropshire as nowhere, but he could understand how Francis might think it so. Francis who lived for society's parties and routs; who held his tailor as dear to his heart as he did his own brother. It was a testament to their friendship that the earl had left London during the peak of the social season to accompany him to the country.

Francis muffled a groan as he squirmed in his seat. 'Twas also another mark of their friendship that the poor old chap hadn't fussed about plans for a morning ride. Lord Merrick was a notoriously poor horseman and was known never to rise before noon.

"What do you think? Should I offer for Charlotte?"

Beneath his fashionably pale complexion, the Earl Merrick flushed. "I don't know. I suppose if you love her . . ."

Had it been anyone but Francis, Richard would have laughed in his face. As it was, in his present mood, he feared he might say something that even the affable Lord Merrick would find unpardonable.

He was definitely in a wicked humor this morning. Not one that made for good company.

Francis stifled another saddle-weary groan, and Richard decided he'd be doing both of them a favor if he sent his friend back to the house.

"See here, Francis, you know that property I've been inquiring about? I'd like to ride out and see where the boundaries meet, but I know you've some correspondence to take care of. What say I meet up with you later in the day?"

Francis nodded, putting a good face on his obvious relief. "Right-o. I do have some letters I must get off. I'll see you at luncheon, then?"

"Yes, I shouldn't be too long."

With an inexpert kick of his heels, Francis turned his mount, gave Richard a brief salute, and headed toward home.

Home. Richard was still having a hard time thinking of that dark little mausoleum as such. His late uncle's residence, Leyton Hall, was a dreary place, completely devoid of charm or warmth. The idea of bringing Charlotte to live there . . . He could not imagine it.

But then again, neither could he imagine living with Charlotte anywhere. Not that she wasn't a lovely girl. Hell, she was almost too lovely—a porcelain doll with delicate hands and empty blue eyes. She was sweet-tempered, soft-spoken and uncomplicated. She would expect very little from him, and he would give her even less. She would never ask where he'd been or whom he'd been with. No questions, no demands. All in all, she would make a damned fine wife.

Then why was he hiding away in Leychurch, putting off the inevitable?

He nudged his mount forward, slowly weaving his way down the hill, as the question played through his thoughts. Why was he so reluctant to do what he knew had to be done?

Sex, he decided, was not the obstacle. Even if Charlotte was lacking in passion—which he strongly suspected she was—he was not marrying her for her ability to pleasure him. A mistress was meant to fill that role, not a wife.

And he could not blame Charlotte for the fact that she bored him to tears. Most women did, as well as a good number of men. For this reason, Richard's acquaintances numbered many, but his friends few. It was simply that he did not enjoy most people's company for more than an hour or two. He grew bored, impatient.

A discussion of horseflesh could only hold his interest for so long. Gossip and idle chatter had him yawning behind his hand within minutes. Granted, his friend, the Earl Merrick, could hardly have been described as an intellectual or a man of superior wit, but at least Francis felt matters deeply. If not clever, he was sincere, unlike the pretentious and false who comprised the better part of the *ton.*

Francis, too, understood better than anyone else what made Richard tick. He was a good enough friend not to discuss it, though an occasional word or gesture—like the significant glance he'd given Richard's leg—revealed a certain insight. Yet even Francis, a man closer to him than any other, was not privy to all Richard's secrets.

Like Francis, Charlotte Wetherby was innately honest, although profundity did not favor her thoughts or emotions. If obliged to marry—and Richard was if he wanted that bloody inheritance—he could do a far sight worse than the fair Miss Wetherby.

Then why delay? Typical bachelor jitters? Or, God help him, did Francis have the right of it? Did his wound reach deeper than the scar on his leg?

Richard tugged open his cravat with a vicious yank.

"That's better," he muttered. The blasted thing had been suffocating him.

Taking a deep breath, he focused on the land rolling out before him, returning his thoughts to the task at hand. If he remembered correctly, his property ended at the Severn. The neighboring property . . .

"Stop, you beastly creature! Stop, I say!"

The frantic plea made Richard pull up sharply on his

mount. He held still for an instant, gauging the cry's point of origin, then jerked his horse toward the river.

Blast, but he wasn't in the mood for rescuing fair damsels. Most likely, some country wench had lost her nerve after leading a bloke on a merry chase. Poor bastard.

Nonetheless, he'd better have a look. A man who'd been teased and then left frustrated could become rather disagreeable.

He slowed as he approached the Severn, realizing that the cries had ceased. Perhaps the girl had only been putting up a token resistance and had been persuaded by her lover's caresses.

He brought his horse to a standstill behind a clump of oak trees. Although he didn't want to be caught spying upon a tryst, he owed it to the girl—and to his conscience—to make certain naught was amiss. He swung down from his mount and silently walked around the thicket of low-spreading branches. The smell of mint, crushed beneath his boots, scented the air.

He pushed aside a thickly leafed limb and peered through the foliage, unprepared for the sight that met him. Expecting two sweethearts caught in a fiery embrace, his gaze instead settled on a moss-covered, fully clothed chit standing waist-deep in the middle of the river.

Drenched from head to toe, the girl was spewing water from her mouth like a fountain while shoving clumps of wet hair from her eyes. Moss draped her in gooey-looking ropes of green. Further downstream, her riding hat could be seen floating away to parts unknown.

Once the young woman had emptied her mouth and cleared her vision, she turned to a horse drinking a few feet away, and said with an astonishing amount of dignity, "Licorice, you are an accursed animal."

Richard huffed a sardonic laugh. So here was the

"beastly creature" she'd been rebuking. Not some spurned beau. Realizing that she was in no danger—except for perhaps catching a chill—Richard decided to retreat. As he started to turn away, the girl reached for the buttons of her riding habit.

Richard froze.

This could get interesting, he thought with a devilish smile. He decided to linger another minute or two.

As she worked at the buttons she labored to drag herself from the water, but the rocks at the river bottom must have been slick. She slipped and thrashed about. Richard thought her one of the most graceless women he'd ever seen. Of course, she did appear to be severely weighed down by her wet jacket and skirts.

"Fustian," he heard her mutter in her low, cultured voice—a husky purr that made him think of well-aged brandy and cigars.

She stopped trying to climb from the river and concentrated her efforts on removing her jacket. Her buttons had been misaligned but, after a minute's fumbling, she managed to peel the dripping garment from her arms.

Richard caught an appreciative whistle between his teeth. The naughty little Naiad wasn't wearing a corset and her wet blouse clung to her like a second skin. Her breasts, small yet high, were clearly outlined, and crowned by two rosy, tasty-looking buds.

She twisted the jacket in her hands, and wrung about a gallon of river water from it. Raising her arm overhead—and affording Richard another pleasing eyeful—she heaved the coat onto the grass. She then bent forward, and it looked as if she intended to remove her skirt. Alas, Richard's mount chose that most inopportune moment to announce their presence with a loud snort.

The girl straightened, her eyes as round as shillings. She

looked toward him and their gazes met. Richard stepped out from behind the foliage, annoyed by a vague sense of embarrassment.

"Pardon me, 'gentle nymph,' " he mocked. "But it seems I've caught you 'swaying the smooth Severn stream.' "

The young woman grew stiff. "Do I know you, sir?"

"I think you do not."

"But apparently *you* know of *me*. Where did you learn my name?" she demanded.

He frowned, wondering what made her believe that he knew her name. Then he recalled the next line of the verse he'd been quoting: *Sabrina is her name, a virgin pure*

"Sabrina?" he questioned, nonplussed by her familiarity with Milton.

"Miss Simmons to you," she corrected sternly. "And kindly answer my question."

" 'Twas but a fortunate guess."

She glared at him, patently suspicious, then gave him her back as she made another attempt to lumber across to the riverbank. By an ungainly combination of lunging and swimming, she scrambled to the other shore and dragged herself onto the grass. Her breath was coming hard, and Richard felt his loins stir as his gaze fixed on the rise and fall of her chest.

A whiff of interest stirred more than his loins. Who was this girl? She couldn't be a servant as he'd first thought, for her speech was too refined and she knew her poetry. But if she were quality, she must be a singular chit to be sitting on a riverbank, pouring water from her boots.

"*Are* you a virgin pure?" he asked with deliberate provocation, again referring to the poem.

To his surprise, she did not blush or feign offense, but regarded him with a level eye and an equanimity that almost made him smile. He wasn't sure how she managed it, but plopped down in a puddle of mud, with her hair down and her breasts virtually bare, she looked as prim and practical as a schoolmarm.

"You seem fond of quoting poets," she retorted, dropping her gaze as she fought to drag on a boot. " 'Percontatorem fugito; nam garrulus idem est.' "

Avoid a questioner, for such a man is also a tattler. He tipped his head in mocking tribute. Horace. In flawless Latin, no less.

How very intriguing.

"Well done," he commended. "But what if I promise not to tattle? It can be our little secret."

Pausing, she glanced up at him through her lashes. Richard debated crossing the narrow band of river to determine the color of her eyes.

"I do not share secrets with strangers," she said.

"Ah, my oversight." He bowed. "Richard Kerry, Viscount Colbridge, at your service."

Her hands stilled for a moment as she was pulling on the other boot. "I cannot say I care much for your 'service,' Lord Colbridge. You could have proven more helpful in assisting me from the river."

A smile tugged at Richard's lips.

"My apologies, dear lady. The services I am accustomed to providing young women are generally of a more"—he leered at her—"personal nature."

His bait was not taken. On the contrary, she gave him a look that was at once censuring, aloof, and amusingly tolerant.

She finished fastening her boot and stood, clearly preparing to leave. Richard had the irrational desire to stay her, for he was rather enjoying their exchange. He wanted to learn more of this unusual Latin-spouting female.

"Wait," he said. "Now that we are no longer strangers, aren't you going to appease my curiosity, Sabrina?"

"Permit me to remind you, Lord Colbridge, that curiosity did not well serve the proverbial cat."

Picking up her jacket, she thrust her arms into the dripping-wet sleeves.

"But curiosity has its benefits," he argued, reluctant to let her go. "Did not Hume write that 'curiosity is one of the permanent and certain characteristics of a vigorous mind'?"

She walked to where the horse was grazing at the river's edge, her boots making a *squish-squish* sound with each step. With her hair hanging about her, and her wet clothes clinging to her slim frame, she reminded him of nothing more than a drowned rat. Yet, in spite of this, he felt himself swell in his breeches.

Picking up the reins, she turned to look at him over her shoulder. "Hume did not say that," she calmly rebutted. "Samuel Johnson did."

Richard's brows angled to a vee. *Damn.* Damn if she wasn't right. That had been Johnson.

She led the animal up the embankment and Richard had the uncanny sense that the tables had been turned. Where previously he had been the one taunting and teasing, playing with words, now he felt as if she'd just issued him a challenge. As if she, this curiosity of a female, had just thrown down the gauntlet.

Chapter
Four

Sabrina didn't rattle easily; she was far too levelheaded for that. But as she rode home, shivering and shaking, she could not help but wonder if it was her wet clothes or her jangled nerves that had her quaking like a poorly set pudding.

After all, how much could a girl—even a sensible one—endure in a twelve-hour period?

Last night, she made the acquaintance of a ghost . . . and today, she meets up with the devil himself!

For there really was something diabolical about the Viscount Colbridge. Something dangerous.

Pulling her arms in tight to her sides, she sought to warm herself. She was so very, very cold. A bone-deep chill—almost like a premonition—had settled over her as soon as she'd learned the identity of the dark mocking stranger with the pronounced limp.

He had taken her by surprise, no question about it. For in her mind she had pictured him quite differently. His hair was supposed to have been fair and curly, not an inky-black mane that fell to his shoulders like some sixteenth-century pirate. And instead of being comely as she'd assumed, he was harsh-featured and lean, with a nose that looked as if it had been broken once or twice. More than likely that limp of his had been acquired in a pubroom brawl or perhaps at the hand of an enraged husband.

Her fingers cramped on the reins.

Blast the man. He was not at all what she had expected. She had imagined him to be uneducated, but he had quoted Milton with an ease wholly inconsistent with his libertine reputation. And had it been coincidence that he'd cited that particular verse? Or had he known her name and merely been toying with her?

She squinted into the sun. How irksome, too, had been his attempts to trip her up, playing with the words she so dearly loved. To confuse Hume with Johnson . . . Honestly.

Nonetheless, that he was familiar with either philosopher gave her pause. Quite obviously, the Viscount Colbridge was not a dandified twit. He was, however, pompous and insolent. Everything about the man bespoke boldness.

The way he had looked at her with those eyes, eyes as bleak and black as mortal sin . . .

She shuddered. She would have sworn they were without a soul. Never had she known a regard so unnerving and, yet, at the same time so compelling.

And his voice. Its timbre had been almost hypnotic. Many an unsuspecting female must have been lured to her doom by that voice. And to the viscount's bed.

Doubt crept into Sabrina, winding its way around her

confidence. It had been fairly easy to imagine surrendering herself to a faceless man, one that had been no more than a name. But now. Now that she'd come face-to-face with the genuine article . . .

With a brisk mental shake, she took hold of herself. *Chin up, Sabrina.* No getting weak-kneed now. Her responsibilities were as they'd always been—to her brothers.

Yes, Lord Colbridge might be the closest thing to the devil that she'd ever met, but it mattered not. He could truly be Satan himself, and it would not change her plans.

Only one question raised by their encounter was of any real consequence The viscount had obviously made a marked impression on her, but *how had she impressed him?*

She made a face as she glanced down to a ribbon of moss clinging to her riding skirts. 'Twould be safe to assume that she hadn't bowled him over with her grace and beauty. In fact, although she did not know a great deal about it, she would not say that their meeting had been an especially auspicious beginning to a seduction.

She ought to have been more pleasant, more cordial. But she'd been taken off guard. Lurking about in the trees, spying on her, he'd made her uneasy. And then, once she knew who he was, she'd had to fight for her wits.

If only she could remember all that she'd said to him. Flustered by his innuendo and too-bold stares, she'd not known how to respond. Had her gaucheness been revealed? Had she already botched any hopes of seducing the arrogant rogue?

"Nell," she whispered.

Nell would know what to do.

For the first time, Sabrina actually felt grateful for the ghost's appearance. Undoubtedly a woman of Nell's experience would know how to repair the damage she might have done during this morning's interlude. Or, at least, she hoped she would know . . .

As she approached Simmons House, Sabrina swung down from Licorice and, with a swat to his flank, sent him in the direction of Hattie's husband, Peter, who was working in the stables. The couple's devotion to the family continued to be one of the happy constants in the Simmons' ever-changing circumstances.

Sabrina let herself in the front door, wishing she might enjoy a nice, hot bath before she sought out Nell. But she dared not. This chance meeting with Lord Colbridge required immediate consultation. Besides, she needed to reassure herself that Nell had not been merely a figment of her imagination.

She passed into the front hallway, and a high-pitched squeal arrested her step. The gleeful cackle had come from her library. *Her* library.

Someone had invaded her sanctuary, and that someone sounded very much like Teddy. Teddy, who frequented only rarely the room with all the "hateful, boring" books.

With a sense of foreboding, Sabrina dripped across the foyer and opened the library door a crack. Her breath caught in horror.

Sprawled on his stomach, with his chin cradled in his hands, Teddy was lying on the rug in front of the fire, his eyes glittering with an eight-year-old's delight. Beside him sat Andrew, his legs neatly crossed, his mouth slightly open. Even from this distance, Sabrina could see the enraptured look in his bespectacled gaze.

Both were staring up at their resident ghost who was apparently in the midst of telling a tale.

" . . . *then ole Smitty pulls out his dagger and rams it up 'gainst Billy's gullet. 'Ye've played me false once too often, Billy me lad,' he growls. 'Now ye're goin' to pay.' And as*

Billy prepares to meet his Maker, Smitty draws back the knife and—"

"Madame deNuit!"

Three pairs of guilty eyes turned to her.

"Sabrina!" Teddy jumped to his feet. "You've interrupted our story."

Sabrina slipped into the room and pressed back against the closed door, as if she could keep the rest of the world out.

"I . . ."

"But how famous of you to bring us a ghost," Teddy went on, fairly dancing a jig. "Nell's a real trump, she is."

Oh, Lord. So much for hoping that the boys wouldn't be able to see their resident spook.

"Good morning." Sabrina nodded uncomfortably, searching for words. "I . . . I see you've all met."

"It was me who found her," Teddy boasted. "I came looking for you and found her in here, floating about."

Yes, of course. How easily Teddy accepted it.

"Then Andrew came in and oh, I wish you'd seen him, Rina! At first, he couldn't see Nell, but when I made him look real close . . ." Teddy giggled. "He turned white as chalk, his knees got all wobble-like, and I thought for certain he was going to swoon."

Sabrina glanced to Andrew, expecting him to object to his brother's ridicule, but Andrew was paying Teddy no mind. His attention was fixed firmly on Nell. If Andy had been pale earlier, as Teddy claimed, now two bright red flags shown in his cheeks, and his mouth hung slightly ajar.

Sabrina frowned. "Well, now that you've met, I want you to run along, boys. I have some urgent business to address with Madame deNuit. We can discuss our ghostly visitor later, but in the meantime, I think we should keep this to ourselves. Understood, Theodore?"

Teddy looked disappointed, but nodded.

"Andrew?"

He didn't even glance at her.

"Andrew?" she repeated, more sharply.

"Eh, what's that, Rina?"

"I need to speak privately with Madame deNuit," she re-iterated, jerking her head in the direction of the hall.

"Oh." He slowly clambered to his feet.

Sabrina held the door open for them and as they filed out, Teddy turned and asked, "Nell, later on can you finish telling us what happened to Billy?"

"Sure I ca—"

"Madame deNuit is going to be very busy, Teddy. I doubt she will have time for storytelling." Sabrina's tone brooked no argument "Now go see if you can lend Peter a hand in the stables. You both could benefit from some fresh air. And remember—not a word to anyone!"

She closed the door on Teddy's grumbling

"I didn't think that you cared for children," she said to Nell as the door clicked shut.

Nell lifted a plump shoulder. *"I don't as a rule, but those two seem all right."*

"Yes, they are 'all right,' " Sabrina agreed with deliberate tact. "But it might be best if you limited your time in their company They're very impressionable, particularly Teddy."

Nell sashayed toward her in that gliding-floating way she had of moving. *"Don't much matter to—"* She pulled up short. *"Cooee! What 'appened to you?"*

Sabrina pursed her lips, knowing she must look like a piece of flotsam. "I was making the acquaintance of the Viscount Colbridge."

"And just who is this viscou—" Nell's hand went to her

mouth. *"Oh, blimey, Sabrina, don't be tellin' me this bloke's the one?"*

"The one?"

"The one you want to bring to yer bed."

Sabrina winced. Must the woman put everything so starkly? A mental image of that abominable man laid out in her bed with his chest bare . . .

"Yes, he is the man I must seduce."

"Gawd, and he saw you lookin' like this?"

"Well, yes. I'd just fallen into the river."

"Oh, for the love of . . ."   Nell threw up her hands in a gesture that suggested all was already lost. *"Did you talk to him?"*

Sabrina nodded, wishing that she could recall their conversation more clearly. But she'd been so very unsettled by his mockery and soulless eyes.

"And what did you say?" Nell prodded.

"Um . . . I cited Horace—"

"The horse?"

"Horace, a Latin poet from the first century B.C."

"Aagh!" Nell slapped a hand to her ghostly forehead. *"Oh, luv, you've dug us a hole to begin with fer sure."*

Sabrina glanced down at herself. "That bad?"

"It's not just how you look, Sabrina. You've committed the gravest of all sins!"

Sabrina curled her toes in her boots, fighting a sense of the ridiculous. Who would have ever thought that she would be getting a dressing-down from a dead brothel owner?

"Girl, you never, ever let a man believe you've got, learnin'. Why, a mort with brains'll shrivel a bloke up faster than a cold dunkin'."

Shrivel him up?

"Oh, luv." Nell shook her head disconsolately, and Sa-

brina noted how her accent was growing thicker in her agitation. *"You've got no choice now, dear. Ye're goin' to have to let me help you, now you've gotten off to such a bloody wretched start."*

Sabrina pulled in a deep breath. "As a matter of fact, Nell, I had already decided to make use of your offer. To quote Virgil: 'We are not all capable of everything.' Since I fear I am not capable of seducing Lord Colbridge on my own, 'twould be foolish of me to spurn your offer of assistance."

It was not an easy admission to make, for Sabrina was proud and liked to think of herself as an independent woman. However, circumstances being what they were—and Lord Colbridge being who he was—she had to concede that she needed help.

"Well, I'm that glad you're going to let me teach you what I know . . . but first things first. You 'ave to stop talkin' like a bluestocking, girl. It's all right with me, I figure, but when you're with yer viscount, you must be more careful. A man don't want no scholar in his bed. He don't want to have be thinkin' while he's tuppin'."

Sabrina opened her mouth to ask what "tupping" meant, then thought the better of it.

"I see," she said slowly. "So you are concerned that I might have given the viscount the impression that I'm educated?"

"Well, with all this talk of Latin horses . . ."

"And he would find that feature repulsive in a mistress?"

"Most men would, luv."

Drat! Drat that unfortunate meeting!

Sabrina walked over to the divan and sat herself on the seat's edge, twining her fingers together. "What shall we do, then?"

Nell paced the floor in front of her. Pacing, floating, gliding.

"Let's start by tellin' me what you know of this fella. A viscount. Plump in the pockets, I suppose?"

"I cannot speak to his circumstances, but yes, I do believe Lord Colbridge is comfortable."

"Hmm-mm." Nell arched a thin brow. *"And do you know if he's the sort who fancies keepin' a lady for his pleasure?"*

Sabrina stiffened. "The viscount is purported to be a hopeless rake. According to gossip, he only recently gave his latest mistress her *congé.*"

"Ah-hah!" Nell seemed to find that bit of news especially interesting. *"Do you know anything of the canary he let go?"*

"Canary? What canary?"

"The girl, the bit o' muslin."

"Oh. No, I know nothing of her, other than that she was French."

"You don't know if she were dark or fair?"

"No, I don't."

"Hmm-mm." Continuing to pace, Nell casually reached into her overflowing décolletage and adjusted her bodice.

Sabrina blinked, glad that Teddy and Andrew had left the room.

"What does he look like then, this viscount?"

"He's tall and lean, with black hair and black eyes. He's not handsome, not at all, but there is something oddly compelling about him. Something attractive but sinister that draws you to him, like the flames of a fire. You know you shouldn't get too close and yet you cannot resist . . ."

Her words trailed off under Nell's piercing scrutiny.

"Sabrina, luv, there's one thing you must understand 'fore we go any further. When a girl accepts a man's pro-

tection, 'tis business, nothin' more. A gent might be good with the pretty speeches and fill yer ears with promises, but there ain't no place for foolishness in this work. If you want to set yourself up as the viscount's miss, the first rule is you can't be lettin' yerself fall in love with him."

"Fall in love with him! Good heavens, you needn't worry about that, I assure you. If my reading has taught me anything, 'tis the folly of putting credence in such a false emotion as love."

Her vehemence must have convinced Nell, for the ghost's frown eased, and she glanced curiously at the library's shelves.

"They teach you that in books? Blimey, per'aps there's some good in readin' after all."

"Oh, yes. Mary Wollstonecraft says . . ."

Nell extended her palms in a staying motion. *"Now, now, you needn't preach to the choir, girl. I couldn't agree with you more. I've always figured that men must 'ave made up this idea of love just so's they could lead us women 'round by our noses."* She clicked her tongue. *"A pity, too, let me tell you. I've seen many a girl lose her 'ead over a bloke and never with a 'appy ending."*

"Well, please don't worry about me. All I require for a happy ending is being able to keep Simmons House. And that means seducing Lord Colbridge."

"And we'll make sure that you do," Nell promised. She walked over to the window, and Sabrina could almost see the thoughts spinning through her ghostly head.

"First," Nell said, *"we'll 'ave to invite the viscount over for a visit. We can't let him go on thinkin' you're some kind of bookish Long Meg."*

Sabrina flinched. A bookish Long Meg? Was that what she was?

"And I've got to teach you the tricks o' the trade—well,

at least a few of 'em. We 'aven't got time to go through 'em all." She turned away from the window and floated over to where Sabrina still sat, shivering and wet. *"And, 'course we'll need to fix you up. Do you even own a dress that ain't black or gray?"*

"Why, yes. I had been in mourning, you see." She shrugged apologetically. "I guess that I simply never bothered to come out."

"Well, now's the time, luv, now's the time." Nell rubbed her hands together and Sabrina thought the madam must enjoy the challenge of making over the Simmons ugly duckling. *"You run off and 'ave a hot bath and we'll start your lessons straight after. We've got a lot to cover 'fore the viscount comes to tea tomorrow."*

"Tomorrow!" Sabrina jumped to her feet. "Why, that's far too soon."

"Sabrina, luv, we've only twenty-nine days left to convince yer viscount that you'd make him a proper mistress." Her pitying gaze said it all. *"We 'aven't a moment to lose."*

"Simmons. Of course. Why didn't I put the names together?"

Richard stared down at the invitation in his hand, dismayed by his lack of perception. How had he failed to connect the girl in the river with Simmons House, the property he was seeking to purchase?

"Eh, what's that?" Francis peeked his blond head over the latest edition of the *Post*. Although they'd only been a week from London, already the earl pined for news from Town.

Richard indicated the note he held. "I've been invited to tea at the home of my neighbor, Miss Simmons."

"A country spinster?" Francis shuddered. "I don't envy

you one jot, old fellow. I suppose you must go to be polite, but I hope that you weren't counting on my company."

Richard smiled slightly, seeing no reason to disabuse Francis of his faulty deduction. Sabrina Simmons could not yet have seen twenty-one, hardly an age to qualify for spinsterhood.

"Not to worry, Francis. I would scarce submit your refined sensibilities to such an ordeal. She's probably learned of my inquiries about Simmons House and wishes to discuss the matter with me."

"Oh, God. Worse yet," Francis groaned. "Poor thing will most likely cast herself at your feet, weep all over your boots, and beg you not to evict her from her home." He shook out his paper, adding dryly, "Lucky for you, you've a heart of stone, Colbridge. I daresay there's nothing the old girl could do to sway you."

Richard's eyes narrowed as he looked over the crisply lettered message. Was that indeed Miss Simmons's purpose? She would be in for a disappointment then, for Francis was right—he was not a man easily swayed. Once he'd set his mind to something, nothing—especially not a woman's tears—would keep him from his course.

"At the very least, I'll drink her weak tea and munch on her dry biscuits, and have a look at the house. The banker described it as pleasant, but naturally I'd wish to decide that for myself."

"Naturally," came the mumbled reply.

Richard was preparing to rise from the table, leaving Francis to enjoy his gossip in peace, when the earl suddenly let out an excited "By Jove!"

His color was high as he reemerged from behind the newspaper. "You will not believe what extraordinary news is hinted at here, Richard!"

"Let me guess. Lady Jersey has developed freckles?"

The sarcasm passed right over Francis's head.

"No, no," he said with an impatient wave of his hand. "It is suggested here that certain persons have learned the identity of the infamous Ennui!"

"Really?" Richard cocked an intrigued brow. "Do they name him?"

"No, but the article strongly hints that he will soon be exposed."

"Interesting. What else does it say?"

"Apparently a few ladies of the *ton* were so enraged by Ennui's most recent leaflet that they prevailed on their husbands to unmask the"—Francis bent over and squinted at the print—" 'perpetrator of these callous and cruel attacks on womanhood.' "

"Goodness. Was his last circular so very shocking?"

Francis puffed out a surprised breath. "You should know better than to ask me of all people! You know that I don't go in for radical thought. Never actually have read any of Ennui's treatises."

Richard forced back a smile. "No, of course not."

"It does say here, however, that the article in question strayed from his usual satire."

"Hmm?"

"Evidently his latest pamphlet argued that it was time for women to shed their roles as 'ornaments to society' and to begin to be productive," Francis read. "And by productive, Ennui meant in more than a *procreative* sense. My word!"

"Radical, indeed." Richard poured himself another cup of coffee, as Francis laid down his paper, sporting the look of a man thoroughly scandalized.

" 'Tis obvious Ennui does not travel about in good society," Francis said. "For never could he question the value of a gentlewoman if he were familiar with a true lady such as Charlotte Wetherby!"

Richard refrained from commenting on the 'value' of his intended. "You think then that he must be of the lower class?" he asked, sipping at his coffee.

"Do you disagree?"

"He could as well be or not, I imagine."

"Well, I think he's full of rot. And I'm glad I haven't tortured my brain, laboring over his essays."

Richard grinned behind his cup. "Wouldn't want to overtax the poor organ, would you, Merrick?"

"I see no reason to," Francis huffed. "Deep thinking is hard enough without wasting my time on Ennui's nonsense. Besides, I would maintain that the man does not believe half of what he writes. I think he just enjoys causing a stir is what I think."

Richard tipped his head thoughtfully to the side. "You know, Francis . . . I think you might very well be right."

Chapter
Five

"So you see, boys," Sabrina finished explaining, "since only we three can see Nell, it might cause undue speculation as to our, uh, mental stability if we told others about our ghost."

Teddy pushed out his lower lip and rolled onto his back. Two skinny legs poked out from under his nightshirt. "But it's such a plummy secret, Rina. It's too good not to share."

Sitting at the head of Teddy's bed, Sabrina tossed a pillow at her younger brother, which he easily dodged. "Nonetheless, Teddy, it must remain our secret, or I might well get carted off to Bedlam and then where would you and Andrew be?"

She was only half-joking.

Andrew looked over his shoulder from making his bed and scowled at his younger brother. "You must think of what's best for everyone, Teddy. Sabrina is doing all she can for us, you know."

Sabrina sent Andrew a grateful glance and folded her hands in her lap. "There is one more thing," she said. "Over the next few weeks, you might notice that I am somewhat . . . changed."

"What do you mean?" Teddy asked, scrambling to his knees.

"Well," she said slowly. "You know how I've been working on a plan to keep Simmons House from falling into Lord Colbridge's hands?"

Teddy nodded, his wheat-colored hair flopping into his eyes.

"At any rate, while implementing this plan, I might seem to be behaving differently or speaking in an unusual manner. You might notice that my attire is altered, that I am acting altogether unlike myself."

"You will be in disguise?" Teddy asked brightly, appearing rather pleased at the idea.

"In a manner of speaking, yes, I will be disguised. Now, I've already advised Hattie that things might be a little odd around here, so she is prepared. But it is very important that I can count on your assistance, the both of you, in carrying out this project."

"Naturally, you can count on me," Andrew declared, directing a significant look in Teddy's direction.

"Me, too!"

"Splendid. Then your first commission is to remove yourselves from the house today at teatime. Hattie will pack you a basket and you can have yourselves a picnic out in the field."

"Oh, jolly!" Teddy cried. "Are we to have cakes?"

Andrew appeared less delighted, as he solemnly set his

glasses onto his nose. "Are you having someone to tea, Sabrina?"

She lifted her chin, wishing her brother weren't always so perceptive.

"Yes, Andrew, I am. I've invited the Viscount Colbridge."

"Balderdash!" Teddy looked as affronted as an eight-year-old can look. "How could you invite that ogre here, Rina? The man's a beast. I refuse to let him step foot into this house!"

Sabrina pursed her lips. She feared that she was raising a miniature tyrant.

"Pardon me, Master Simmons, but I don't believe it's within your authority to refuse anyone admittance to this home," she gently reprimanded. "And I give you fair warning: should you, by chance, occasion to meet up with Lord Colbridge, I would expect you to be the very picture of politeness to his lordship, a veritable model of gentlemanly behavior. Do I make myself clear?"

Teddy's famous lower lip made another appearance.

Sabrina ignored it and turned to Andrew.

"Andy?"

Though he nodded his assent, Andrew did not look pleased. "I would like to know just what kind of man would send three orphans to live on the streets," he muttered unhappily.

Sabrina knew, but refrained from saying.

The kind of man whose eyes had no soul.

Hours later, Richard Kerry was riding toward Simmons House, having accepted Sabrina Simmons's invitation to tea.

The day was beautiful, the sun shining as radiantly as a freshly minted guinea, the breeze alive with the scent of new-sprung greenery. It was the type of bucolic splendor that elevated the spirits of those persons who had spent too many months in the soil and soot of a decaying London. That is to say . . . most persons.

With vague detachment, Richard acknowledged that the sun was shining and the weather was warm, but he wasn't inclined to wax rhapsodic over a pansy or a cloudless sky. Particularly today when he was otherwise preoccupied.

As he rode along toward Simmons House, an unfamiliar sensation tugged at him, a heightened awareness he could not define. This feeling continued to prey on him until, at last, he was able to recognize it. It was, to his astonishment, curiosity. A condition he had not experienced for a very long time.

Not only was he curious, he realized, but he was actually looking forward to another interview with Miss Simmons. For some reason, the sharp-tongued, sharp-witted Sabrina of the Severn had kindled his interest. Richard had to ask himself "why?"

She was unusual to be sure. She was graceless. She was outspoken. She was nervy.

She was different.

Yes, that was it. No wonder he found her mildly interesting. Sabrina Simmons stood out like a sore thumb when contrasted to the ladies of his acquaintance.

Dear Lord, he could still laugh at her regal manner as she had stumbled about in the current like a drunken sailor. And, when most women would have fled shrieking to discover a man spying upon them, *she*, the singular female, had quoted him Horace.

Yes, it was the unexpected that intrigued him—the unpredictability of her actions. Little wonder he was curious then. Little wonder, indeed.

Cresting the hill that sloped up from the river's valley,

Richard had his first good look at Simmons House. He was impressed, but not overly so. The manor was grand, and yet not too grand; pretty without being precious. It did appear larger than his uncle's home—he estimated between thirty or forty rooms. The grounds were pleasant; the park modest, but adequate.

As he approached the front, an unliveried groom materialized from nowhere to take his horse.

"Good day to you, m' lord."

"Good day."

"They're expecting you," the man said, gesturing to the front door where a maid stood waiting like a mobcapped sentinel.

Richard's lips twitched. Either the Simmons didn't receive much company or his visit was of uncommon consequence. He rather suspected it was the latter.

The maid ushered him in, and bade him follow her to the drawing room. He trailed her little pigeon-like steps across the foyer, while quickly scanning the front part of the house. The hall was spacious and light; elegant in construction in a way that was lacking in his uncle's home. Lemon oil sweetened the air and the woodwork glistened with fresh polish. He nodded with satisfaction.

It might do very well.

The maid pushed open a door and gestured for him to go in. He did and the door was pulled shut behind him. He thought he was going to have to wait, when a movement caught his eye. A woman stood by the window.

Her silhouette was accentuated by the afternoon sunshine streaming in through the glass . . . and not to her disadvantage. The thrust of her breasts, the curve of her hips—the gown's sheer fabric left just enough to the imagination to tantalize.

Cynically he wondered if the woman's revealing pose was a calculated one. It was effective, nonetheless.

She swung around.

"I beg your pardon," he said. "I was shown in here to await Miss Simmons."

"Lord Colbridge."

The husky voice arrested him halfway into a bow. He jerked aright.

"Miss Simmons?"

As she slowly walked toward him, Richard's sole acknowledgment to having been caught off guard was a wryly raised eyebrow. This was the watery waif he'd met just yesterday?

The outdated riding costume had been replaced by an extremely low-cut gown in a shade of yellow that complemented her light brown curls. When last he'd seen her, he hadn't been able to identify the color of her hair, since it had been hanging in stringy, wet clumps about her shoulders. Its current arrangement was a marked improvement.

"My lord, I am delighted to see you again," she purred.

"I assure you, ma'am, the pleasure is all mine." Richard accepted the hand she offered and bowed over it. He was surprised when she gave his fingers a light squeeze.

"Won't you please sit down?" she said.

She preceded him to a sofa of crimson damask, its upholstery worn and patched. He joined her, taking the opportunity to study her as she settled her skirts about her ankles.

At least he had remembered one thing accurately about the girl: She was no beauty. With her sharp cheekbones and large eyes, she could more precisely be described as arresting rather than handsome.

Swiftly his gaze swept over her profile, detecting the blackening around her eyes and the sheen of rouge upon her lips. The cosmetics had been applied with too heavy a hand, somehow making her appear both experienced and vulnerable at the same time.

"I am so pleased you could come today, Lord Colbridge. After our first meeting, I was hoping for the chance to show myself to better advantage." She fluttered her lashes in an awkward and rapid sequence.

His lips itched to smile but he mastered the temptation. He was too curious to see what this transformation was about. Yesterday by the river, Miss Simmons had been blunt and outspoken; her demeanor had been stiff, if not downright prudish. This simpering painted lady was not at all what he had expected.

"Shall I ring for our tea?" she asked with another flap of her lashes.

"Please."

Leaning forward—so far forward that he could not but appreciate her *belle poitrine*—she rang the silver bell resting atop the tea table.

And then realization dawned, hitting him like a load of bricks. The plunging neckline, the cosmetics, those bizarre veiled looks. The chit was attempting to flirt with him, in the hopes that a flapping of lashes and a peek of cleavage might dissuade him from purchasing her home!

His lips thinned and he wasn't sure if he was more disappointed or amused. He'd been looking forward to a stimulating interview, the same verbal contest that they'd engaged in yesterday. He'd hoped to amuse himself with Miss Simmons if for nothing else but a short respite from his constant state of boredom.

Alas, Francis's predictions had proven all too accurate. Except that in place of an old maid's tears, he was to be tormented with a green girl's coquetry.

She fussed with her skirts again, and he saw that she was more revealing her ankles than concealing them.

The transparent ploy provoked a small smirk. Perhaps there was some sport to be had here, after all. If the girl desired a flirtation, two could play this game. . . . And he could damn well play it better than she could.

"Tell me, my lord, how long have you been in Shropshire? Have you only recently arrived?"

"I came up from London a week ago," Richard answered. "You might have heard that my uncle bequeathed me Leyton Hall."

As he spoke, he turned toward her and languidly stretched his arm across the sofa's back, so that his fingertips hovered only an inch above her shoulder. She sent a hasty glance to his hand.

"My, yes." Her gaze furtively darted to his hand again. "Please accept my condolences on your recent loss."

"My thanks, though since I'd never even met the old prig, I've hardly been weeping buckets of tears over his passing. Calhoun didn't approve of me, you know. I suspect that he only left me the house out of some misplaced sense of familial obligation."

"Oh, I see," she responded uncertainly. "Well, at least, my lord, you've—"

"Please. Call me Richard. After yesterday's meeting, I feel we are well enough acquainted for such familiarity."

"Of course." She licked at her too-shiny lips "And you may call me Sabrina."

"Sabrina," he echoed softly, caressing her name with his best bedroom voice.

Nervousness flashed in her eyes—eyes that began as a pale blue around the pupil and gradually darkened to a deep forest green. Nice, he had to admit.

"It is such a lovely place though, Leyton Hall." She flashed him a vacuous smile. "I've often admired how it is situated so conveniently near the river, and its lands are so extensive and so pleasing. Why, it must be one of the nicest homes in this part of Shropshire."

She looked at him expectantly. He said nothing, but allowed his hot eyes to drift over her suggestively.

"And how very fortunate for you to visit for the first time during spring," she said, forging ahead as if he had responded to her inane prattle. "Spring in Shropshire is the most agreeable of seasons. The weather is so temperate and the flowers are beginning to bloom and . . . and . . ."

She paused, her eyes almost pleading with him to say something. But he merely leaned closer and gave her a practiced look that had burned the pantalettes off many a more experienced woman.

"I . . ." She licked at her lips again. "I do hope you plan to stay in the neighborhood."

Richard smothered a spurt of desire as he followed the path of her tongue flicking across her mouth. She was holding up well, considering that his eyes were virtually ravishing her. But he could do better.

He allowed his gaze to fall to her décolletage. "With such enticements so near at hand . . . I cannot see why I should ever wish to leave."

She blinked and glanced down to her chest as if unsure what he was staring at.

He choked back a laugh. The girl was in over her head. It was time to put this charade to an end. . . .

Slowly his fingers drifted lower, just far enough to graze her shoulder.

At his touch, she jerked away and the mask crumbled. Once again Sabrina Simmons was sporting that school-marmish demeanor he remembered so well from yesterday. "Lord Colbridge! You—"

How he would have loved to have heard her response, but Sabrina fell silent as the door swung open and the plump pigeon-maid bounced into the room with the tea tray.

He shot Sabrina a sidelong glance. Her spine was ramrod stiff and her eyes were sparkling with blue fire.

Perhaps he was behaving badly, he thought without remorse, but the chit had brought it on herself. Such amateurish flirtation would not succeed with the greenest of country bumpkins. And her motive could not be plainer if she'd embroidered it on the goddamn sofa cushion!

As the servant set out the refreshments, he heard Sabrina mutter something beneath her breath, as she tried to collect herself. He couldn't be certain, over the tinkling of silver and the clatter of plates, but it sounded like she murmured testily, "Yes, I know. I know."

He wondered what she could mean.

The maid exited and Sabrina began to pour out. He had to give her credit. It had taken her only a matter of seconds to recover her equilibrium; unusual self-control for a woman.

She passed him a cup and he could tell that she was deep in thought. He decided to try an experiment of his own.

"Sabrina, I am curious as to your remarkable facility with Latin. Where did you happen to learn?" he asked idly.

She dropped a third lump of sugar into her tea. "I would scarce call it remarkable. I've reasonable knowledge of Latin, French, Ital . . ." Her cup and saucer abruptly rattled in her hand.

"Did I say reasonable?" she hurried to amend, fluttering her lashes. And just like that, the frivolous mask was back in place. Richard's jaw tensed. Evidently he hadn't sufficiently shocked her with his own brand of flirtation.

"You must pardon me, Richard, for overstating my talents," she cooed. "I vow that you must be far more accomplished than I could ever hope to be. Not only in languages, but I'm sure in all other areas as well." Reaching over, she lightly touched his thigh and his muscle clenched in response. "I am but a simple girl with simple thoughts."

He narrowed his eyes, resisting the urge to shake her. To shake some sense back into her silly little head. Could he have been wrong about her? Or was this all part of some puzzling masquerade?

Hooking one ankle over his knee, he leaned back against the cushions and watched her prepare a plate of tiny cakes and biscuits, as if the fate of the world hung on the exact placement of each bloody biscuit.

"Do your simple thoughts generally lean toward Milton and Horace?" he asked her, determined to get to the truth.

"Oh, Richard!" She tittered. And not very well. "I must have given you such the wrong impression of me yesterday. I assure you I am no different than any other woman."

He regarded her impassively, wondering if it were so. Was she no different?

And yet. . . . Something niggled at him, leaving him dissatisfied, unsure. Why was he not repelled by her? She did not offer much in terms of beauty. Why then was he so intrigued by her, despite her feigned vacuity?

Because it was feigned, he realized. She was intentionally trying to pass herself off as dimwitted, even though anyone with sense could see the truth in those discerning blue-green eyes. But for what reason? Did it again concern Simmons House?

His annoyance eased and he actually smiled as he drained his teacup. Miss Simmons had not proven a disappointment after all. She'd presented him a mystery to solve, a new game to play. And he was intrigued enough by her—and bored enough with himself—to play it.

A clock chimed the hour and Richard knew he should take his leave.

He would have liked to have lingered, to have learned more of her intentions, but etiquette demanded he not overstay this first visit. Besides, a small part of him perversely enjoyed the fact that there were limits within which he would have to work. For what fun was a game without a few rules?

Setting his teacup on the tray, Richard rose.

"Leaving so soon?" Sabrina asked. Her disappointment appeared genuine.

Richard bowed. "It has been lovely." *Entertaining as well.* "I hope I might call again?"

"Please do. And soon," she fervently urged. And then, as if it were an afterthought, she jumped to her feet. "Allow me to show you out."

Richard followed her into the hall, moving quickly to keep up with her no-nonsense gait. She didn't walk like other women but strode along as if she were headed somewhere with a purpose. He'd become so accustomed to his own indolent limping swagger that he had to hurry to keep up with her.

The maid appeared with his hat, then proceeded to open the front door.

Richard executed one last bow to Sabrina who was worrying her lip with her small white teeth.

"Richard," she suddenly blurted out, and clutched at his sleeve as he made to go. "There is to be an assembly in town Wednesday evening. I rarely attend such affairs, but thought that I might . . . this time. That is, this Wednesday." Her cheeks had taken on the same hue as her rouged lips. "D-do you think I might see you there?"

Her forwardness surprised them both, he thought. Releasing his coat sleeve, Sabrina hurriedly dropped her gaze. He surveyed her bent head for a moment, maliciously wondering what she might do if he refused. Would he be foiling a key gambit in her stratagem?

But the temptation to see her again was too great for him to refuse. He smiled slightly. "That sounds . . . interesting. Perhaps I shall see you there?"

She nodded, not meeting his eyes.

"Good day, then," he said.

His horse was ready and waiting and he pulled himself into the saddle, sending a curious glance back to Simmons House. What had he been thinking? Normally a visit to a country dance would have appealed to him about as much as a bath in boiling oil. But how could he have resisted the pathetic desperation in her plea?

He nudged his mount with his heel and started off toward home when suddenly a high-pitched *thwang* vibrated through the air. An object smacked sharply into his temple.

"Damn!"

His horse tossed its head, and Richard grabbed at the reins as he spun around in time to see a small white-haired boy disappear around the corner of the house.

Richard's fingers automatically flew to the injury, and when he pulled them away, his glove was stained and slick with blood.

By God, he'd been beaned with a slingshot!

Chapter Six

"I am sorry, Nell. I know I didn't perform very well today."

Flopping back onto the library sofa, Sabrina sent a disgusted look at her exposed stockings, wondering wryly if the viscount had duly appreciated her trim ankles. The man would have had to have been blind not to notice them the way she'd been baring them to him every few minutes.

"Now, now, luv, you didn't do as bad as all that."

Sabrina closed her eyes and rested the back of her wrist against her forehead. "Thank you for the lie, but you needn't sugarcoat it for me. I was awful. And I let that despicable man get under my skin."

A sudden chill told Sabrina that Nell had sat down next to her. She still hadn't gotten used to the frostiness that seemed to surround the ghostly madam.

"Well," Nell said archly, *"that one would get under any-*

one's skin, my dear. He's a shrewd one, your Richie. Cunning as a fox. We might 'ave to rethink our plan."

Sabrina chuckled softly. "Her Richie" indeed. "Tell, me the truth, Nell. Do you think it hopeless?"

"Blimey, no! I can tell he rather fancies you."

"Nell, please . . ."

"No, 'pon my honor," the ghost insisted. *"If there's one thing I know it's men, and I tell you that Lord Richie looks at you the way a hungry man ogles a steamin' bowl of mutton stew."* She flashed her gap-toothed smile and Sabrina rolled her eyes.

Faith, but she would like to believe Nell. She'd like to think she was making some progress with that horrid, horrid man. Not only was this seduction business more difficult than she'd anticipated, but, even more frustrating, she was obviously not well suited to it.

If only there might be another way. But she'd examined her options a thousand times over—especially since actually meeting Lord Colbridge—and every time she had come up empty. There was simply no other way to secure the amount of money necessary to pay off the mortgage short of thievery. And stealing was both illegal and immoral. What she had planned was only immoral.

"The assembly wasn't a good idea, was it?" she asked.

Nell dabbed at her nose with a ghostly powder puff. *"Not one I'd 'ave chose."*

Sabrina threaded her fingers through her hair, dislodging all Nell's carefully constructed curls. "I must have been daft to even suggest it. How can I go into Leychurch made up like some cheap trollop—"

She caught herself. Too late.

"Oh, Nell, I didn't mean—that is to say . . ."

The ghost waved her off with a perfumed hand. Frangipani. Sabrina was getting to know it well.

"Go on," Nell said, graciously indulgent. *"I'm not ashamed of what I am. Never 'ave been. A girl does what she 'as to and that's what I did. I got meself off the streets."*

Sabrina regarded her with a faint frown. Nell as a flesh-and-blood woman? She hadn't given much thought to what the ghost's earthly existence had been like. But now it seemed important to her that she know.

"What happened?" Sabrina asked. "How did you become . . . what you became?"

Nell idly fingered the scarf looped around her neck. *"Oh, I started off like we all did. Sellin' me services on the streets—"*

"How old were you?" Sabrina interrupted, ashamed of her prurient interest.

"Oo, lemme think. I must 'ave been thirteen, I guess."

"Thirteen?" Andrew's age? Sabrina's stomach wrenched with shock and pity. "My God, Nell, where were your parents? How could they allow a child to . . ."

"Didn't 'ave a mum. No dad, neither." Nell shrugged as if it meant nothing to her, but Sabrina suspected it did.

"But you must have had parents," she argued.

"I must 'ave, but I never knew 'em."

"You never knew the love of a mother or father?"

Nell's features hardened almost imperceptibly. *"I'm like you, Sabrina. I don't believe in what I can't see and I never saw nothin' in all me years that made me believe in that rot they call 'love.'"*

A tightness filled Sabrina's throat. Although she didn't believe in romantic love, love for family was something else entirely. She could hardly credit that Nell had no experience with love. Not a mother or brother. A friend. No one.

"What about yer *mum and pa?"* Nell asked. *"Did ye rub 'long with 'em all right?"*

Frowning, Sabrina drew back, as if she could physically retreat from the question. Perhaps she hadn't exactly "rubbed along" with her parents, but she had loved them. And, more painful yet, had understood them.

But could she explain it to Nell? Explain the fence she had been forced to straddle her entire life? At once shying away from her father's emotional recklessness, while fighting not to become her mother—a woman terrified of life's passions? Yes, she had loved her parents. Loved them dearly. But above all else she feared becoming them.

"We got on," Sabrina answered evasively. "I did love them very much."

Doubt, tinged with something like envy, colored Nell's smile. It hurt Sabrina to see it.

"But you haven't yet finished your story," she prodded. "How did you get by all on your own?"

"Well, me earliest memories are of workin' the Strand, pickin' pockets. I did that 'til I was thirteen or so, and soon after, I was lucky 'nough to get into a shop."

"A shop?"

Nell lifted a brow. *"An academy, bawdy house. The abbess took a shine to me 'cause I was sharp. So she taught me to read and let me 'elp with the books, so I didn't 'ave to work upstairs. I'm telling' ye, gettin' off the streets saved me life, it did. Anyhow, when old Rosie cocked up 'er toes, I took over. I must 'ave been eighteen or there'bouts."*

Nell's gaze had grown distant and cloudy as if she were looking back to her years on earth, and suddenly it struck Sabrina that her own situation could have been much graver than it was. How could she bemoan her circumstances when the fates had been so much kinder to her than they'd been to poor Nell?

At least she had Simmons House. She had grown up in comfort, not in the back alleys of London. And if she had to give herself to the Viscount Colbridge, it could not begin to compare to what Nell had been forced to do merely to survive, to keep food in her mouth.

But, above all, Sabrina, unlike Nell, knew what it was to love and to be loved. She had Teddy and Andrew. And the memory of her parents. Nell had had nothing.

Remarkably though—and Sabrina honestly thought it remarkable—despite all the adversity life had meted out to her, Nell seemed neither bitter nor mean-spirited. She was a bit rough around the edges but, at heart, she was a good soul. Or spirit.

Nell had weathered life's hard knocks—and death's—and still could smile.

Sabrina suddenly felt ashamed of herself. Instead of looking down her nose at Nell, she should be following her example. Endure. Persevere. Strive.

Renewed with determination, Sabrina sat up straighter, slamming her fist into her palm. "Well, to borrow from Shakespeare's Ulysses, perseverance keeps honour bright. If I am to be honorable in this endeavor I *cannot* give up so easily."

"*Right you are,*" Nell agreed with a firm shake of her head. Her bonnet bounced, swaying faux pearls and ribands. "*We'll simply 'ave to keep workin' at it.*"

The ghost folded her arms across her massive bosom and looked Sabrina over like a butcher sizing up a side of beef.

"*Tonight, now, I want you to soak yer head twice as long as you did last night, Sabrina. The lemon juice is doin' some good, but your hair isn't as shiny as it ought to be. And 'ow are you doin' with those bosom exercises?*"

Sabrina placed her palms together in front of her chest. "I did two hundred this morning, as you ordered."

"*We better make it three 'undred,*" Nell said flatly.

Sabrina nodded.

"And we'll need to spend some time practicin' your coy glances. I feared you was goin' to sprain an eyelid the way you was goin' about it earlier."

Sabrina blinked, testing her lids. Maybe she had sprained something.

"All right, luv, watch close," Nell ordered. *"You tilt your head just so. Right, that's it. Now, slowly lower your lashes . . ."*

"I haven't seen you tip so heavily since you lost that thousand pounds to Mills last year," Francis commented, as Richard replenished his wine glass yet again.

" 'Twas a damn foolish wager," Richard conceded. He emptied the claret bottle and shook it a few times for good measure to ensure that every last drop had fallen into his glass. Three other bottles had already been drained and removed from the table.

"Oh, I don't know. I might have taken that wager myself if I weren't such a cautious fellow. Who'd have thought old Mills could actually stuff his foot into his mouth?" Francis wagged his head in disbelief. "Does make one wonder how the blighter passes his time, doesn't it?"

Richard grunted. "Well, being cautious must have its advantages. One need only look to your finances in comparison to my own for proof of that."

Francis squirmed self-consciously. He hated to discuss his wealth. "Oh come on, now, Richard. Once you marry and take control of the rest of that inheritance, you'll be well enough off. It's a tidy sum you're looking at. Most respectable."

Richard dipped his head in acknowledgment. "Thank you, Francis. 'Tis so reassuring to know that all I must do is sell myself like any good prostitute and the money is mine."

"Sell yourself? Confound it, you and the institution of marriage! If you're so damned opposed to it, forego the inheritance then, won't you?"

Richard glowered at him. Francis had an uncanny knack of hitting to the heart of a matter. He *could* forego the inheritance; he didn't need riches. He could get by on what he had. But for some reason it seemed spineless to choose bachelorhood over the money. As if he were not able to face up to his fears.

"I say, I'm sorry I snapped at you," Francis apologized. Richard flinched, unable to remember the last time he had begged anyone's pardon.

"But in my defense, I must say that you have been intolerably churlish this afternoon." Francis regarded him questioningly. "I did happen to notice that you received a letter from Miss Wetherby today. No unfortunate news, I trust?"

"Hardly. Just the typical drivel."

Francis set to studiously filling his pipe, not even glancing up to ask, "Nothing of interest then? She didn't happen to mention or write about—"

"For heaven's sake, you can read it if you're so blasted interested." Richard jammed his fist into his pocket and produced the letter.

Francis eyed it with caution. "Oh, I don't know. Probably not good form to read someone else's . . ."

Flicking his wrist, Richard tossed the note across the table where it landed beside the earl's wine glass. "I told you, it's nothing but gossip. A narrative of Lady Dayton's rout, I believe."

Gingerly Francis picked the letter up from the table. "Well, if you have no objection . . ."

With an indifferent shrug, Richard dismissed him and Francis quickly tucked Charlotte's correspondence into his own coat pocket.

"So if it wasn't unhappy tidings from Town, what *has* put you into such a foul humor? . . . Ah-hah!" Francis lifted a finger as if struck with inspiration. "Tea at Simmons House. Pray, don't tell me that old lady Simmons performed a miracle and actually stirred up feelings of guilt in you?"

Richard tipped his wine glass and let its contents flow down his gullet.

"No. No guilt," he answered. No guilt, but a lot of other unfathomable emotions he could not name. He'd had a deuce of a time thinking of anything but Sabrina Simmons since he'd returned from Simmons House. It had to be her novelty, he decided, the challenge she presented. What could the silly wench be up to?

Richard glanced to the earl, who was drawing contentedly on his pipe. Francis understood the female mind. He might he able to shed light on Richard's senseless preoccupation with the girl.

"I don't suppose," Richard asked with studied indifference, "that you'd have any interest in accompanying me into the village Wednesday evening?"

"And why should I wish to do that?"

"Well, I understand there is supposed to be some type of assembly. It might prove diverting."

"A country assembly? Rubbing shoulders with the masses?" Francis wrinkled his nose. "Sorry, but I'm scheduled to have my eyes gouged out on Wednesday; a much pleasanter pastime, I'm sure."

"Come on now, Francis, consider it a good deed on your part. You can educate the provincials as to the latest fashions while taking the opportunity to display your fancy plumage."

Francis pursed his lips. "I suppose it might not be too wearisome."

With a faint grin, Richard raked his fingers through his hair, inadvertently scraping the scab that had formed at his temple.

"Damn," he muttered. A warm stickiness began to drip down the side of his face and he blotted it with his napkin.

"Are you bleeding?" Francis demanded.

"Mmm. I had a run-in with a pint-sized David this afternoon. I should thank my stars that the urchin didn't take out my eye."

"Now this sounds interesting. Who was the child?"

"I would guess he was Miss Simmons's brother."

"Brother?" Francis sat back in his chair. Richard followed the progression of his thoughts, determining the exact moment the earl realized his error. "Wait here now. Just how old is our neighboring spinster?"

"Twenty. Twenty-one."

"And you didn't tell me?"

"Do you care?"

Francis's affronted expression went blank. "No, I suppose not. But I still think it bloody odd you didn't tell me."

He cast a curious glance at Richard, who kept his features bland, wary of Francis's bursts of insight. He didn't want his friend to ask—nor did he wish to ask himself—why he hadn't told him about Sabrina.

"So, pray tell, what did you do to the lad for him to draw your blood?" the earl asked. "Or was it rather something you did to his sister?"

"I assure you the attack was wholly unprovoked."

Francis's nose twitched like a hound picking up a scent. "I see. And is the sister equally as hot-tempered?"

Richard didn't care for his friend's tone. Merrick was on to something and he knew it.

Richard fabricated a yawn, stretching his arms to his sides. "You know, old man, I believe the claret has finally caught up with me. I'm going to stumble off to bed while I can yet walk. Good night, Francis."

He pushed away from the table, refusing to meet Francis's eye. Though the veriest dandy, the Earl Merrick could be as clairvoyant as a carnival gypsy when he set his mind to it.

A half hour later, Richard sat at a writing desk in his bed chamber, whittling at a pen. He was cloaked in a sinfully luxurious velvet robe, a gift from one of his lovers—not one of his mistresses, but a lady he had been involved with last year. Who had it been? Lady Chattington, perhaps?

Richard shrugged and shaved another bit from the pen. He couldn't say why he was squandering his time trying to remember who had given him the nightrobe. It didn't matter. It was only another aimless question to occupy his thoughts. To keep them from straying to Sabrina Simmons.

He had been planning to write about her. Her gauche endeavors this afternoon would have made fine fodder for Ennui's next essay, what with the unsophisticated flirtation and glaringly conspicuous motive. It could have made for an amusing article.

But though he had hoped that in writing of her he might exorcise her from his mind, he hadn't been able to do either. Intent on sketching a blistering portrait of a provincial coquette, he had picked up his poison pen and encountered a mental block as thick as a stone wall.

He'd jotted down a few sentences, then scratched them out. He'd started afresh on a clean sheet of paper, only to toss it into the fire, and repeat the process with a third. The problem lay not in his choice of words, but in his subject. How could he describe her when she was as unclear to him as the muddiest waters of the Severn?

She was intelligent, yet behaved as if she hadn't a brain in her head. Her conduct vacillated between that of a nun and that of a demimondaine. She was not beautiful or even pretty, but she aroused him more than any woman he could remember meeting in years.

What was it? Was he just so bored that one contrary country chit could tie him up in knots? Lord knows, he'd been sinking steadily into a life of monotonous decadence and depravity, where even the smallest item was seized like a lifeline if it offered a momentary break from the mind-numbing tedium of his existence.

Sabrina offered such a break; she was a moment's respite in a lifetime of ennui.

Whereas his father—may he rot in hell—had successfully battled boredom with whoring and booze, Richard had not been so lucky. He'd tried, by God, he'd tried. He'd experimented with all the stimulants: drink, drugs, danger.

During the past dozen years, he'd downed oceans of gin, dabbled in opium, and laid his life on the line in the seediest brews of London. Nothing had worked. Granted, sexual diversion had been useful in keeping the boredom at bay for a short time; but even in that, Richard resented that he required someone else—especially a woman—to drive away his demon, Apathy.

He just didn't give a damn. About much of anything.

Until now his writing had been his only outlet, his satirical attacks on society serving to feed a bitterness he refused to examine too closely. But he knew from where it came. He could not delude himself that easily.

Richard threw down his pen in disgust, knowing he would be unable to write.

Staring at the ink-splattered page, he told himself that if he had any sense, he would throw down his pen for good. Not that it mattered, but if Society were ever to learn of his identity as Ennui, there would be serious hell to pay. That piece he'd written last year had even had Prinny calling for his head. Something about the gouty Regent wielding his fork more productively than his scepter . . .

Richard shrugged. What should he care? Undeniably his unmasking would result in a scandal, but 'twould not be the first the Kerry name had suffered. The scandal his mother had brewed so many years ago still haunted the memories of a few people—he glanced to his maimed leg—and scarred the memories of others.

Linking his fingers behind his head, Richard leaned back in his chair and brushed aside unwanted remembrances. His thoughts drifted again to Sabrina.

Really, he thought, he should be grateful to the girl for providing him a distraction. At least, he could look forward to one evening where he would not expire from boredom.

But which Sabrina Simmons would appear at the country assembly Wednesday? Would it be the straitlaced scholar or the incompetent coquette?

Chapter
Seven

"Nell, please stop nattering at me so," Sabrina whispered behind her fan. "I can scarce think with all your talk."

Though invisible—per Sabrina's request—Nell hadn't stopped prattling since they'd left Simmons House.

"I weren't natterin'," the ghost's disembodied voice protested. *"I was just sayin' that a wee bit more rouge wouldn't 'ave killed you none. Your color is off, Sabrina luv, and we both know you've got to look your best for Lord Richie."*

"And I explained to *you*, Nell, that Leychurch is a far cry from London. I've made a big enough stir as it is, showing up here tonight. Have you not heard their whispers? 'That dowdy Simmons girl?' 'The book-loving bluestocking?' I cannot imagine what all they must be saying to see me in a gown like this with my face powdered and painted." She self-consciously lifted her fan higher, her gaze nervously scanning the half-empty assembly room.

In spite of the whispers, Sabrina knew that she could not blame her discomfort on her Shropshire neighbors. The people of Leychurch were, for the most part, pleasant enough folk who enjoyed a spot of harmless gossip now and then. Naturally, Sabrina's gussied-up appearance was going to be commented upon.

And she would not have to feel so ill at ease, if only she were more comfortable in this milieu. But when it came to being a social butterfly, Sabrina thought of herself as more of a . . . moth.

Because of their mother's affliction, her parents had rarely entertained, so Sabrina had never learned the oh-so-important art of meaningless conversation. Idle chitchat and insincere flattery did not trip easily from her tongue. Often at gatherings like these, she would forget herself and answer a question about weaving with a passage from *The Odyssey*. If the discussion around her turned to hunting, she would somehow end up relating the story of Actaeon in all its gruesome detail. She could not seem to help herself.

Tonight, however, she had her very own Cyrano, in the shape of a ghostly madam, lurking behind her and dispensing the appropriate inanities.

"Now, remember, luv," Nell prompted. *"When Lord Richie shows up, I want you to bloody well tip over the butter boat on 'im. Believe me, there's nothin' a bloke loves more than a pretty word about his manly shoulders or shapely calves."*

Shapely calves? Sabrina wrinkled her nose, wondering whether Madame dePompadour had been obliged to praise Louis the Fifteenth's limbs in order to curry his favor. She suspected not.

Tucked in her corner, Sabrina watched the musicians

preparing, their randomly plucked notes dotting the conversational buzz. The dances would be beginning soon and Lord Colbridge had yet to appear. In fact, many local residents were absent tonight. According to the sisters Glanding, who were serving as Sabrina's chaperones this evening, the assembly's attendance was poor due to a recent outbreak of mumps.

Though Sabrina felt sorry for those afflicted, she was just as glad not to have to face the entire village. Her transformation from ugly duckling to passable sparrow had generated sufficient talk.

"Cooeee!" Nell suddenly murmured in Sabrina's ear. *"Would you take a gander at the fella who just walked in!"* The ghost made a throaty sound of approval. *"Mmm-mm, if he ain't as pretty as one of them museum statues."*

Sabrina turned toward the door. An impeccably dressed man of obvious breeding had entered, his London elegance a striking contrast to the Leychurchians' rustic attire. With hair the color of pale ale, a straight nose, and a square jaw, the stranger was pleasing to look upon, Sabrina had to admit. But he could not hold her attention once Richard appeared in the doorway behind him.

In fact, the entire room seemed to grow smaller when Richard stepped into it. Or so Sabrina felt. The musicians suspended tuning their instruments, the drone of voices faded into quiet. Like the blast when opening an oven door, Richard's presence swept through the chamber—dark, hot, and dangerous—reaching into every corner. Her corner.

His gaze lit on her and all the moisture in Sabrina's mouth abruptly evaporated. She felt herself trapped, ensnared. But then he released her, his eyes shuttling past.

Lord Rand, an impoverished baron and the self-appointed master of Leychurch's thin society, hurried forward to greet the patrician guests. The musicians resumed their tuning as conversation resumed, and Sabrina swallowed to moisten her dry mouth.

"Pike my peepers if I've ever laid eyes on such a comely bloke," Nell purred, still rhapsodizing over the fair-haired stranger.

"I wonder who he is?" Sabrina idly asked.

"A chum of Lord Richie's. Known each other since they was in leadin' strings together."

Nell's certitude surprised her. "How on earth do you know that?"

"To tell you the truth, I don't rightly know how I know. Some kind of feeling I've picked up. Must 'ave somethin' to do with bein' a ghost, I imagine. Just came to me."

"Ghostly intuition?" How very interesting. Every day it seemed that Sabrina and Nell learned one more feature of the spectral condition. "Do you sense anything else? About Richard in particular?"

"Sorry, luv. The feelings just sorta pop up. Can't explain 'em or govern 'em."

With a small disappointed frown, Sabrina snapped shut her fan. She could have used a little supernatural advantage in her dealings with Richard Kerry; any insight into that very disturbing man's character would have certainly been of use to her. Especially tonight, when she had vowed to do a better job of flirting than she'd done the other day at tea. Hours upon hours, she and Nell had worked diligently as Sabrina had tried to master the intricacies of seduction.

"Oh, look, 'ere he comes."

Sabrina's pulse instantly quickened, before she saw that Nell referred to Richard's blonde companion, not Richard. While the viscount conversed across the room with the aged war hero Captain Quinn, Lord Rand was circling the floor with Richard's friend, making the introductions.

As Lord Rand approached with his disinterested-looking

charge, Sabrina could not help but appreciate the irony. *This* was how she had initially pictured Richard. A fair-haired fop. Right down to the elaborately coiffed curls and cinnamon-brown eyes.

"Lord Merrick, may I introduce Miss Simmons, one of our locale's lovely and learned ladies?"

Sabrina smiled, reminded of Lord Rand's fondness for alliterative effect.

"And Miss Simmons, the *Earl* Merrick"—Lord Rand savored the word "earl" as if it were a particularly delicious treat—"who does us great honor tonight with his presence. Lord Merrick is a houseguest of our newest resident at Leyton Hall, the Viscount Colbridge."

Sabrina heard Nell's blissful sigh sound behind her.

"This is a pleasure, Miss Simmons. Lord Colbridge had mentioned to me our great fortune in neighboring such a charming lady and I heartily second his opinion."

Though doubtful that Richard had ever described her as charming, much less spoken of her, Sabrina refrained from saying so aloud. She was too busy wondering if Lord Merrick's presence at Leyton Hall would have an impact upon her plans.

As the earl bowed over her hand, the musicians began to play in earnest as couples moved toward the center of the floor.

"A reel, how jolly," Lord Merrick said. "Will you stand up with me for the first set, Miss Simmons?"

Oh, no. Even Teddy danced with more elegance than she. "I'm not much of a—"

"You bet your sweet arse, you will!" a familiar voice blustered in Sabrina's ear, making her wince.

With a strained smile, and a vow to leave her opinionated ghost home next time, Sabrina corrected herself. "I'd be delighted."

The earl led her out to join the other couples while Sabrina surreptitiously searched for Richard. Easily identified by his coal-black shoulder-length hair, he stood with his back to the dance floor, still in conversation with Captain Quinn.

Without thinking, she asked the earl, "Does Lord Colbridge not dance?" As soon as she said it, she recalled his limp. "Oh, how thoughtless of me. His infirmity . . ."

"No, Miss Simmons, not thoughtless of you at all. In fact, Richard dances and fences and rides. He's a remarkably skilled athlete. I assure you his leg bothers him not one whit." He then added enigmatically, "At least, not in the physical sense."

Sabrina's eyebrows lifted. She would have liked to have questioned the earl as to his meaning, but the dance called for her to swing away and circle. When they rejoined hands, she returned to the subject, hoping she did not appear overly inquisitive, "How did the viscount happen to come by his injury? The war?"

Lord Merrick hesitated. "A carriage accident," he briefly offered. "But I warn you that Richard does not like to speak of it."

Curious, Sabrina again let her gaze drift across the room. She would not have believed the cavalier viscount to be self-conscious about anything, much less such a relatively minor affliction. Had he, after all, an Achilles heel?

"Pssstt." Nell's sibilant whisper caused Sabrina to lose a step and stumble. *"Go on,"* the ghost instructed from an invisible point somewhere to Sabrina's left. *"Say somethin' flatterin'."*

"Not Lord Merrick," Sabrina whispered out of the side of her mouth. "I am not trying to seduce him, for heaven's sake."

"Blimey, why not? He looks rich as Croesus and tasty as a quince tart."

Tasty as a— Sabrina rolled her eyes, waiting until the dance called for her to spin away from the earl before quietly murmuring, "Simmons House, remember?"

"Pooh," she heard Nell scoff. *"A bloke with that kinda blunt can set ye up wherever he pleases. Go on, luv, why don't ye tell 'im . . ."*

"Would you let me be?" Sabrina blurted out.

The earl's fingers stiffened in hers. "I beg your pardon?"

Blast and double blast. Mentally shooting daggers at Nell, Sabrina scurried to cover her gaffe, flashing the earl her most brilliant smile. "Would you let me be . . . so forward as to compliment you on your pin, Lord Merrick? The setting is most unusual."

To Sabrina's relief, the earl gobbled up the flummery hook, line, and sinker. "Why, thank you, Miss Simmons," he preened, clearly gratified by her praise. "I take great care in the selection of my jewelry, you know. Only one or two London establishments carry the quality of . . ."

Sabrina didn't know the first thing about gems or baubles, but smiled politely as the earl discoursed. Albeit proud in his appearance, Lord Merrick did not strike her as an arrogant man. And in spite of his dandified ways, she rather liked him.

"Alas, my sartorial interests are not shared by my friend," the earl sighed, his eye falling critically on the plainly dressed Lord Colbridge. "Many is the time I think the man would prefer sackcloth and ashes. Might ease his conscience," he mumbled as if to himself.

Sabrina's eyes widened. Richard Kerry, the notorious rake, possessed a conscience?

Unhappily the dance concluded before she could pry further into Lord Merrick's intriguing comments and, when next she glanced up, she realized that the earl was leading her toward Richard. Captain Quinn had gone to join the second set of dancers, so the viscount stood alone as they approached.

"Richard," the earl hailed him. "See what fortune follows us. Our neighbor, Miss Simmons."

Curling her fingers, Sabrina steeled herself to meet Richard's eyes. Those unfathomable, soul-penetrating eyes. Still, when their gazes locked, she could not stop the physical jolt that shook her.

"Sabrina," Richard greeted, inclining his head and somehow turning even that gesture of courtesy into an act of mockery.

"Richard." She curtsied.

"Lower," Nell's voice urged. *"You want to make sure he gets himself an eyeful."*

Obediently Sabrina deepened the curtsy enough to display her meager bosom.

"Already dropped the formalities, have we?" Lord Merrick piped in, appearing inordinately pleased with the discovery. "Well then, I daresay you'll want to have a turn around the dance floor, Richard, before the enchanting Miss Simmons finds her dance card full."

Sabrina blushed and the ghost instructed in a whisper, *"Giggle."*

Sabrina obligingly produced a titter that was more nerves than flirtation.

"Not bad," the ghost opined.

Thanks, Sabrina thought wryly.

Waving his hand, Richard indicated the couples pairing off for the next set. "Shall we?" he asked, without any real enthusiasm.

Sabrina faltered. The prospect of being held in Richard's arms . . . A sharp, ghostly poke between the shoulders reminded her of her mission. As she accepted Richard's hand, his touch sent an icy shiver tingling up her spine.

"Remember your lessons now," Nell hissed as Richard led her onto the floor. *"And no talk of Play-toe!"*

Right. No Plato. Only simpering, cooing, and eyelash batting.

The opening notes of the quadrille set them in motion. Sabrina noticed that Richard did not seem at all hindered by his limp—of course, she would notice since she had yet to raise her gaze from his shoes. With enviable grace, he spun and twirled, accommodating his weaker leg with subtle shifts of his weight.

"Are you enjoying yourself?" she asked, daring to lift her eyes as high as his neckcloth. "You do not find our little gathering too unimaginative for your taste?"

"Unimaginative? On the contrary, Sabrina, rarely have I witnessed such *novelty* as I have in this room."

A small frown creased her brow and she deliberately smoothed it out. Must he always taunt her with his riddles?

Forcing her gaze to his, she dipped her lashes to seductively shield her eyes. Just as Nell had taught her. "Whatever could you find novel here in Leychurch? I would have thought you'd miss the many diversions of London."

His lips quirked. "I assure you, I find sufficient diversion right here."

Though breathless beneath his scrutiny, she made herself contrive another giggle. "Why, Richard, if you continue to look at me so, I will think it is *I* you find so intriguing."

She waited expectantly for him to answer. Surely a gentleman would cough up the required flattery.

"In truth," Richard answered, sidestepping her ploy, "I find the quiet of country life surprisingly refreshing. I long not at all for London."

"Oh." Deflated, Sabrina tried again. "But you must miss

your friends. Aren't you afraid that you might become . . . lonely at Leyton Hall?"

The faint narrowing of his eyes suggested that now *she* had confused *him*. "No."

Sabrina's courage began to slip. This tactic was getting her nowhere. Pour on the compliments, Nell had said.

"You dance beautifully, Richard. You are very light on your feet."

Then, curse the fates, she chose that precise moment to miss a step and tread firmly across his toes.

"Oh." She felt herself pinken.

"And you are remarkably light on my feet, as well," he countered dryly.

Her cheeks flamed even hotter. Far be it for the fiendish man to let her blunder pass without comment.

"Tell 'im he has fetchin' eyes," a voice breathed in her ear.

Sabrina jerked her head to the side as if to discourage a bothersome insect.

"Tell 'im he's the spankin' finest figure of a bloke you've met . . ."

"Spanking—" Sabrina sputtered.

Richard's black brows curved up. "For treading on my toes?" His eyes glinted wickedly. "A bit harsh perhaps but I'd be happy to oblige."

A humiliated gasp was all Sabrina could manage.

In the background, she could hear Nell chortling. Above her, Richard's eyes were gleaming with devilish amusement. Beneath her, her knees were threatening to give way, weakened by mortification.

Every instinct told her to flee. Every bit of her cried out for her to run from the room as fast as her spindly legs would carry her. But *no.* She categorically refused to be cowed by this man.

She was going to seduce Richard Kerry if it killed her! And the way matters were progressing, she thought she might very well expire of embarrassment before this seduction was complete.

Struggling for composure, Sabrina glanced over Richard's shoulder, noting the many heads bent in whispered conversation. Her flaming red face must have drawn their attention.

Gather your wits, Sabrina sternly counseled herself. But 'twas difficult to think with any sense of logic once her mind had formed a picture of her sprawled across Richard's knees, her bottom bared, . . .

"Ah," Richard groaned softly.

Sabrina winced. Faith, but she had trounced on Richard's foot yet again. And then she realized why. He had stopped dancing and she was still moving. While she had been lost in her thoughts—utterly shocking thoughts—the music had come to an end.

Richard released her hand. "A pleasure, Sabrina. If a painful one."

She had botched the flirtation again! By Jove, she simply could not let him walk away without . . .

"Richard!"

He turned to her, his expression hinting of impatience.

Now, what should she say? It was too difficult to invite him to Simmons House with the boys about . . .

"M-might I see you at the fair this weekend?" she suddenly asked, giving him a desperate, simpering smile. She knew that he must think her the most brazen of women. "I would greatly welcome your company if you would care to meet me there?"

Richard's brows hitched together and beneath his gaze, Sabrina felt as if she were being stripped bare. His response sounded almost angry.

"I do not see how I will be able to resist."

* * *

On the ride home, bouncing along in the borrowed carriage, Nell could tell that her pupil was battling a severe case of the dismals.

"Come on, luv. Give us a smile. I think you did a bang-up job t'night."

A dispirited sigh fluttered the lace around Sabrina's collar. "I am quite sure that Richard finds me a dreadful ninny, Nell. He is not stupid, you know. The only reason I can fathom why he prizes witlessness in a woman is that he is too lazy to exercise his own intellect.

"I must have been mad to ever believe I could pull this off. I will never be able to make myself into a proper seductress."

"Gor, luv, you've only been at this seducin' business a few days. Give yerself some time. You're cottonin' on."

"I am not so certain time is the answer." Sabrina's lips pursed together ruefully. "Nell, I fear there is something I have overlooked, some crucial element of my education. For instance . . ." Nell could hear a blush steal into Sabrina's voice. "The jest that Richard made about . . . spanking. You and he seemed to find it ever so entertaining, whereas I—"

Nell shook her head in a flash of understanding.

"Sabrina, luv, you're a clever li'l piece and you read books and all that, but . . ." Nell gave her a hard look. *"When you first called on me to teach you 'ow to seduce a fella, did you know just what it was you was askin'?"*

Sabrina sat up straighter against the squabs, her eyes growing round. "Oh. Well. I am not exactly familiar with all the particulars."

"Hmm-mm?" Nell prodded.

"Yes, ah. I believe a bed is involved. And, um, there is kissing." She glanced up hesitantly. "Is there more?"

A sly grin slipped out. *"Oh, there's more, all right. A fair sight more. But we're better off stickin' with the basics, and savin' the finer points fer later."* Nell tugged at the tops of her gloves. *"Now listen close, luv, you'll need to pay attention. Have you ever seen a man without 'is knickers?"*

"Teddy, when he was a baby."

Nell chuckled to herself. *"Blimey, Sabrina, somethin' tells me yer Lord Richie ain't goin' to look like no baby. No sirree, not that fella. You see, luv, a man's put together different-like . . ."*

Chapter Eight

"He's a real stud, this one is. On a good day, he can cover six mares in a single afternoon."

Sabrina flushed and glanced to the animal under discussion, a proud-looking stallion with a glistening black coat. Pawing impatiently at the ground, the animal seemed eager to be about its business. Or on to another mare.

The two gentlemen farmers praising the horse stood with their backs to Sabrina, obviously not aware that she'd come up behind them.

Before she could announce her presence, Mr. Davis sent a familiar jab into Mr. Jensen's side.

"From what I hear, Jensen, the new lord of the manor would put this horse of yours to shame. Rumor has it that six a day is standard fare for the Viscount Colbridge."

The two men burst into laughter as fire coursed into

Sabrina's cheeks. She backed away, nearly tripping over a willow crate housing a pair of geese. The geese honked, but their protest was drowned out by the general hubbub of noise, laughter, and animal cries that charged the air.

Hastily she opened her parasol and hid her burning face behind it. *Six a day?*

Ever since Nell's edifying lesson on bedroom intimacy, Sabrina had been spending far too much time trying to picture what the ghost had described. She'd lain awake nights, trying to envision herself with Richard . . . doing *that*.

To her mind, it seemed implausible, if not downright impossible. The logistics alone . . . But Nell assured her that not only was it possible, there was more than one way to go about it! She just couldn't see how—

"Miss Simmons."

Sabrina jumped guiltily, especially mortified at her thoughts' direction, when she recognized the voice and its owner, Mr. Hurley, Leychurch's vicar.

"Mr. Hurley," she greeted, and lowered the parasol to further shadow her face. Although she'd insisted that Nell not make her up so heavily today, the change in her appearance was bound to draw notice from those who'd not seen her at the assembly.

And she was right.

The vicar's gaze dipped to her neckline, lingering until Sabrina cleared her throat.

"Ahem."

He directed his ferrety eyes higher. "Miss Simmons, you *are* looking well."

"And you, sir," she lied. Frail and pasty-complected, Mr. Hurley appeared more bilious than customary today. Even his breath had an unhealthy odor to it. She sidled back a step.

"We have missed you these past months. I hope your brothers are well?"

"Very well, thank you," she said, refusing to make excuses for their Sunday absences.

In fact, it had been nearly a year since she and the boys had last attended a service; since the day of their father's funeral. The earth was still being shoveled onto her father's grave when Sabrina had stumbled upon a group of parishioners gossiping. Gossiping about them. About their unfortunate circumstances, and their father's financial failings. About her poor marriage prospects. She had not since set foot in All Saints Church.

"You must let us know if we may be of any assistance to you," Mr. Hurley said. "After all, our mission is to serve our congregation. Particularly those of our flock who have fallen on hard times."

Sabrina clenched her jaw. "Thank you, Mr. Hurley, but we are doing well. Very well."

"Oh." His puff of foul breath forced Sabrina back another step. "I had heard differently. Well, if there is anything, anything at all, that *I* might do to—"

"Here you are, Miss Simmons," a deep voice interrupted.

As if from nowhere, Lord Colbridge materialized at the vicar's side, looking even more disturbingly masculine than Sabrina had remembered him.

He had removed his coat and draped it over one shoulder, hooking it by a negligent thumb. Hatless, with his midnight hair loose and his cravat rumpled, and his eyes narrowed into the sun, he appeared rugged and robust. And dangerously appealing.

"Lord Colbridge, how nice to see you again," she said, nonplussed to realize that she meant it. At least, to some degree. "Have you made the acquaintance of Leychurch's vicar, Mr. Hurley?"

The two men exchanged brief nods. Mr. Hurley's was notably reserved.

"I understand, Lord Colbridge, that you've only recently come to our part of the country," the vicar said in an accusing tone. As if arriving uninvited to Leychurch were a sin in and of itself.

"You understand correctly."

"Well, I should warn you, my lord," the vicar said, clicking his tongue, "that Shropshire is *not* London."

"I had noticed the difference."

"We have certain standards here in the country, certain principles to live by. I am sure that a man of your position appreciates the importance of setting a good example for the community."

Richard merely shifted his weight from one foot to the other and Sabrina thought he looked excruciatingly bored.

Mr. Hurley persisted. "I might then hope to see you at next Sunday's service?"

Staring past the vicar's shoulder, Richard said blandly, "You might hope, but it would not be of much use."

Sabrina had to press her lips together to keep from grinning at the vicar's affronted expression.

"I . . ." He gaped. "Well!"

He stiffened and turned to her. "Miss Simmons, I must bid you good day, but before I go I feel it my duty to speak to you as your spiritual counselor." Sliding his gaze meaningfully in Richard's direction, he lowered his voice. "Be on guard, I urge you. A young woman alone, and in your unhappy circumstances, cannot be too cautious of her reputation, you know."

"I wouldn't worry if I were you, vicar," Richard taunted. "Miss Simmons is in capable hands."

He held up his large gloved palm and smiled slowly.

"Indeed!" Mr. Hurley gasped. He sent her one more weighty glance before he pursed his lips and stalked away.

Although Sabrina knew firsthand how cutting Richard's sarcasm could be, she could not feel sorry for the vicar. He was really a rather odious man with his roaming eyes and feigned solicitude. And what was this about being her "spiritual counselor?" Why, to her mind, Nell, a confessed prostitute, was better qualified to act in that role than the insincere Mr. Hurley.

"Charming fellow," Richard murmured as the clergyman disappeared from sight. "May I?" He offered her his arm.

Sabrina hesitated only a second, thinking of the impression Richard had just given Leychurch's vicar. Following their dance together at the assembly—and her fiery blush that had been noticed by all—Sabrina had assumed that half the town would be speculating on her relationship with the Viscount Colbridge. And gossip was sure to be fueled by her appearance with him today at the fair.

But, she told herself stoutly, there was no point in acting the hypocrite. As much as she might prefer to be discreet, the gossips' tongues did have reason to wag.

She mustered her courage and laid her fingertips on Richard's shirtsleeve. His skin felt hot, the muscles in his forearm flexing at her touch. She barely stopped herself from jerking her hand away.

Why? she asked herself. Why did she always react so strongly to this man? For some reason, when she was with Richard, she felt achingly aware of both him and of herself. He made her feel almost too alive, too sensitive to every sound, every touch. She found this heightened awareness disconcerting in the extreme.

Together they began to stroll toward the central part of the fair, to the brightly colored booths lined up in the distance. The aroma of pies and sweetmeats mingled with the scent of hay and livestock, perfuming the warm day with a spicy sharpness. The hum of fair activity was punctuated every few minutes by the plaintive call of a penned animal.

"I had begun to wonder if you'd decided against coming," Sabrina said, uncomfortable with their silence.

"And miss the opportunity to see you again, sweet Sabrina?"

Mockery faintly stained his voice, and she peeked at him beneath the brim of the parasol. He was looking straight ahead so that she could tell nothing from his expression.

"I questioned whether you would want another opportunity after my mistreatment of your feet the other night." She tried to give him a flirtatious smile, but her lips were trembling too violently.

"A little trodding of my toes is not likely to keep me from what I want," Richard answered.

Sabrina's ears grew hot. *What did Richard want?*

"And where is Lord Merrick?" she asked, searching for a safe topic. "Did he not join you?"

Richard smiled faintly. "Lord Merrick draws the line at rural assemblies. A common country fair would have Francis abed for weeks."

Unsure of his meaning, Sabrina remained silent.

"Did you come into town alone?" Richard asked as they passed by the first booth.

Most of the crowd had gathered near the roundabout where the games had begun, so that only a handful of fairgoers milled about at this end of the grounds. "No, our servant Hattie came with me. She is helping at her sister's booth, selling jams and pickles."

"So it's just the two of us for the afternoon?"

Sabrina's toes curled. "Y-yes."

Although their party might have been a threesome, if she hadn't convinced Nell to remain at Simmons House. The ghost had wanted to tag along, but Sabrina had persuaded her to stay home. It was simply too distracting the way Nell floated about, continually dropping tidbits of advice into her ear.

She surreptitiously tugged at the lace fichu in her bodice. As they drew nearer to the fair's main festivities, she was beginning to recognize people. Her Leychurch neighbors. Mr. and Mrs. Pointeaux, Sir Wesley, the Glanding sisters . . .

Some nodded cordially; some forgot to nod, they were so busy staring slack jawed at the sight of the bluestocking Simmons girl walking with an infamous rake; and some brave souls actually stopped to obtain an introduction.

"Sabrina, is that you?" Mary Kingston waddled toward them, her bright eyes snapping with interest. "Why, I hardly recognized you, dear."

Sabrina summoned a wan smile. Although she'd always enjoyed Miss Kingston's company—the spirited spinster held interesting and progressive views on women's rights—Sabrina cursed the fact that their paths should cross today. Last year, Sabrina had helped transcribe a book Miss Kingston had written, one advancing her radical feminist theories.

The spinster smiled and indicated Richard with the point of her cane. "And who is this?" she asked bluntly.

Sabrina was obliged to make the introductions.

"Colbridge? I think I have heard of you, young man."

Richard's mouth twisted. "I would urge you not to believe everything you hear."

"Hmmph." Mary Kingston's gaze swung back and forth between Richard and Sabrina. "I do not usually, I assure you."

With her sharp eyes still lingering on Richard, Miss Kingston said, "Sabrina dear, did you happen to read that rogue Ennui's most recent essay in the *Post*? Though I think the man's a scoundrel, I did find that many of his arguments correspond with my own views on the emancipation of women. Wouldn't you agree?"

Queasiness churned Sabrina's stomach. "I-I wouldn't know," she stammered, though she had read the article. Miraculously, she conjured up an insipid little laugh.

Miss Kingston drew back with a puzzled air. Then that puzzled air cleared.

Oh dear Lord, if only the ground would open up and swallow me whole. For there in the spinster's eyes, Sabrina saw it. The woman *knew* precisely what Sabrina was about.

"No. Of course not," Miss Kingston said, shrugging a shoulder. "Don't know what made me ask. Well, children, enjoy yourselves today. It's bound to be an interesting one."

With a wave of her cane, the spinster bid them good afternoon and trundled off.

Sabrina chewed at her lower lip, not meeting Richard's gaze. She had been fortunate to dodge that bullet. Now what about those yet remaining?

Somehow Sabrina did manage to survive the following hour, thinking that it could have gone far worse. No one they met openly accused her of being a fallen woman—or of aspiring to be one—although rampant curiosity was stamped across more than a few faces. The rumors that had begun with the assembly would be in full bloom before nightfall, she knew.

Richard, while not radiating warmth and affability, was restrainedly polite throughout the many introductions. Only Sabrina detected the glint of sardonic amusement in his fathomless black eyes.

After making an initial circuit through the booths and suffering the gawkers and simpering for Richard, Sabrina felt as if her nerves were about to burst into flame. Richard's presence had been wearing at her, heightening her senses until his every touch, his every glance had her as skittish as a kitten.

When he cradled her elbow in his hand and steered her to the shade of a spreading elm, her arm stung as if, instead of merely cupping it, he had landed a blow to her funny bone. What on earth was wrong with her today? Something had changed since the assembly. But what?

Richard left her beneath the elm as he went to seek out two mugs of cider. Watching him saunter lazily away, she asked herself with every ounce of her objectivity: What had changed?

She still thought Richard Kerry unnerving, his arrogance insufferable. He was sardonic and irreverent and self-absorbed. But now—and here came the revelation—now, thanks to Nell, she was seeing him as a man. . . . As a potential lover.

She cast a thoughtful look to Richard's retreating back. Logically speaking, she knew it would be easier for her if she were not repelled by him. Even if she found his lifestyle repugnant and the squandering of his intellect shameful, she could not say he was wholly abhorrent to her.

She folded her hands in her lap. Perhaps she ought to look at this development as propitious. Anything that aided her mission, that facilitated the surrender of her virtue to this man, should be seen as a boon from on high. So, she decided in her eminently practical way, she ought to regard her new awareness of Richard Kerry as a blessing.

"Thirsty?"

She looked up, startled. "My, you're quick," she said.

One side of Richard's mouth lifted as he handed her a fragrant mug. "Not always, I promise you."

Gracefully, he lowered himself to the ground beside her.

His coat he'd insisted she use as a blanket, although she suspected that her two-year-old dress was worth probably one-tenth of what he'd paid for the London-tailored jacket.

Sipping at her cider, she eyed him from under her lashes, silently reviewing her lessons with Nell. The ghost claimed that a man's favorite topic was himself and had advised her to steer the conversation as frequently as possible to Richard's interests.

Sabrina tilted her head, smiled softly, and gave Richard the look she'd practiced a thousand times in the mirror since the assembly.

"Richard." His name now came easier to her lips. "You know that I've never been to London. I'd like very much to hear about it."

"What would you like to know?"

"What is it you enjoy doing when you are there? What are your hobbies, your interests?"

He eyed her evenly. "When in London, I drink, I gamble, and occasionally I go to Gentleman Jack's and blacken someone's eye."

"Oh." She averted her gaze so that he would not see her disdain. "How entertaining."

"That is what I *do* in Town," he said. "I did not say it's what I enjoy."

Confusion wrinkled her brow. Always mocking, teasing, speaking in circles. Why couldn't he just speak plainly?

"Well, then," she persisted, forcing another coy glance. "What *do* you like to do?"

"I enjoy toying with people."

Her breath caught somewhere near her ribs. That was plainly put. "Do you toy with me?"

He smiled, the empty smile that reminded her so much of the frozen Lucifer from Dante's *Inferno*. "I ask you the same: Do you toy with *me*?"

She stared at a blade of grass, a frail thin spike of green that fixed her attention more acutely than any of the hundreds of blades of grass surrounding it.

"What do you mean?" she asked, hoping her voice didn't sound too strangled.

"I mean that I believe you enjoy playing games as well as I do, sweet Sabrina."

"Why . . . why do you say that?"

He reached over and smoothed the cuff of her gown, his fingers lingering on her wrist. Her gaze darted to his.

"Intuition?" he asked.

Her breath was becoming a stitch in her side. She released it in a weak giggle.

"How do you know me so well, Richard? You are right, of course. I love games. Piquet and Pope Joan. Cap-verses and speculation. I . . . I just adore all sorts of games. In fact"—she leaped to her feet, feeling her courage dry up like her cottony mouth—"what do you say we try our hand at some the fair has to offer?"

She gazed down at him, privately cursing her loss of nerve, even as she babbled on. "There is bowling and skittles. I daresay you wouldn't be interested in catching a greased pig, but there are other diversions I'm sure you'd find diverting."

Dear God, did she sound like the veriest peagoose or what?

Unwinding his long legs, Richard grabbed his wrinkled jacket and stood. His eyes, as dark as a winter's night, held hers, probing, alive with unspoken questions.

She thought he stood too close.

"I think," he said quietly, bending over her, "that 'twould be easier to pin down the greased pig than you, sweet river nymph."

Chapter
Nine

Richard watched her ogle the satin ribbon with the same intensity with which he was ogling her. Her desire for the scrap of material was so obvious, he could not fathom why she simply didn't purchase it. It was but a shilling.

As she stood over the colorful display, frugally deliberating, she reminded him of one of those queer, white-capped Quaker women. Self-disciplined. Serious. A frown wrinkled her brow as her small white teeth worried at her lower lip.

Absorbed with the ribbons, she did not realize that her mask had slipped to reveal an intelligent thoughtfulness; a pensive sobriety that was in sharp contradiction to the cosmetics and coquettish affectations. The rouge and eye blacking, the giggles and insipid smiles—they were not Sabrina. What he saw now was the real woman hiding behind the faux flirt: an oddly appealing, earnest-faced, skinny girl.

"Go on," he urged, indicating the ribbon. "The color will suit you."

The vendor, a shrewd-eyed fellow, followed Richard's lead and held aloft the turquoise trimming that had taken Sabrina's fancy. "It would look fine on ye, miss. Match your eyes nice it would."

"Thank you, it is pretty . . . but no."

As she began to turn away, the muted regret in her eyes triggered a realization Richard had failed to consider—the silly girl could not afford it.

"Wait." On impulse, he grabbed hold of her arm. "Allow me. Please."

Sabrina glanced uncomfortably to the booth vendor. "I don't think it would be proper—"

"We'll take it." Richard snatched up the ribbon, then carelessly tossed the man a coin. With a commanding hold on her arm, he maneuvered Sabrina away from the booth before she could offer further protest.

Instantly he wondered why he'd done such a foolish thing. Frivolous acts of gallantry were not his style. He never bought trinkets for his lovers although, from time to time, he would purchase favors with an overpriced piece of jewelry. But even in those cases both parties understood that no sentiment was attached to the bauble. It was merely payment for sex.

He realized that he'd bought the damn ribbon out of guilt, thinking that the cheap scrap of satin would somehow serve as consolation to her when he bounced her from Simmons House. His lips twisted with cynical rationalization. After all, there was nothing quite like a turquoise rag to assuage the disappointment of losing one's home, was there?

"You should not have done that," Sabrina whispered, stave-stiff beside him.

Angry with himself that he had, Richard growled, "It was a bloody shilling. It was nothing. Like tossing a child a candy."

Under his hand, he could feel Sabrina's outraged gasp shudder through her and he felt perversely glad. She tried to pull away, but he held her arm tight, knowing that he must be bruising her.

"Release me," she hissed.

He didn't, and she ceased to struggle when a group of passersby crossed in front of them.

He led her away from the booths toward a thick cluster of trees and shrubs. Fury and frustration egged him on as he relentlessly pulled her into the brambly maze of scotch broom and overgrown weeds and squat brush oaks.

Up until today, he had been enjoying her games. But no longer. He was weary and irritated—annoyed by the dual faces she presented. He wanted to test her, to push her. Push her hard enough to see exactly what was behind this act of hers.

Dragging her between the brush, he found an open spot no larger than a closet. He gripped her wrists and drew her close, the accursed turquoise ribbon tumbling between his fingers.

"Why?" he demanded.

He expected her to rage at him, to condemn his boorishness and his unforgivable manhandling of her.

But no.

In those few short seconds while he hauled her into the trees, she had managed to bank the anger he'd felt pulsing beneath her skin. Calmly and with dignity, she looked up at him, only a slight quavering of her mouth evidence of her recent emotion.

"What do you mean?" she asked.

Damn her and her self-control.

He closed his eyes. Why didn't the stupid wench just come out and ask him not to buy Simmons House? Her masquerade concerned the property . . . did it not? What was she waiting for, for God's sake?

Of course, a voice chided him, he could end it himself if he would only inform her that the purchase was virtually a *fait accompli*. That he had already determined to buy Simmons House and all the cleavage in the world would not alter his decision.

But he would not tell her. To do so would be to admit defeat in this absurd little chess match they played.

Rather, he wanted her to confess, to expose herself and her motive. He wanted to push her into baring herself to him.

"Why," he asked, "do you behave as if . . ."

A giggle and a rustling of leaves checked his words. He looked over his shoulder and saw that a clearing opened up on the other side of the brush. A pair of intertwined lovers, young and impatient, had taken refuge in the open space, evidently oblivious to Richard's and Sabrina's presence only a few yards away.

Locked together, the two young lovers were devouring each other with their mouths, their hands working feverishly, their whispers unintelligible.

Richard glanced back to see that Sabrina had also discovered the amorous pair. Her sea-green eyes were enormous, dominating her small face, as she looked past him to the clearing. With her wrists still clenched in his fingers, he sensed the abrupt acceleration of her pulse. The tiniest hint of conscience told Richard he should take Sabrina away. But another, more dominant part of him insisted on keeping her here. As punishment?

She looked up at him and tugged at her wrists, her eyes beseeching. *Please let us go.*

Knowing himself for the very devil, Richard shook his head slightly. *We stay.*

In the clearing, the girl's bodice and shift had already been pushed to her waist. Her lover's palms were kneading her naked breasts with breathless fervor.

The lovers sank to their knees on the spring-crisp grass and Richard deliberately drew Sabrina more firmly against him. Her efforts to pull away stirred the surrounding branches and she stilled. For fear of discovery, he assumed.

In the clearing, the young man grasped the girl behind her waist as she arched against him, throwing her head back. Her full breasts gleamed like the sun's reflection off a bucket of creamy milk and her lover bent over her, pulling one pink-tipped mound into his mouth.

Sabrina's breath caught and Richard looked down at her face hovering but inches from his shoulder. Her expression looked agonized—as if she knew she should not watch, but was powerless to resist. He found her torment more arousing than the tableau on the other side of the bushes.

Behind him, the girl's husky whimpers carried on the air like the rhythmic call of a morning dove. Richard's gaze slid to Sabrina's throat, picturing how it might look working with such sounds of pleasure. The long expanse of ivory convulsing and throbbing . . .

He glanced back to the lovers. The young man had removed his shirt and the girl was clutching at his shoulders as he suckled her, her fingers digging into his bunched muscles.

Richard looked to Sabrina, and his member stretched, growing heavy and hard. With her cheeks flushed and her lips open, she could have been the woman whose breasts were being laved and licked with such tender care. Beneath his fingers, her pulse danced frantically and the air about them was warm and close.

Sudden and irrational desire possessed him: He wanted to see Sabrina's mouth pull taut with pleasure, to see her small pert breasts naked beneath the afternoon sun. The strength of his fantasy surprised him and it was all he could do not to throw her onto the ground and have his way.

The girl's cries became higher and more urgent, a soft keening that floated on the wind. Richard's eyes did not leave Sabrina. He brushed his hips against her, purposely, but she did not spare him a glance. Her tortured gaze clung to the young couple.

Never had he seen such an erotic combination of shocked purity and enthralled sensuality as was written across Sabrina's features. Her body, pressed against him, was taut and quivering like his straining manhood.

A shift in Sabrina's expression made him turn again to the clearing. The girl now lay on her back and her lover was pushing her skirts up her legs. Past her ankles, then her knees, until her skirts were a frothy peach pile around her waist. The man feathered his sun-dark hands up and down his lover's pale thighs as the girl thrashed her head from side to side on the grass. Both were panting loudly and Richard thought it a good thing or else they surely could have heard Sabrina's labored breathing.

With one hand, the young man reached for his pants and Sabrina tensed. Her chest looked ready to burst from her bodice, her exhalations were so sharp.

Unable to deny himself, Richard leaned forward and pressed his lips against the exposed column of Sabrina's throat.

She jerked her gaze up and, for a brief moment, he felt himself caught and held. Suddenly he saw himself in her eyes as clearly as if he were looking at his reflection.

It immobilized him. It terrified him.

And then, with a burst of strength, Sabrina wrenched from his grasp and was gone. He heard her crashing and stumbling through the brush at the same time he heard the lovers' startled whispers. He did not turn around but slowly followed Sabrina's path until he emerged from the brush.

She was nowhere in sight.

He remained where he stood, silently raging at what he had seen. Of himself.

Sabrina splashed water into her face, careless of the fact she was wetting her gown. She was hot, so very hot. Perspiration trickled down the back of her neck, running like a fiery stream over the length of her spine.

Hattie had said nothing when she'd appeared in her feverish state, merely pointing her toward the rear of the booth where Sabrina had found the water. Although only tepid, against her cheeks, it felt refreshingly cool.

Her fingers shook as she scooped another handful from the bucket. She was shaking from reaction, she knew.

Never had she experienced such . . . *tension*. Every muscle, every organ, every inch of her skin felt tight and tingly. Even her insides had clenched up in some invisible fist.

Staggering over to a crude plank bench, she sat herself down. *Be careful what you wish for . . .*

The old adage echoed in her head like a child's taunt. *Be careful, be careful.*

Curiosity had been her downfall. For days, she had been trying to visualize, hoping to understand, the intimacy that Nell had described. When Richard had insisted they remain in seclusion and spy on the young couple, Sabrina had been stunned. But then she had thought, *This is my opportunity to learn. To see what lovemaking is about.*

'Twould be educational, she had told herself with unassailable logic. Merely another exercise in her training, she'd argued with her conscience.

Dropping her head into her damp palms, she groaned.

She had failed. She hadn't had the fortitude to see the lesson through. When the bare-chested young man had begun to unfasten his trousers, Sabrina had felt as if she might snap. That if she remained and watched, she might in truth split into two wholly separate persons—the Sabrina she had been her entire life and the one she was trying to mold herself into now. A woman who could sacrifice her body, yet hold onto her honor . . . and not hate herself for it.

Weakly she pushed herself to her feet. She wanted to go home, to see Andrew and Teddy. She needed to remind herself why she was doing this, why she was allowing Richard Kerry to lay claim to her soul. It was for her brothers, wasn't it?

The door closed behind Mr. Bardwell with an ominous *clunk*.

Nell looked across the foyer to Andrew, who was still standing on the parlor threshold, wearing the same concerned frown he'd worn since he'd admitted the banker into the house. Magnified by his spectacles, the worry in his eyes looked too enormous a load for one so young.

Poor little chap, she murmured. In spite of herself, Nell had developed a soft spot for the stoic, sober-as-a-judge Andrew. He wasn't like most children, and certainly not like that scamp Teddy. He was quiet, considerate—and treated Nell as if she were a goddess come to earth.

She floated over to him, materializing as she approached.

"Gor, you look blue-deviled," she said cheerfully. *"Why so glum, little fella?"*

"Didn't you hear?" Andrew jerked his head in the direction of the parlor.

"Oh, that?" She made a dismissive sound. *"I wouldn't fret over that greasy-faced banker if I was you, Andy luv. He's just doin' his job."*

"But thirty days, Nell." He leaned his shoulder into the door jamb and sighed. "We have only thirty days to pay the arrears on the mortgage before they throw us out."

Thirty? She wished she had that many. Twenty-two days were left to her. Twenty-two days to complete her mission before she was called back. To God only knew what fate . . .

"Sabrina is seein' to it, Andy, don't you worry. You can trust your sister to take care of this, can't you?"

He peered at her over the top of his glasses, resembling more a man of seventy than a mere lad of thirteen. "What is her plan, Nell? How does she think we can hold on to Simmons House?"

Nell eased back a step, fending off his questions with upraised palms. *"Now, now, you know I can't go blabbin'."*

"But I might be able to help her if only I knew what she intended," he argued with a passionate sincerity that touched her long-dead heart.

He was just like his sister, she thought. The two of them managed to make everything sound so logical and sensible; they could talk themselves out of the hangman's noose, those two could.

Nell shook her head. She couldn't do it. If she ever were to tell Andrew of his sister's plans, Sabrina would personally escort her into Hell. The girl was determined that the boys not ever know of her sacrifice.

"It's not my place to talk to you of this, Andrew."

"But I want to help. We are running out of time."

Nell's lips tightened as she floated past him into the parlor. Time *was* a factor. She could appreciate Andrew's frustration because it so closely matched her own. She hated this feeling of helplessness, knowing there had to be something more she could do to serve Sabrina's purpose. And serve it quickly.

She drummed her fingernails atop the hearth's carved mantel, though no sound issued from her ghostly tapping. Only the clicking of Andrew's heels sullied the silence, as he paced back and forth, his fingers linked behind his slim back.

"If I but knew how to speed matters along," Nell muttered beneath her breath.

As she saw it, Lord Colbridge was the sticking point in all this—the great unknown in their carefully crafted scheme. A tough bloke to figure with his dark smiles and evil eyes, he reminded her of a man haunted. And haunted by more than a well-meaning ghost like herself.

Nell knew why Sabrina had settled on him as a protector—because he had a notion to buy Simmons House—but Nell was beginning to think they might need to switch their attentions to a more suitable prospect. If she could study Lord Richie alone and decide on her own his suitability . . .

"Come to think on it, Andy, there might be something you can do to help."

"What? What can I do?" He strode into the drawing room, eagerly smoothing his sandy blonde hair back from his forehead.

"You do know I'm helping your sister in this undertakin' of hers, right?"

Andy nodded.

"Well, you might not know this, but 'though I'm a ghost and capable of all manner of wondrous tricks, I've got my limitations, sad to say. I can't just go gaddin' about wherever I want, like simply fly off to London or float away into Leychurch whenever the whim strikes me."

"You can't?"

"No. There are rules aplenty to being a ghost, let me tell you. And I'm kinda learnin' 'em as I go. I'm here on a mission, you see."

"A mission?"

Nell toyed with the locket around her neck, sliding it absently up and down the cleft of her bosom. She had to be careful what she told Andrew; the little man was a downy cove.

"I've been sent to help yer sister. If it goes off all right, then I get me angel wings and can move on to heaven." At least, that's the way Nell figured it. No one from on high had ever told her flat-out what she had to do.

"At any rate, luv, bein' a ghost, I can only get around and go places with Sabrina or . . ." She winked at him, causing a rush of pink into his fuzzy cheeks. *"Or with another earthly being who can see me."*

"You m-mean with m-me?" Andrew went from pink to scarlet.

"Hmm-mm. You and Sabrina and Teddy are my connections to the physical world. Where one of you goes, I can go."

"And where are we going?" he asked warily.

"I think we need to pay Lord Colbridge a visit."

Andrew's youthful brow puckered. "I take it we would make this visit without asking Sabrina's permission?"

Nell lowered her voice to a confiding tone. *"To tell you the truth, Andy luv, I don't think she'd take kindly to the idea, so I figure we'd have to do it on the sly."*

Indecision flickered behind the spectacles. The obedient little bloke.

"Now, don't forget we'd be helpin' her," Nell argued. *"I can have a look-see at how this viscount fella lives. And"*— she sidled closer—*"I sure could use a man's opinion in all this business."*

"A man's opinion?" Andy looked to grow six inches before his voice suddenly dropped two octaves. "Right." He rubbed at his chin as if checking for new growth. "When do you think we should try to see him?"

Nell smiled to herself. *"Isn't tomorrow the day Sabrina goes and reads to those two widow ladies?"*

Andrew nodded. "Every Monday afternoon like clockwork."

"Well, then, tomorrow, my friend, you and I will pay Lord Richie a visit."

Chapter
Ten

"Who?"

"Mister Andrew Simmons, m'lord."

Seated behind his uncle's plain yet serviceable desk, Richard tipped back his chair and raised his gaze to the ceiling. A smirk pulled at his lips.

He had half anticipated this visit, had almost been waiting for it. After his thoroughly debauched behavior yesterday, Sabrina would have run home weeping buckets of affronted tears. So what would she have done? Sought out some doddering old uncle to come defend her honor and demand satisfaction. And for what? Richard tried to rationalize. A chaste peck on the neck?

He sat forward, and the chair's front legs slammed to the floor. He rotated his neck first to the right, then to the left, to release the cramping in his shoulders.

Having spent the morning reviewing his finances, he was not in the most jovial frame of mind. Although not yet in dun territory, his assets required a careful eye if he were to maintain his preferred style of living. His bills piled high, but they could have been higher. Many of his creditors were lying low on their demands, banking on his impending inheritance.

He clenched his fists.

Damn his self-righteous uncle. That bequest hung before Richard like a maddening carrot, tantalizing him with its promise of financial security. Its allure grew stronger with each passing moment as time continued to tick down to his thirtieth birthday.

He glanced at the calendar. Less than two months remained. Two months before he either had to march Charlotte down the aisle or else forfeit the bloody money.

"Hell."

"Beg your pardon, m'lord?"

Richard's gaze snapped to the waiting servant. *Ah, yes, the outraged Simmons relation.*

"Send him in," he ordered. "And see that we are not disturbed."

"Yes, m'lord."

Linking his fingers together on the paper-strewn desk, Richard steeled himself for the forthcoming unpleasantness, conscious of the fact that he probably deserved a good tongue-lashing. If not worse.

He couldn't honestly say what had gotten into him yesterday, but in retrospect even he had to admit that he had crossed over the line; a line of conduct he'd liberally drawn for himself, which normally spared him from twinges of guilt like the one he was currently experiencing.

He did not know why he had done it. Something about Sabrina had goaded him into it, pushed him to act beyond the pale. Forcing her to play voyeur with him had been completely unfair and unprincipled of him . . . even if wildly stimulating.

But dammit, he had been so bloody furious. Furious at Sabrina for stringing him along with her ludicrous pretense—but most of all furious with himself for letting the wench get under his skin.

The door to the study opened and in walked a child. A boy, actually, in a hideously ugly jacket many sizes too small for him.

Just as Richard began to take note of the resemblance— the dark blonde hair, the grave demeanor—Dekes announced him.

"Mister Andrew Simmons."

So she's sent a boy to do a man's work. . . .

Richard rose from behind the desk and extended his hand. The youngster stepped forward and shook his fingers with such vigor that his spectacles bounced on his freckled nose.

"This is a pleasant surprise . . . Mr. Simmons." Richard invited him to sit as he took his own seat. "To what do I owe this honor?"

The boy cautiously perched himself on the edge of the caned-back, craning his neck as if his cravat were suffocating him. Which it probably was. It was so poorly knotted.

"I thought a call in order," the lad said in a voice cracking with the onset of puberty. "Since we're neighbors, I thought the proper thing to do would be to come by and introduce myself. Especially under the circumstances."

Richard did not need to ask what circumstances, though he did think the boy was being unusually polite.

"So you reside at Simmons House?" Richard asked, wondering if this was the young David who had wielded the slingshot last week.

"Yes. I believe you've already made the acquaintance of my sister, Sabrina?"

Richard answered carefully. "I have had the pleasure."

The word "pleasure" caused the boy's gaze to sharpen, piercing Richard with its clear, blue-eyed candor. Richard gave a bland smile, confessing nothing.

"To tell you the truth, Lord Colbridge, it's Sabrina I have come to discuss."

An indifferently raised brow constituted Richard's sole reply.

"She is bearing a heavy burden, my lord, what with caring for me and Teddy . . ."

"Teddy?"

"Oh, um, my younger brother. He insisted on tagging along today, but I've ordered him to remain in the stables. He's playing with some kittens." The boy gave a nervous poke at his spectacles. "I-I hope you don't mind."

"Did he bring his slingshot?"

"Uh, no. I don't think so."

"That's fine then."

The boy slid a finger under the edge of his neckcloth and tugged. "Anyhow, Lord Colbridge, as I was saying . . . Sabrina is very distressed."

"And this distress concerns me?" Richard asked, injecting an impatient annoyance into his words.

Andrew did not back down, but cocked his fuzzy chin.

"Yes, my lord, it does."

The lad's courage stirred a faint admiration, reminding Richard of another time and of another boy who had stood uncertainly, yet boldly, on the threshold of manhood.

"Just how old are you, Andrew?"

He blinked, evidently unsettled by the non sequitur. "Thirteen last October."

A spurt of emotion tensed Richard's jaw. He'd been the

same age when his mother had set into motion the scandalous events that had . . .

"You're damned presumptuous for one of your years, showing up here like this."

"My apologies, Lord Colbridge, I do not intend to be impertinent, but I am the man of the family now and I have certain obligations in that role." His expression became severe. "About Sabrina . . ."

Oh, hell. Was the pup going to demand pistols at dawn?

"She is most concerned about your interest in Simmons House, my lord."

"Simmons House?"

"We understand from our banker, Mr. Bardwell, that you are considering assuming the mortgage. I would like to know if this is true, Lord Colbridge. Do you plan to oust us from our home?"

Richard could not contain his wry smile. So the little soldier wasn't here to demand satisfaction, after all.

"Excuse me, my lord, but I do not find this a subject for levity," Andrew protested. "This is a serious matter. Most serious."

"Don't get your feathers ruffled, my good man. I assure you I do not jest at your expense." He smiled reassuringly and some of the starch went out of the boy's spine.

"Tell me," Richard said with more than idle curiosity. "Does your sister know that you are here?"

"No. She is away from home this afternoon visiting friends. If she did find out I'd come, though, she would be frightfully cross."

"Is she cross often?" Many times, Richard had found himself admiring her unusual self-control.

"Sabrina? Good Lord, no. She is uncommon, even-tempered, if you ask me. Nothing seems to provoke her anger. Unless, of course, you mistreat one of her books."

"Her books?"

"Her library. It's her sanctuary."

Richard twirled a letter opener through his fingers. So, he had not been mistaken. Sabrina *was* well read yet purposefully concealed her learning.

"She reads a great deal then?"

"All the time. She's read everything we own at least twice." Andrew shrugged. "I think she feels guilty that she hasn't sold the books since we're so hard up . . ."

He caught his indiscretion by biting into his lip. Richard pretended to take no notice.

"About Simmons House," Richard said. "Has your sister not discussed the matter with you? In light of the fact that you are the man of the family?"

"She has, but she's not provided me with the specifics. She merely says she is working on arriving at a resolution."

"I see. Well then, speaking man to man, I think you should know that your sister and I are in the midst of . . . negotiations." If their bizarre game of masks and minds could be called such a thing.

"Oh." Andrew blinked like a confused baby owl. "So nothing has yet been resolved?"

"No. Not yet."

The denial caught Richard by surprise. What was he saying? Of course he had decided to buy the property. Why was he lying to the child?

The answer was in Andrew Simmons's face. The patent relief beneath the boy's grave countenance made Richard want to squirm. Made him feel like the heartless son-of-a-bitch he knew that he was.

Come on now, a dark inner voice taunted, *it's not as if I'll be casting the Simmons family into the street.* Surely they could take refuge with some far-flung relation somewhere.

Besides, if their circumstances were as dire as all that, he'd be doing them a favor by ridding them of the house's upkeep. They must be squeezing blood out of every pence to try to maintain that large home on their limited means.

Richard cast Andrew an uneasy eye. The boy was trying to cross a leg over one knee, but his gawky limbs seemed too long for him to manage. It was painful the way he reminded Richard of himself at that age—tottering awkwardly between infancy and adolescence, while struggling to find his way as a man.

An unfamiliar disquiet settled in Richard's gut. He hated the feel of it.

"Look here, Andrew," he heard himself say. "We're going to do some target shooting this afternoon. Why don't you stay and join us?"

Andrew's eyes widened in that owlish way of his. "Me, my lord?"

"Why not? Do you know how to fire a weapon?"

He shook his head.

"Then it's high time you learned." Richard stood, turning away from the restrained delight in the boy's eyes. Somehow the sight of it made his gut tighten up even worse.

"I . . . is it all right? I mean I have Teddy with me—"

"Oh, right. Teddy." Richard straightened a pile of letters. "Well, as long as we make sure he remains unarmed, I don't imagine he'll prove a nuisance."

Andrew's mumbled response drew Richard's gaze.

"What?"

"Nothing, my lord. Nothing important."

"Very well then. Let's hunt up Francis and see just what kind of shot you're going to make, Andrew, my boy."

Nell glared at Teddy, who glared back with all his ferocious eight-year-oldness.

"Listen, Lord Troublesome, I'll see you get a good chivey if you don't heed your brother. Andy said you was to stay here and play with the kitties and that's what just ye're goin' to do."

"But I want to look around," Teddy argued in a plaintive whisper.

"That weren't the bargain and you know it. You black-mailed us into lettin' you come along, so you're here. But I don't want you causin' no trouble for Andy. You are to stay put."

Nell jabbed her finger toward the stable floor where six gray and white kittens tumbled in the hay at Teddy's feet. Next door to their stall, an inquisitive mare peeked her head over the slats to investigate the ruckus.

"Why can't you stay with me?" Teddy asked, propelling his lower lip out past the upper, then batting his lashes with an artlessness his sister could not match.

Nell clenched the muscles in her cheeks. If she hadn't, she would have been grinning from ear to ear. Teddy was a monster the likes of which she had never seen. Not that she'd known many children in her time, mind you, but this towheaded scamp had no equal. He was incorrigible, will-ful, and wily. He could tell the most spanking clankers and butter wouldn't melt in his mouth. As far as Nell was con-cerned, a ten-day-old trout was less spoiled than Theodore Simmons.

She could not tolerate him.

She thought he was delightful.

"What do I look like?" she huffed. *"A bloomin' nurse-maid? We're here on business, Mr. Nibs. If we're goin' to help Sabrina, we've got to do some snoopin' around."*

"I want to snoop. Why can't I snoop?"

"'Cause Andy said you can't. He doesn't want you

*muckin' things up and you're the bloodiest mucker I've
ever seen."*

"I'm not a mucker," Teddy grumbled, but he plopped
down into the hay, conceding defeat. The kittens instantly
scrambled onto his lap.

"We won't be long," Nell said. *"The stablehands'll keep
an eye on you."*

"You better not be long," Teddy retorted. "Or I'll come
looking for you."

Heaving an exasperated sigh, Nell exited the stables,
wrinkling her nose at the lingering odor of horse and ma-
nure. She was dabbing her perfumed handkerchief to her
nose when she saw him.

"Coo-eee!" she murmured with relish.

That devilish handsome Lord Merrick was striding
across the lawn toward her, whistling a cheery tune.

Instinctively Nell glanced to her bosom to make sure it
was adequately exposed before she remembered he couldn't
see her. He couldn't appreciate the sight of her apple
dumplin' shop because, to him, she was invisible.

Disappointment hit her right between the eyes. A fine-
lookin' gent like that and she couldn't do a blasted thing
about it. When she'd been alive, maybe only two or three
times had she wanted a man simply for the sake of wanting
and no other reason. But now, here was a bloke who was
settin' her on fire and she might as soon be dead. Hell, she
was dead.

He circled around the house and Nell followed him, realizing that she really ought to check on Andy. Her argument
with Teddy had delayed her at least ten or fifteen minutes
and she knew she shouldn't miss the interview with Lord
Richie.

But, as the earl continued to the back of the house, Nell
figured that a few extra minutes wasn't going to make a

difference. Besides, 'twouldn't hurt any to find out some more about this fella. She still thought Sabrina should at least consider setting her cap for him.

The rear of the house opened onto a large field where Nell was surprised to find Andy and the viscount standing in the thigh-high grass. Actually, the grass was only thigh-high on Andy; reaching just below the knees of Lord Richie and the earl, who went over to join them. At the other end of the field waited a pair of servants in scarlet and black livery.

As she drew nearer, Nell anxiously scanned Andy's face, wondering if it were a good sign or an ominous one that the meeting had been so brief. But Andy was smiling. Looking downright chipper. And . . . his cravat had been retied.

Despite the fact she desperately wanted to hear Andy's report, Nell hesitated to reveal herself. After the night of the assembly, Sabrina had read her a nasty scold about materializing in front of other people. She said it was too unsettling for those who *could* see her.

That girl sure did like to lecture. Nell suspected that Sabrina didn't exactly approve of her, although she tried not to show it. Nell felt her disapproval nonetheless. She liked Sabrina—liked her a lot—but sometimes the girl tended to judge others a bit too harshly. Nell supposed that when you were as smart as Sabrina and read as much as she did that maybe you had a right to be uppity.

"Francis, this is Andrew Simmons," Lord Richie said. "My neighbor at Simmons House."

Francis smiled—*ooh, if his teeth ain't as white as a baby's bum!*—and gave Andy's hand a hearty shake.

"Andrew, allow me to introduce my good friend, the Earl Merrick."

Nell decided to indulge herself and dove in for a better look.

Running her fingers down Francis's coat sleeve, she appraised the expensive fabric. First-rate this was. Superfine crafted by a top-notch tailor. Solid gold watch chain, cravat pin sporting an oversized pearl, soft-as-butter leather gloves. This gent lived in Swell Street.

Her scrutiny extended higher, past his cleft chin to a well-shaped mouth that looked to smile often. Next came a pair of soft brown eyes that stole her ghostly breath. A master of studying men, Nell could tell by his face that Francis was a kind man.

She glanced from the viscount to the earl and back again. Blimey, there was no comparison. A better title, three times as handsome, and money pouring off him like sweat. What was Sabrina thinking? The girl was wasting her time on Lord Richie—who was a hard nut to crack if ever she'd seen one. The Earl Merrick, now he was their man!

"Andrew has flattered me and requested a few pointers in his shooting technique," Richard said. "I thought since we had already planned to practice that this would be a perfect opportunity for us both to share our expertise with him."

Francis nodded his agreement. "Famous. Good to meet you, Andrew."

Six long-barrelled weapons were spread out on a plaid blanket next to Richard. He picked one up.

"This is a Baker Flintlock Rifle, Andrew. The weapons you see here are already loaded so we'll need to be very careful handling them. After the first round, I'll show you the proper way to load one from beginning to end."

Richard handed Andrew a rifle, spending a few minutes explaining its workings.

As Nell listened with half an ear, she gnawed at a fingernail, wondering if Sabrina would ring a peal over her head when she heard about this. Why, just yesterday, Nell had got herself tossed in the suds when Sabrina walked in and found her teaching the lads how to chisel at cards. She couldn't rightly say how Sabrina would feel about Andy playing around with rifles.

"What are we using for target practice?" Francis asked.

Richard grinned. "Uncle Nigel's china. Ghastly stuff. I've rigged a device to hurl the plates into the air for additional challenge."

"I say, that's clever. Where'd you come up with that?"

Richard jerked his head to Andrew, who was studiously examining his weapon. "From his younger sibling," he said. "The brat with the slingshot."

Richard gave the sign and downfield the servants loaded the plate-flinger. He raised his rifle, speaking quietly to Andrew.

"The target will follow the path of a bird in flight, so you need to be ready to swing the rifle in time to the target's course. In this case, a horizontal arc from north to south."

A disk sailed through the air. A blast followed and whitish fragments drifted to the ground. Lord Richie had just blown a china dinner plate to smithereens.

"Now you give it a go, Andrew," he said.

The boy raised the rifle to his shoulder, then glanced anxiously at the viscount. Richard urged him on with a bob of his chin.

The plate was launched. Andrew aimed. Lifting his gun in a smooth arc, he fired. The recoil sent him stumbling back a step.

"I hit it! By Jove, I hit it!"

Andrew looked to burst as Francis applauded him with a slap on the back.

"You're a natural, Mr. Simmons," Lord Richie said. "You've got a steady hand, 'tis obvious."

"May I fetch it?" Andrew asked, pointing to the other

end of the meadow. "I know that I only nicked it, but I'd like to"—he ducked his head—"to keep it if I may."

Nell saw Richard and Francis exchange an amused look over Andrew's bent head.

"Of course, you may keep it," the viscount said. "For your first effort, it was a damned fine shot."

Richard cupped his hands to his mouth and yelled to the servants to hold up as Andrew headed down the field in hot pursuit of his souvenir. His spectacles skipped around on his nose as he gamboled through the tall grass, his face aglow with pride.

Watching Andrew sprint across the pasture, Nell's chest filled with a strange fullness. An aching happiness that she could not name. All she knew was that in three weeks, she was going to have to say good-bye to this little family. And she didn't for a moment think it was going to be easy.

Ka-boom!

The deafening gunshot exploded practically in Nell's ear, nearly throwing her from her feet. The acrid smell of gunpowder pinched her nose.

That had been close.

She whirled around to find both Francis and Richard staring at a smoking hole in the earl's coatflap.

"Blimey," Nell breathed.

However, as the earl remained steadfastly on his feet, she realized that he was not bleeding. Evidently, by some miracle, the ball had missed Francis by less than a hair's breadth.

Suddenly all eyes turned as one toward the house from where the shot had originated. Nell's hand flew to her chest.

"Teddy!"

The youngster stood about fifty feet away, one of the

enormous Baker rifles, nearly as long as he was tall, clutched between his fingers.

No one moved or spoke or breathed for many seconds. Then Nell saw Andrew racing across the field, waving his hands frantically above his head.

"Dear God, Teddy, are you daft?" Andrew bellowed as he ran. "What are you doing shooting at Lord Merrick?"

The rifle slipped from Teddy's hands and fell into the grass. Raising a slim finger, Teddy pointed directly at Lord Richie and, in the loud, vibrating high-pitched voice of a child, he clarified, "I was trying to shoot *him*."

Andrew staggered to a halt. Nell looked fearfully to the viscount. The silence hung like a pall around them.

"Well," Richard said dryly. "For *his* first effort, it was a damned fine shot as well."

Chapter
Eleven

Sabrina could not recall the last time she had been in such a white-hot rage. In fact, she doubted whether she had ever known such an anger in all her twenty-one years.

Staring fixedly at the bald spot at the back of Peter's head as he drove them toward Leyton Hall, she did not dare spare a glance to the penitent little figure sitting at her side. She knew that his cornflower-blue eyes would be sparkling with unshed tears, and that his pouty lips would be atremble with pleas for forgiveness, but she was not yet ready to face him. At least, not until she brought her anger under control.

Teddy, Teddy, Teddy. So much like their rash and reckless father. How could she blame the child for his daring spirit when it was as much Papa's legacy to him as the dimples in his cheeks?

Of course, she felt partially responsible. She'd been so careful, so cautious, in learning to control her own reckless passions, that she hadn't had the heart to curb Teddy's impetuous nature. Much could be forgiven in a child of eight. But not attempted murder.

Good Lord, what if he had killed Richard?

What if he had injured himself?

The carriage lurched and Teddy's hand grabbed at her arm for support. Expressionless, she glanced down at the short grubby fingernails that didn't look as if they'd been washed in a week when she herself had scrubbed them spotless only last night.

At least he hadn't blown off his own fool head, she thought with a sense of relief, realizing that a measure of her anger sprang from fear. Fear for her hotheaded Teddy.

She placed her gloved fingers over his hand. He squeezed her arm in silent thanks.

"Teddy," she said a minute later when she trusted herself to speak. "I am disappointed that you did not confide in me last evening. To have this secret hanging over you all night and then to ask Andrew to confess your sins . . . I wish that you had told me straightaway what you had done."

His tiny voice quavered. "I know I should have, Rina."

"Then why didn't you?"

"Well, the way Andrew jumped up and down and screamed and tore at his hair, I figured I must have done something pretty awful."

"Yes. Attempted murder is pretty awful, Teddy. Death is permanent, you know, not a mistake you can correct."

"Then how come Nell isn't dead permanent?"

Sabrina grimaced. Leave it to him to conceive of the unanswerable question. "Nell is an exception, Teddy. I cannot exactly say why, and I don't know if she can explain it either, but you could ask her about it if you want."

Another jolt rocked the poorly sprung carriage, jarring Sabrina's teeth together. "Do you know where we are going?" she asked.

"Lord Colbridge's?"

"Hmm-mm. And what are we going to do there?"

Teddy's chin sunk into his chest. "Apologize," he mumbled.

"That's right, young man. Although I daresay an apology is meager reparation for nearly having a bullet shot through you."

"But I didn't hit . . ."

Sabrina silenced him with a look that, for once, kept Teddy's overactive tongue between his teeth. He set to studying his shoes with particular interest.

Let him stew for a while, Sabrina thought. She had enough on her mind to keep her occupied. Like how in the world she was going to face Richard after what had happened at the fair.

She had not told Nell about seeing the lovers. She hadn't been able to speak of it or of Richard's lips caressing her neck . . .

Memory sent a warmth into her throat, a thickness that made it difficult for her to breathe. Unconsciously her hand rose to rest at the base of her neck, her thumb gently massaging the spot that Richard had claimed for his own. The worst of it was not the fact that she had spied upon two strangers' intimacy. Granted, it had been sinful to do so, but the experience had benefited her purpose from an educational standpoint.

No, what Sabrina found twice as disturbing as the voyeurism was how her imagination continued to distort the scene. How, as she lay in her bed at night, her mind persisted in envisioning her and Richard as the primary players in the erotic exhibition. His hands roaming her, his mouth suckling at her breast . . .

The pulse in her neck pounded, throbbing against her fingers. She dropped her hand limply into her lap.

Dear God, what was happening to her? She didn't even like the man! How could she secretly wish for him to touch her, to do those things to her?

Perhaps she ought to talk to Nell. Perhaps a logical explanation existed for the shocking turns her bedtime dreams had taken. But deep down in her heart of hearts, Sabrina suspected that she already knew the truth. That the only logical answer to the source of her inner turmoil was . . . desire.

Desire? her intellect mocked her.

To think that she, an enlightened woman who could recite Mary Wollstonecraft, pages at a time, was still vulnerable to the most basic of human yearnings. . . . Or should she say human failings?

Yet have I in me something dangerous. Though Hamlet's something dangerous had not been desire, Sabrina knew her frailty, knew what it was in her that placed her at peril.

And how very ironic. At the fair, she had been comforted to realize that she was not repulsed by Richard. She had thought her tolerance of him a happy turn of events. Now, panic assailed her with the knowledge that not only was she not repulsed by Richard, but that she actually felt a strong attraction for him.

Ironic indeed.

As the carriage emerged from the woods at the base of the hill, Leyton Hall came into view. From recently acquired habit, Sabrina hastily scanned her toilette. She'd been in such a state this morning, she had not applied the cosmetics Nell had taught her to use nor arranged her hair in anything more becoming than a simple knot.

Her dress, however, would have met with the ghost's approval—if Nell had been in a position to comment on anything so banal during the morning's chaos. One of the three gowns that she and Nell had refurbished, the blue-sprigged muslin bared her arms and bosom in a manner that even Sabrina admitted flattered her.

Filling her lungs slowly, she prepared herself to confront Richard. Would he openly ridicule the way she'd fled him at the fair or would he already have dismissed the incident? A rake probably didn't give a second thought to a stolen kiss. And, for all she knew, Richard might consider voyeurism as inoffensive a hobby as needlepoint.

She smiled wryly. Not to mention the fact that her brother's attempt on his life might have distracted him from their little interlude the other day. According to Andrew, Richard had not so much as raised his voice at Teddy following the shooting. He'd simply retrieved the weapon and allowed Andrew to rush the homicidal youngster home.

Would he be angry today? Would he ever forgive them? Most importantly, had Teddy's blunder ruined her chances of becoming Richard's mistress?

Peter pulled the carriage up to the house and, from her brother's expression, Sabrina thought Teddy wished he might evaporate like the fog hovering above the river. He sent Sabrina a pleading glance, but she clamped her lips together and forced him out of the carriage with a stern look.

At the door, she feared that the sour-faced butler would not admit them. The servant regarded Teddy with the same enthusiasm one would grant a slug upon one's dinner plate. After a pause, and while maintaining a cautious distance, he ushered them in.

The drafty and shadowy hall sent chills through Sabrina as she and Teddy were left to cool their heels in the foyer. The house was quite similar to the way Sabrina had pictured it. Lord Calhoun had been an austere man, and the stark surroundings reflected his temperament.

The butler returned. "This way," he unceremoniously invited them.

They followed him down the corridor, Sabrina insisting that Teddy precede her. At the end of the hall, the servant pushed open a door. The glare of the sun's rays momentarily blinded Sabrina since her vision had been adjusted to the tenebrous foyer. They'd been brought to a breakfast room. A pretty, little breakfast room with east-facing windows that admitted the morning light.

Sabrina's gaze swept the room. She found Richard before Teddy did. Standing in the corner with a china cup in his hand, he was watching them from hooded eyes. His satanic resemblance was underscored this morning by unrelieved black attire.

She shivered, instinctively responding to the contrast between light and darkness. Between the cheerful morning sunshine and the enigmatic inky-haired man who seemed to radiate danger.

Teddy had frozen directly before her. Sabrina nudged him forward with the tips of her fingers, empathizing with his trepidation. She, too, felt jittery under Richard's intense regard.

She placed her hands on Teddy's shoulders, and physically turned him to face Richard.

"Lord Colbridge." Her voice sounded huskier than normal. "We appreciate your indulgence in allowing us to call so early. Urgency demanded that we impose on you."

Richard set his cup down, his eyes smoldering like coal. "Good to see you again, Miss Simmons."

Beneath her palms, Sabrina felt her brother grow as rigid as a board. He would bolt if she released him.

"Theodore has something to say to you."

She cued Teddy with a squeeze to his shoulders. He remained mute. She squeezed a bit harder.

"I . . . I'm sorry I shot at you," he blurted.

Richard inclined his head. "I accept your apology."

Teddy craned his neck around and looked up at her pleadingly. "May we go now?"

Before Sabrina could answer, Richard intervened. "A moment, please."

Teddy paled to another shade of white as he turned toward Richard.

"In light of the circumstances," Richard said ominously, "I would ask something of you, Master Simmons."

It was all Sabrina could manage to hold the rascal in place.

"W-what?" Teddy croaked.

Richard folded his arms across his chest. "My ostler informs me that we have a surplus of kittens cluttering up my stables. I might hope, that as a gesture of good will, you would relieve me of the responsibility of one."

From holding him in place, Sabrina now had to clutch at Teddy to keep him from sagging.

"You want me to have a kitten?" he squeaked.

"If it is not too much to ask."

"Too much to ask?" Teddy straightened, his customary bravado surfacing. "Nah, I can help you out with a kitten," he said magnanimously.

Sabrina didn't know whether to laugh or to box the scamp's ears.

"I'll go choose one right now." And before she could stop him, Teddy was streaking out the door like a blonde comet.

And she was alone with Richard. Dark, dangerous Richard, whose show of compassion had surprised her.

"That was kind of you," Sabrina said.

A corner of his mouth lifted. Not in a smile. "I am not known for acts of kindness, Sabrina."

"Nonetheless, it was good of you," she breathlessly insisted. "I hope you will accept my apology as well."

"Why? Did you put him up to it?"

"No!" Her hand splayed across her chest. "Why would you think so?"

Without seeming to move, Richard closed the distance between them. His hooded gaze held her in place. "After the way I behaved at the fair," he said softly. "It would not have been unreasonable for you to want to put a bullet through me."

She swallowed. "'Twould seem extreme retribution."

"Oh? What would you consider a more fitting punishment?"

His ebony eyes glittered like black ice.

Sabrina struggled for words. How could she tell him she did not want to punish him? That instead she wanted him to teach her more?

"Richard," a man's voice called from the corridor.

Sabrina whirled around as the golden-haired earl walked into the room. He skidded to a stop when he saw her.

"Oh, I say, I'm sorry to barge in. Didn't know we had company. Good to see you again, Miss Simmons." Francis broke into a wide grin. "So, you're the sister of the atrocious Teddy, are you? Just saw the nipper in the hall and came to warn Richard. The little man did beg my forgiveness quite sweetly before he dashed off like a dervish."

"You're very gracious," Sabrina said, "considering that he almost killed you."

"Pshaw. Never really cared for that coat anyway. Gives me an excuse to buy another when we get back to Town."

Sabrina went as still as a statue. "You're headed back to

London?" she asked. She hadn't the courage to glance toward Richard.

"Right-o," Francis blithely confirmed. "Richard's finally had enough of rusticating. In three days' time, I'll be back in the welcoming arms of my tailor. Which reminds me," he said more to himself than to her, "I'd better check up on my valet. I never have cared for the way the man folds a shirt. Entirely wrong and the stupid creature can't seem to learn to do it right."

He extended his hand. "Take care, Miss Simmons. And best of luck with your high-spirited charge."

"Thank you," Sabrina said faintly as Francis saluted her.

With a departing wink to Richard, he left.

Sabrina could not move. She felt as if a whirlpool were sucking her down, pulling her into the bowels of the earth. Richard was leaving. Her plans. Oh God, her plans were unraveling like thread from a spool.

She had to say something.

"I should go."

And yet her feet remained rooted to the floor.

"Sabrina."

His voice commanded her gaze. Reluctantly, she turned to him.

"You still haven't told me my punishment."

"Punishment?" she feebly echoed. *Oh yes, the fair.*

Her thoughts reeled in dizzying circles. What could she say? Richard was leaving. Going away.

His fathomless black eyes searched her expression and she wondered what he saw there. Did he see her panic? Did he see her disappointment?

"You look different today," he said.

In a self-conscious gesture, she touched the side of her face. "I do?" she said inanely.

He frowned, the wrinkles in his forehead bearing down

on his thick ebony brows. His eyes continued to scour every inch of her face, giving no quarter.

"You look," he whispered darkly, "as if you need to be kissed."

"I do," she repeated.

In wonder, she watched his hand slowly lift from his side. With extraordinary clarity every detail of that hand imprinted itself into her memory. The long fingers, lightly brown and weathered. The few dark hairs curling beneath his knuckles. The small scar looping up from his wrist.

His palm cupped the back of her head. Gently he pulled her to him. Her gaze fixed on his lips, so lush with their Cupid's-bow curve. Warm and velvety, his breath washed over her with promises of what was to come.

Her heart slammed against her chest as his lips tentatively grazed her mouth. Then again, just skimming the surface, a mere brush of breath and firmness.

More, something inside her cried, afraid that he might stop.

He must have heard her.

His next pass was more definite, his lips traveling from the edge of her mouth across her lower lip to the other corner. He reversed direction, the tip of his tongue joining the assault.

Sabrina made a sound at the back of her throat. He answered her with a soft growl, his teeth capturing the fleshiest part of her lip and pulling it into his mouth.

Her fingers somehow found themselves clinging to the lapels of his coat. A distant part of her questioned how she was still able to stand.

With his teeth and tongue, he urged her mouth to open to him, capturing her tongue with his when she acquiesced. Startled at his intimate invasion, Sabrina gasped lightly. He took advantage of her surprise and set a rhythm of possession with his tongue that thrummed through Sabrina's blood.

She tentatively explored him as well. He tasted wonderful and wicked and somehow she knew he would taste like this. Forbidden.

His fingers threaded through her hair, massaging her scalp and melting her bones. He pulled her more tightly against him and her head fell back, giving him greater access. His mouth left hers, gliding across her jaw. When he thrust his tongue into her ear, something scalding shot through her abdomen.

She gasped.

Again he seized her mouth, sucking as if he might pull her soul from her body. She honestly believed that he could.

Her breasts began to swell and she rubbed them against his chest, instinctively trying to assuage their need. Her heart was beating in her ears so loudly she could hear nothing else. Nothing but the sound of her own panting.

"Richard. Richard," she moaned into his mouth.

His name must have broken the spell. He raised his head, his midnight eyes wild, untamed.

Sabrina's fingers ached to caress the swollen flesh of his mouth.

"This," he breathed hoarsely. "This was punishment enough."

Then he was gone.

Chapter
Twelve

Richard was counting the stitches in his shirt cuff. *Thirty-seven. Thirty-eight.*

"And it was so sad to see her given the cut direct like that. It was a frightful misunderstanding and dear Letitia did not deserve it. In front of Lady Kinnard and half of London society!" Charlotte's voice filled with genuine sympathy. "I nearly succumbed to tears myself I felt so wretched for the poor darling."

"Oh, you are too good, Miss Wetherby. So charmingly compassionate." Francis handed her one of his five-shilling handkerchiefs and Charlotte daintily dabbed at her eyes.

"Oh, goodness, have I . . . have I made a spectacle of myself?" Charlotte cast a soft, anxious glance at Richard, who pretended not to see it.

"Not at all, dear lady," Francis hurried to assure her. "I,

for one, find it mighty refreshing to see a lady of your refinement capable of such feeling."

"Your admiration, Lord Merrick, is generous but sadly misplaced." Charlotte sighed and glanced to the drawing room window, where a light drizzle speckled the glass with silvery raindrops. "If I weren't cursed with timidity, I should have spoken up for Letitia, defended the unfortunate girl. But I . . . I was too shy to say anything."

"You cannot fault yourself for that," Francis protested. "Why, no one would expect you to lay yourself open to public scrutiny on behalf of a virtual stranger. Don't you agree, Richard?"

"Certainly not," he said, glancing at the pocket watch tucked into his palm. Faith, they'd only been here twelve minutes?

"Mama says I would be invited out to more parties if I weren't so bashful." Her eyes abruptly widened and Richard felt them alight again on him. "Oh! Oh dear, I didn't mean to say that I feel the need to make new acquaintances of gentlemen in particular or . . ."

"We understand precisely what you mean," Francis soothingly intervened. "Don't we, Richard?"

"Hmm-mm."

Richard's gaze drifted lazily to the window. Well, he couldn't offer for Charlotte today. Not that he could specifically recall, but he was fairly sure there was some superstition that maintained it was unlucky to propose during inclement weather. Besides, he wasn't convinced he wanted to spring it on her only his second day back in Town. Seemed hasty. Didn't feel right.

Doesn't feel right. Richard chuckled humorlessly to himself. Who was he trying to fool? Marrying Charlotte had never felt right. But damned if he wasn't going to do it anyway.

From the corner of his eye, he watched her as she walked across the room to fetch Francis some sheet music. Odd. He didn't recall Charlotte being so plump. She wasn't overweight by any means, but she did look rather round when compared to . . .

Richard's fist spasmed around his watch as he realized where his thoughts had been taking him. *When compared to Sabrina.*

Damn it to hell! What was it about that fine-boned paradox of a female? It was that blasted kiss, that's what it was. He shouldn't have done it. He knew better than to dally with innocents. Especially the home-grown, provincial sort.

If she hadn't looked so unbelievably disappointed to learn that he was leaving Shropshire . . .

But he'd had to leave. He'd had to get away while he still knew who the hell he was.

Assuredly, Sabrina's game had been fun for a while. She had made for an entertaining country diversion. But when he found himself starting to question whether or not to buy Simmons House after he'd already made his decision. . . . When her gangly bespectacled brother began to remind him of a period of his life he'd just as soon forget. . . . When he was wasting far too much of his time thinking about her and actually beginning to *trust* himself with her . . .

He checked his watch again.

At least Sabrina didn't bore him. She might switch back and forth between a priggish governess and an amateurish coquette with each swing of the clock's pendulum, but she held his attention. With her brandy-husky voice and her prim pursed lips that tasted like heaven . . .

He lurched to his feet.

"Richard?" Charlotte's voice rose with concern.

"A drink," he said.

"Shall I ring for tea?" She glided toward the bell pull.

"No. A brandy will do fine." He strode over to the sideboard and poured himself a healthy portion from the decanter. Pivoting around, he silently dared either of them to comment on the early hour.

Hell, you better get used to it, Charlotte. If I want a brandy at one o'clock, I'll have one. If I feel like a bottle of gin before breakfast, I'll damn well drink it.

In reality, he wasn't a heavy tippler. But perversity made him spread his legs wide and throw back the brandy in one fiery gulp. He leaned back against the wall and crossed his ankles in indolent challenge.

Charlotte edged uneasily back to her chair as Francis rushed in to cover Richard's rudeness. "I say, Miss Wetherby, I hear Lara Howard has finally drawn Roylett into the parson's mousetrap."

Charlotte gratefully availed herself of Francis's conversational distraction. "Yes, is it not splendid news? She's very fond of him, I understand, and her mother is simply delighted."

Silence yawned before them again.

"My eyes," Francis said a shade too loudly, "how could I have forgotten? At my club last night, just as I was leaving, I heard murmurings of some terrific bumblebroth concerning Edgerton. Do you know what that might be about?"

"Why, I'm surprised you haven't heard of it. It's all the talk. Very sad, though. Very, very sad. I probably shouldn't speak of it, but my heart does go out to Lady Edgerton in spite of . . ."

Shaking her head, she lowered her voice to a respectful whisper.

"Evidently Lady Edgerton found herself in a 'delicate condition' that in no way could have been Lord Edgerton's responsibility. Naturally no one would have known or suspected if the dear lady hadn't tried to—I beg your pardon, is something amiss, Lord Merrick?"

The muscles in Richard's jaw stung he was clenching his teeth so hard, while Francis's eyebrows were dancing across his forehead as he labored to alert the oblivious Charlotte.

"As I was saying," Charlotte went on. "In desperation, I assume, Lady Edgerton attempted to run away with the—"

"Miss Wetherby!" Francis burst out.

"Lord Merrick, whatever has come ov—" Charlotte's eyes rounded to the size of sovereigns. "Oh, my. Oh, my. The scandal—"

Richard met her horrified gaze with a tense stretching of his lips that might have passed for a smile on any other day. He raised his empty glass to her in mocking tribute. "That's right, Charlotte. The scandal."

"I-I . . . I did not mean . . . Oh, Richard, I never intended, oh—"

Francis quickly passed her another handkerchief.

Richard pushed away from the wall. The anger was rushing over him anew as if it had all happened yesterday.

"Merrick, old man, I'm going to need to shove off. You can find your own way home, can't you?"

Francis did not look at him. "Yes," he said curtly.

"Good day then, Charlotte. Francis."

With a negligible dip of his head, Richard turned and sauntered out of the drawing room as if he had not a care in the world.

He was standing on the street in front of the Wetherby town house when he realized he was still holding the empty brandy glass in his fist.

"I cannot believe I let you talk me into this," Sabrina grumbled, shaking out her gown with enough force to rip open seams. "My first trip to London and I am staying in a brothel!"

Paula's Palace of Pleasure, no less. Honestly!

Sabrina glanced up with a nervous scowl. "And would you please come down from there? You know I don't care for your levitating like that."

Nell obligingly floated to the floor and perched herself at the foot of the chipped iron bed. Sabrina made a mental note to check the bedding for vermin.

"Gor, you're in a nasty mood," the ghost said, pouting in a way that forcibly reminded Sabrina of her youngest brother. *"And here I figured I was doin' you a favor by helpin' you find a place to stay."*

Nell *was* trying to be helpful, Sabrina told herself with a guilty grimace.

"Nell, I'm sorry. I fear that the last few days have taken their toll on my nerves. Leaving the boys and then the long coach ride . . ."

Flicking her gaze around the room, Sabrina shoved the folded gown inside a musty-smelling armoire. "I just never imagined when you said I could stay with an old friend of yours that you were talking about another madam."

"Well, it's not costin' you nothin'," Nell pointed out defensively. *"And like she said, Paula doesn't bring gents 'ere any more. She's got a big house over in Clerkenwell that she's usin'."*

With another skeptical appraisal of the bed, Sabrina thought she should be grateful for small blessings. At least, she wouldn't have to worry about strange men prowling the corridors at night, accidentally stumbling into her room.

"Paula was very . . . understanding," Sabrina conceded.

"Ah, she's a gem, ain't she? Paula and me used to be

bosom-bows. I told you all you had to do was mention me name and Paula'd treat you like bloody royalty."

Sabrina's lips compressed into a dubious *moue*. If these were the chambers royalty was given, she'd hate to see where a mere commoner would be lodged.

"Let us hope we won't have to prevail too long on her hospitality. Tomorrow I can call on Lord Colbridge and put forth my proposal."

Nell jangled the locket around her neck, her frustration plain. *"You won't even consider havin' a go at the Earl Merrick?"*

Faith, not again. "No, Nell, I'm not going to 'have a go' at Lord Merrick."

"But if it's blunt you're worried about, Sabrina, he's well to grass. And you got to allow that he's easy on the eyes. A sight prettier than yer viscount."

Sabrina paused in shaking out another gown. Funny, but she hadn't noticed that Lord Merrick was so much comelier than Richard. True, the earl was handsome, but even with his striking good looks, he did not affect her in the same way that Richard did. With Richard, she had begun to feel a bond, an underlying commonality she could not quite explain. Nor, she decided, would she try to explain it to her pig-headed ghost.

"Nell, appearance does not signify. I have already made progress with Richard; I see no reason to begin anew with the earl."

Unless, of course, Richard laughs in my face and turns me down flat.

Nell sniffed. *"All I can say is that I hope you aren't puttin' too much faith in one kiss, luv. A cove like Lord Richie goes about kissin' ladies as often as he spills his water."*

"Really, Nell," Sabrina chided.

The ghost turned her palms up in a gesture of surrender. *"I'm just sayin' that Lord Richie isn't the sort I would 'ave chose. Not when you might 'ave the earl."*

"Logically speaking, however, Richard is the more practical choice," Sabrina pointed out. Quite sensibly she thought. "You see, I won't have to leave Simmons House if Richard is residing virtually next door. When he's in residence at Leyton Hall, I will be close at hand."

Close at hand. The phrase conjured up an immediate vision of those long sun-browned fingers, with their dusting of curls . . .

Sabrina cleared her throat. "The chief difficulty I foresee is that I am bound to appear desperate, chasing Richard to London like this."

"You had no choice, luv. Where was you goin' to find a bloke in Leychurch plump enough in the pockets to set you up as 'is ladybird?"

Nell was right, of course. Leychurch was woefully short of wealthy potential protectors.

After placing the last of her gowns onto the armoire shelf, Sabrina collapsed back onto the bed. She stared up at the cracked ceiling, wallowing in that same sense of fatalism that had dogged her heels since Mr. Bardwell's first visit. No room for second thoughts now. As courageous women had done throughout history, she would rally her nerve and do what must be done.

"I don't know how I'm going to say it, Nell," she confessed.

"I wouldn't beat 'round the bush, that's for sure. Time's wastin'. In seventeen days, I'll be no more than a memory, so if I'm goin' to help you, luv, you're goin' to have to lay it out for him plain-like."

Sabrina swung her head around so that her cheek rested

on the quilted counterpane. "Nell, what will happen to you if we don't succeed?"

A shadow passed over Nell's ghostly countenance. She shrugged and dropped her gaze to her lap. *"I don't know. I s'pose I'll be sent back to Purgatory until another chance comes along."*

Closing her eyes, Sabrina realized that here was yet one more reason that she could not let herself fail. A chill touched her knee. Sabrina opened her eyes to find Nell grinning that wide gap-toothed grin of hers.

"There, there, luv. I know what you're thinkin'. Don't you worry none 'bout me. Nell deNuit's always known how to take care of 'erself. Down here and up there."

"You would like to move on, though, wouldn't you, Nell?" Sabrina asked quietly.

Avoiding her gaze, Nell floated to her feet. *" 'Course I'd like me a pretty pair of angel wings."* She struck a provocative pose and added playfully, *"I think they'd flatter my bubbies real nice."*

Sabrina could not contain her laughter.

"That's better, luv. You ought to laugh more. Lights up your face, it does."

"Thank you, Nell. I will remember that." Rolling onto her elbow, Sabrina propped herself up. "Do you think the boys are well?"

"Ooh, I'd wager they're better than well. You said yerself that Hattie's pert near raised 'em. She'll do just plummy."

"I miss them already."

"Even Teddy?" Nell teased with a wink.

"Even Teddy. You know, since the shooting, he's been as good as gold. I don't know how long it can last but I doubt he'll give Hattie any trouble while we're gone."

Nell rubbed her nose with the heel of her hand. *"He*

does have a bee in his bonnet about Lord Richie, though. Teddy told me that even though the kitten was jolly, he still didn't trust the bloke."

Sabrina smiled softly and looked back up at the ceiling. "That's all right. I'm not sure that I do either."

Chapter Thirteen

Nell was in high spirits. She had a plan.

Sabrina had awakened this morning with a slight case of the chills. Nothing serious. A bit of a red nose and the occasional sniffle. Hardly the sort of thing one would even take notice of.

Unless, of course, you were a ghost with a scheme up your sleeve.

Nell waited until Sabrina came downstairs for breakfast. The kindhearted Paula had left two fresh buns on a plate in the parlor with a note saying she would be out for the day. Fortune was playing directly into Nell's hands.

"Aren't you hungry?" Nell asked.

Sabrina crumbled the roll between her fingers. "I am too nervous for much of an appetite, I think."

"Ooh, I'm not sure it's nerves, luv." Nell fabricated a worried frown. *"You don't look so good."*

"Oh." Sabrina glanced to her gown. "I thought the blue-sprigged muslin the nicest. And Richard seemed to like it. Do you think I ought to change?"

"What? You're thinkin' to visit Lord Richie today?"

Sabrina stared at her blankly.

"Why, your nose is red as a cherry and your color is all off." Nell made a *tsk*-ing sound between her teeth. *"You don't want to go see him, luv, when you aren't lookin' yer best."*

Sabrina raised a hand to her cheek. "I look unwell? I feel in good health but for the . . ."

"Oh, I've seen you look a far sight better."

"But, Nell, you said yourself that time is wasting—"

"One day isn't goin' to make a smidge of difference. You're better off layin' low today and gettin' some rest. Tomorrow you can pay yer visit."

Sabrina chewed uncertainly at her lip. "I hate to squander a full day . . ."

"Don't matter. The important thing is for you to eat some of yer breakfast, have a cup of tea, and rest up for tomorrow."

"Well, I did bring along a couple of books I could read," Sabrina hesitantly conceded. "And a restful day would be nice after our long trip . . ."

"That's the way," Nell encouraged, virtually rubbing her hands together with glee. *"We want you to be at yer loveliest for Lord Richie, don't we?"*

As soon as Sabrina finished her breakfast and went upstairs to fetch her books, Nell put her plan into motion.

The girl might not cotton on, but Nell was about to do Sabrina the biggest favor of her life. The way she saw it you didn't have to be no genius to figure out that a handsome, wealthy earl was a sight finer catch than Lord Richie. Nell just couldn't fathom why Sabrina refused to see it.

And . . . if Nell's ghostly mission was to help Sabrina land a protector, then the folks upstairs in Purgatory would have to agree that she had done a spanking job of it if she helped Sabrina snag herself an earl.

Yes, indeed-ee, Nell thought. She'd be wearin' them angel wings in no time.

Hustling across the parlor, Nell reached behind the divan cushion and retrieved the note she'd written earlier that morning. Although she'd struggled over the spelling of some of the words, she had kept the message brief.

My dear Lord Merrick—
I am in London. Please call on me at Sixty-Eight Camden Street at your earliest convenyence.
                                            —Sabrina Simmons

The tricky part would be determining the earl's address, then arranging for the note to be delivered. Both would take some cunning in light of her spectral limitations.

But like Sabrina said: "Where there's a will, there's a way." And Nell's dream of a heavenly berth made her will strong.

The peal of the doorbell nearly caused Sabrina to leap from her skin. The book she'd been reading fell from her startled fingers onto the carpet.

Dear heavens, who could be calling? Here?

"Aren't you goin' to answer the door?" Nell asked, materializing from thin air.

Sabrina jumped again. "I . . . of course not!" she stuttered. "The caller could be one of Miss Bright's gentlemen friends."

"Oh, pooh. No gent is goin' to call at her home. Why don't you find out who's at the door?"

Sabrina rose to her feet and smoothed her skirts with a nervous movement. "I will *not*! It can't be anyone wishing to see me, since no one knows I'm in London."

The bell chimed again.

"Well, I'm goin' to see who it is," Nell huffed.

In three seconds, she floated back in. *"It's the Earl Merrick."*

Sabrina gasped. "The earl?" Then comprehension bloomed fully upon her. She thrust her fists onto her hips. "What the blazes have you done, Nell?"

Smiling in triumph, the ghost wiggled her fingers at her. *"Ta-ta."* Then she disappeared.

"Miss Simmons?" Lord Merrick's familiar voice called from the hall. "Miss Simmons, are you here?"

Sabrina rolled her eyes heavenward and gritted through her teeth, "Blast you, Nell."

Hurrying across the room, she opened the parlor door. The earl was indecisively surveying the small entrance, his hat in hand. The front door stood ajar.

"Lord Merrick."

He whirled around. "Miss Simmons." Apologetically he waved his hat toward the door. "It swung open of its own accord. I didn't mean to intrude."

Sabrina smiled, though it felt stiff. "The latch must need repair."

She walked past him and, after sending an apprehensive glance to the street, closed the door. Her palms felt damp as she turned back to him.

"How nice to see you again," she said. "I have just made a pot of fresh tea. May I offer you a cup?"

He bent the rim of his beaver in his hands. "That would be lovely. Thank you."

His steps solid and loud in the tiny hall, he followed her into the parlor. As he looked about the room, she thought he did a commendable job of masking his horror.

Stepping into Paula Bright's parlor was like falling into a vat of plum jelly. The entire room had been decorated in varying shades of violet, made worse by a nauseating abundance of lilac ruffles. Although the room was hideous, Sabrina privately thought that the strawberry-pink dining room down the hall exhibited even poorer decorating judgment.

"Please have a seat," Sabrina invited, "while I fetch another cup."

She fairly ran to the kitchen.

"Nell," she hissed as she barreled through the door. "Nell!"

No response.

"By Jove, Nell, this is the outside of enough! What have you done, summoning Lord Merrick? I insist you show yourself to me this instant!"

The ghost did not appear.

"Nell!"

Nothing.

Sabrina narrowed her eyes and grabbed up a cup and saucer, then stormed back to the parlor. As she entered, she found Lord Merrick examining an especially tasteless vase depicting the ravishing of the Sabines. He quickly put it down.

"I must say this is a surprise," she said with brittle gaiety, taking a seat across from him.

His blonde brows lifted. "You asked me to come."

"Oh, yes." Sabrina laughed breathlessly, while vowing to wring a certain ghost's neck. "I meant I hadn't expected you to come so soon. It's very good of you."

"Well, your message did seem urgent. So . . . concise."

"Dear me, did I give the impression of urgency?" Her hands shook as she passed him his cup. "I certainly didn't intend to."

The earl's gaze skirted the room.

"Miss Simmons, it might not be my place to remark on this, but I gather this is your first visit to London?"

Sabrina's cheeks hurt with her effort to maintain a smile. "As a matter of fact it is."

Suddenly the parlor door slammed shut. Lord Merrick's head whirled around.

Under Sabrina's death-like grip, the china saucer should have been ground to dust.

"The wind," she hastily explained. "The house is frightfully drafty."

"Ah-huh." The earl nodded with his mouth slightly open, still gazing at the doorway.

"You were saying, my lord?"

"Go on, Sabrina, girl," a voice whispered in her ear. *"Move in on 'im while you've got the chance."*

Sabrina swatted at her ear.

"What? Oh, yes. Miss Simmons, I hesitate to alarm you; however, I feel duty-bound to advise you of the character of this particular quarter." He ran a hand through his yellow-gold curls. "As you are unfamiliar with London, you understandably would not be aware of the undesirability of letting a house in this particular, ah, neighborhood. An easy mistake to make, indeed.

"I would be honored if you would allow me to assist you in finding alternate—and more appropriate—lodgings."

"My lord, you are very kind. But to be honest, I do not plan to remain in London more . . ." A pinch tweaked her arm and she clenched her teeth. "More than a few days. Two weeks at the longest. And since I've already paid rent

here," she lied, " 'twould not be feasible for me to relo-
cate."

Lord Merrick did not appear satisfied. "Does Richard
know you are in Town? That you are staying in Camden
Town?"

"I have not contacted Lord Colbridge."

Something passed behind the earl's brown eyes. "You do
plan to let him know you are in London, though?"

"Sabrina!" came a plaintive, sibilant, and spectral whisper. *"Show some ankle, luv, bat your lashes. At least give it
a go!"*

Sabrina would have liked to have given something a
"go," but she didn't know how one might murder someone
already dead.

"I had planned on it," she answered the earl, madly im-
provising. "In fact, 'twas the reason I wrote you. I'd hoped
you would provide me with the viscount's direction."

As soon as she'd said it, Sabrina winced, hopeful that he
would not question how she had come upon his address, yet
was unable to find Richard's.

Francis set his cup down, his expression suddenly grave.
"Miss Simmons, may I confide in you?"

"Yes!" Nell's jubilant cry rang out.

"Naturally, Lord Merrick."

"I overstep our acquaintance, and please correct me if I
am wrong; but, might you have an interest in Lord Colbridge that goes beyond the neighborly?"

Sabrina forced back a blush.

Francis turned pink.

"My presumption is unforgivable, however, I ask not
from trivial curiosity."

Sabrina placed her cup upon the tea tray, striving for the
appearance of sangfroid. The earl would believe her inter-

est to be maidenly and romantic. He would not suspect her true purpose.

"Why do you presume so much, my lord?"

"I ask for personal reasons, Miss Simmons. You see, for many years there has been an understanding between families that Richard would wed Charlotte Wetherby."

Sabrina's heart fell like a stone into her stomach.

"For reasons of his own, Richard has not yet formalized the agreement. His uncle's recent demise, however, has forced his hand. He cannot inherit the bulk of Lord Calhoun's fortune unless he weds by his thirtieth birthday, which soon approaches."

Speechless, Sabrina's strained nod encouraged the earl to continue.

"The problem, Miss Simmons, is that I have fallen madly in love with Miss Wetherby." Francis ducked his head. "And I do believe the lady returns my feelings."

"I-I see."

"I refuse to blame myself, for I know that Richard does not love Charlotte as he should."

"He doesn't?"

"No." Francis studied his fingertips. "I have known Richard my entire life, and he would kill me if he knew I told you of this. . . . Nonetheless, I feel you must know if there is to be any hope for your affection."

"Know of what?" Sabrina's thoughts drifted back to the night of the assembly. The earl had made one or two comments during their dance that had piqued her curiosity.

A deep breath swelled in his chest. "No one speaks of it anymore since very few people remember—except for Richard. And God knows, he won't forget.

"You see, Miss Simmons, Richard does not believe himself capable of love. In fact, sometimes I think he truly despises himself, that he's given up on himself. And although

I don't claim to be an expert, I don't see how a man who neither likes nor trusts himself can learn to love someone else."

Taken aback, Sabrina regarded the earl with new and sudden respect. *How very astonishing,* she thought. She had sadly misjudged the foppish Lord Merrick, for beneath all those dandified affectations, the man had an amazingly intuitive understanding of human nature.

"The scandal occurred . . . what?" Francis's gaze blurred as if counting back the time. "Seventeen years ago, I suppose."

"Scandal?" Sabrina asked.

Francis nodded pensively. "It's a tragic tale. I'll try to make it brief. First, you should understand that Richard's parents had a typically modern marriage. They hated one another, but kept up appearances because that's what was expected, you know. His father tippled heavily and his mother was a frivolous woman, flighty even.

"At any rate, Richard was thirteen that year. He and I had just come up from school for the holidays. I don't know exactly how it came to pass, but a day or so after we'd returned home, Richard happened across a note his mother had written. In it he learned that she was . . ." Francis's gaze swerved away. "That his mother was carrying her lover's child. The note also said that she was planning to flee the country with her paramour."

Sabrina stiffened.

"Naturally, Richard was distraught. He couldn't believe that his mother would leave him like that without a word. Naively, he decided to go to his father with the information in the hopes that Lord Colbridge might persuade her to stay."

"Oh, no," Sabrina murmured.

"Yes. Richard's father became furious. He dashed off in

search of his wife, Richard running after him." Francis paused and took a sip of his tepid tea. "His mother lost her head. Confronted by her husband, she panicked and bolted from the house."

Sabrina felt sick, fearing the direction this story was taking. "Richard went after her?" she whispered.

Francis nodded. "They were struck by a passing carriage. Richard's leg was crushed. His mother . . . killed."

"Dear God."

"Yes. To this day, I think that he still blames himself."

"But he was a young boy. He was frightened of losing his mother. Of course, he'd want to tell someone!"

"But you and I are not thirteen years old, we weren't there that day. Richard was the child they had to pry off her bloodied body."

Sabrina turned away, shocked beyond words. The loss of her parents had been painful, but she could not imagine the extent of Richard's torment. Distrust for the mother who'd been prepared to abandon him? Resentment for the father who'd pushed her to it? And his own irrational, yet most likely very real, guilt.

"Why do you tell me this?" she demanded.

"Because for you to have any genuine affection for Richard, you must have been able to see past his armor of bitterness . . ."

"And what makes you believe I care for him?"

The earl shrugged and Sabrina found herself wondering just how discerning a man Lord Merrick really was.

"Let me simply say, Miss Simmons, that if Charlotte ever musters the courage to tell Richard she will not marry him, I would like to think he might find comfort in a friend such as you."

A friend?

Francis stood. "Richard resides at Twenty-Two

Cavendish Square. Please contact him, remembering what I've told you." He turned to leave then paused, bestowing on her a smile that would have melted stone. "You know, Miss Simmons, I suspect you might be hesitant to risk your heart with a man like Richard. But I should tell you that I know him better than most people, and there is one thing I'm fairly certain of: His feelings for you are far from indifferent."

The clock chimed three times. Richard looked up from dotting his last "i" to see that he'd spent half the night toiling at his writing desk.

Prodigious amounts of sweat and ink had gone into this evening's work but, when he'd sat himself down to pen his latest treatise, he had vowed that he would not rise until he'd exorcised himself of one Sabrina Simmons.

Ennui had been silent too long.

Scraping his chair away from the desk, Richard rose and poured himself some claret. He would celebrate.

The wine tasted sour and flat on his tongue, but he emptied the glass anyway, then flung it into the hearth. Caught in the orange flicker of flames, the crystal shards winked up at him, obscenely festive.

He returned to his desk and slowly began to skim through the pages. As he read, he tried to distance himself from the razor-edged words. Ennui had pulled no punches.

'Twas a sight to behold, my friends, a sight to behold. The little provincial pigeon's attempt to transform herself into a peacock would have made even a cadaver roar with laughter. Mutton dressed as lamb, as the saying goes, though this chronicler would have preferred the sheep over the "she."

Eyes and lips painted like a Charing Cross whore, the chit subjected yours truly to an afternoon of the most excruciatingly amateurish flirtation. Rather than stir my manhood, the wench succeeded only in turning my stomach.

And so it went on, page after page. Vile and vicious. Merciless and degrading.

After he'd finished reading, he closed his eyes and rested his head on the back of the chair. Bile had risen in his throat. He thought it little wonder that he could not sleep most nights.

And worse . . . it had not worked. He had hoped that once he'd let loose the power of his poison pen, he would be released. But crucifying Sabrina with his venomous words had not lessened his fixation. On the contrary, it had only revealed more of himself than any mirror ever could. Ugliness. An ugliness from which he had been hiding many, many years.

He pushed to his feet and went to stare out into the black, barren night.

Damn it, if I had any sense, I'd hie off to Leychurch, bed the woman, and be done with her.

But would that be enough?

Spinning around, he snatched up the papers and shoved them into the satchel with his bills. Richard knew he would not be publishing this essay. Ennui had lost his taste for savage mockery.

Chapter
Fourteen

Painfully conspicuous. Sabrina stood on the street in front of Twenty-Two Cavendish Square feeling precisely that. Even in the blue-sprigged muslin and her best cloak—and none of those awful cosmetics—she stood out like a weed in a rose garden compared to the fashionable ladies she'd seen on the street.

She had reluctantly parted with a few of her precious coins in order to take a hackney cab from Camden Town to Cavendish Square. Although she might have managed the long walk, she hadn't wanted to arrive at Richard's front door with the stench of the London streets clinging to her skirts. From what she had seen, pedestrians were hard-pressed to avoid being splashed by the filthy muck fouling the roads and footpaths.

She clutched her reticule tightly to her side, mentally

groping for an appropriate quotation about courage. A word of encouragement from Nell would have sufficed, but the ghost had not shown her face since Lord Merrick's visit yesterday afternoon. Either from disappointment or from embarrassment, Sabrina could not say.

It was too bad, too, for she would have liked to have talked to Nell about this "Charlotte" Francis had mentioned. It had never occurred to Sabrina that Richard might be betrothed. He simply hadn't struck her as a man preparing to acquire a leg-shackle. The knowledge that he might soon be affianced had kept Sabrina up most of the night worrying.

To her mind, 'twas one thing to be the paramour of a bachelor, but quite another to be the woman responsible for a man's dishonoring his marriage vows. Sabrina doubted that she'd be able to go through with her plan if Richard were to suddenly become engaged. She wouldn't feel right about being with a man who was promised to another. Perhaps 'twas a fine line her conscience drew, but one she had fretted over until well past midnight.

Ultimately, if not ironically, she had found solace in the Bible, a copy of which she'd been surprised to find in Miss Bright's small book collection. *Be not troubled, for all these things must come to pass, but the end is not yet.*

"The end is not yet," Sabrina had repeated to herself. Exactly. Richard was not even betrothed, much less married. Why should she worry about that which had not yet come to pass? Heaven knew she had enough worries without needing to borrow additional trouble.

Besides, Francis had intimated that Charlotte would refuse Richard if he should ask for her hand. So, why fret herself silly?

A curricle rumbled by behind her and Sabrina realized she was loitering in front of Richard's house. The last thing she desired was to bring attention to herself, so she lifted her chin, climbed the steps, and raised the knocker.

The servant who answered the door looked her over carefully before asking, "May I help you?"

"You may. Kindly inform Lord Colbridge that Miss Simmons asks for an audience."

Her decisive tone must have prevailed over her shabby attire. The servant admitted her, pointing a surly finger to the foyer's single piece of furniture. Nothing more than a backless x-frame, the chair did not invite one to linger and, as Sabrina seated herself, she wondered if Richard had not planned it that way.

Fortunately, she did not have long to wait before the servant returned and escorted her up the stairs.

This, Sabrina thought, must have been how Marie Antoinette had felt mounting the stairs to the guillotine. She quickly gave herself a firm mental shake. She had not come so far to falter now, to let fear overtake her. She was stronger than that, she knew. In a few minutes, with no more than a half-dozen words, she would do what she had come to do—to offer herself as Richard's mistress.

At the end of the hall, the servant pushed open a door and Sabrina was rooted to the spot.

When she had requested an audience, she had not been speaking literally. Like a fool, she had not anticipated this.

Three faces gazed up at her in curious expectation. No, only two. Richard was not looking at her, she realized. He was staring into the gilt-enclosed fireplace, his saturnine profile reflecting gold and crimson, light and darkness, so that for a second Sabrina fancied he stood in the gateway between heaven and hell.

Pulling her gaze from him, she swiftly took in the room and its other two occupants. Amid the mind-numbing opulence of velvet and gilt and ivory shone a . . . Madonna. A veritable angel sat beside Francis on a sofa so elegant that it alone must have cost what Sabrina owed on Simmons House.

Francis stood. "Miss Simmons, how pleasant to see you again." His phrasing did not give away that they had met only yesterday. His warm welcome should have been a balm to Sabrina's nerves, but she was positively dazed.

The luxury of the surroundings . . . the woman on the divan . . . the shock of not finding Richard alone. Sabrina fought the sting of tears as disappointment swamped her. She'd spent all morning gathering her courage, preparing herself for this interview. And for naught. For nothing.

Francis took her by the elbow and pulled her from the doorway into the drawing room.

"Miss Wetherby, this is Miss Sabrina Simmons, Richard's neighbor in Shropshire. Miss Simmons, allow me to introduce Miss Charlotte Wetherby."

So this was Charlotte. *Damn.*

Sabrina woodenly shook hands and then, guided by the earl, found herself taking the seat beside Miss Wetherby.

Like the fairy princesses in Teddy's bedtime stories, Charlotte Wetherby was a vision of spun sunshine and snow-white lace. She was like a meringue, lovely and frothy, but too fragile to touch. Sabrina felt as plain as brown bread in her simple muslin gown.

"How nice of you to come calling," Charlotte greeted cordially. "It's so very considerate of you to remember Richard."

Her smiling sincerity made Sabrina want to squirm. As if she could think of anything else but that particular man . . .

At the sound of his name, Richard turned from his study of the fire. His jet-black gaze burned into Sabrina, causing her breath to falter. Her mind filled with the memory of their kiss.

"I am surprised to see you in London," he said, almost accusingly.

"I . . . I thought you might be." To Sabrina's shame, her voice wavered.

"By Jove, it *is* fortunate for you to call just now, Miss Simmons," Francis broke in gaily, as if he could not detect the tension vibrating across the room. "We have an appointment at Soane's this afternoon. Supposed to be a fascinating place, like a private museum. You must join us. We'll make a jolly foursome of it."

"Yes, please do, Miss Simmons," Charlotte seconded. "We should greatly welcome your company."

Charlotte's kind entreaty sent another twinge of guilt shooting through Sabrina like a misplaced hat pin. She glanced to Richard, waiting for him to endorse the invitation. He merely regarded her with the faint mockery she remembered so well.

She hesitated. What else might she do? Return home and hope that tomorrow she could call on Richard again?

Her gaze skidded to his, taunting and tense.

"It sounds wonderful," she blurted out, somehow knowing that her acceptance would vex him.

"Splendid!" Francis said. "I'll call for my carriage."

Sabrina could not quite fathom how Francis managed it but, a few minutes later, as they pulled away from Cavendish Square in the earl's barouche, Francis and Charlotte sat in the front-facing seat, while Sabrina shared the rear with Richard. The back-to-back arrangement inhibited conversation between the two couples, creating a false sense of privacy. One that made Sabrina's skin prickle.

Warm yet hazy with clouds, the day did not show London at its best. The grayish sky cast a shadow across the horizon that made Sabrina yearn for the colors of a Shropshire spring. The smell of coal smoke hung thick in the afternoon air.

As soon as the horses set off, Richard—without even looking at her—tersely demanded, "What are you doing in London?"

Taken aback, Sabrina asked, "Are you not happy to see me?" The flirtatious ease she was striving for missed wide. She sounded breathless and nervous.

"My happiness, or lack thereof, is not at issue, Sabrina." He was gazing straight ahead so that she had a clear view of the muscle jumping in the side of his cheek. "I want to know. What brings you to London?"

Sabrina folded her hands in her lap and prayed for courage.

This was it. Now or never.

"You do," she said.

She felt him go absolutely rigid beside her.

The *click-click* of the horse's hooves merged with the cobblestone clatter of carriage wheels. Street voices harmonized together to form one voice that faded under the piercing call of a knife sharpener plying his trade. All the noises of the city's hustle and bustle were magnified in Sabrina's ears as she waited for his reply.

"I see."

That was all. *I see.*

Sabrina licked at her parched lips, but her mouth was too dry to be of benefit. "I had hoped to speak with you . . . privately."

A long pause. "Very well. We can talk. Later."

His curtness disturbed her, but Sabrina had to remind herself that taciturn was virtually Richard's middle name. Always had he mocked her thusly, taunting her with his unsettling word games.

As she and Richard fell into an uncomfortable silence,

Sabrina focused on the couple chatting in front of them. She was unable to make out Francis's and Charlotte's conversation, though she suspected that the earl was carrying on with his clandestine courtship. She wondered if Richard suspected. If he did, would he care? Did he care about anything? Or anyone?

Sabrina cast him a sidelong glance, harking back to yesterday's conversation with Lord Merrick. A glimmer of understanding—and something very close to empathy—stirred within her.

Even prior to her talk with Francis, she had known that there was more to Richard Kerry than the arrogance and contempt he so freely manifested. She wasn't sure how she had known but she had. Deep down, she had sensed in Richard some *thing* that called to her. Some common chord, some basic element of themselves that they shared.

But she had not seen it until Francis had forced her to. Until he'd forced her to envision Richard as a little boy suffering an insufferable loss. Until at last she had understood why a man would need to build walls of scorn and mockery to keep himself safe.

The truth was Sabrina knew about keeping one's self safe. Her mother had used illness to hide from a world she hadn't the strength to face. Even as a young girl, Sabrina had understood why Mama hid upstairs with her pills and possets and smelling salts. Life was just too frightening for some people.

And Sabrina was not so full of conceit that she didn't recognize the shield she herself used every day. She fortified herself with other people's words. Her quotes. Everyone had a trick, a device they used to protect themselves from their fears. Teddy had his bravado, she and Andrew their education and logic. It was simply human nature.

From beneath her lashes, she snuck another peek at

Richard. His profile revealed a steely indifference. But now she knew. Like her and everyone else on God's green earth, Richard Kerry had his fears. His just might be a little scarier than most.

The barouche pulled to a stop with a gentle swaying. The coachman assisted her down and she joined Charlotte on the footpath in front of the Lincoln's Inn Fields house, a three-story structure of classical lines.

Francis and Charlotte preceded them inside, and as Sabrina followed them up the four short steps, she felt Richard's hand lightly graze the small of her back. Her heartbeat quickened and she pulled away from the unexpected intimacy.

Would it forever be like this? she wondered helplessly, willing her pulse to slow. Would she always feel ten times more alive when in Richard's presence? Or once she'd given herself to him would she cease to be so . . . aware?

They entered the front hall, where they were greeted by a youthful, scholarly looking guide. The young man led them to the first chamber on the right, the library.

Sabrina could not restrain her quiet sigh of delight. Not only did shelves and shelves of glass-enclosed books line the walls, but filling the room were her heroes, the figures of history and literature, in the form of antiquities and pieces of statuary.

An Egyptian bronzed figure of Isis was perched beside a plaster cast bust of Flora, which in turn sat next to a palm-sized figurine of Mercury. . . . Hundreds and hundreds of artifacts ranged from full-sized statues to plates to sixteenth-century stoneware tankards.

"I say, it's quite the crush, isn't it?" Francis murmured. "Very like a *tonnish* rout."

"It does seem like a party for old relics," Charlotte concurred with a delicate wrinkling of her nose.

It was almost too much to take in. Sabrina did not know where to look first.

"I say," Francis said with a laugh. "This poor fellow being attacked by the boar looks a bit like me, don't you think?"

Sabrina pivoted around and smiled at the scene painted on an Italian majolica plate. "You do not recognize Adonis, Lord Merrick? I would imagine that you've often been compared to the handsome youth. The story goes that Venus loved him so that after he was killed by the boar, she changed his blood into a flower—the anemone."

"How charming! Francis, you're an anemone," Charlotte said, clapping her hands.

"Really?" the earl asked, appearing pleased.

"Really indeed?" came a wry voice from behind her.

Sabrina started. She'd been so enraptured by the antiquities, she'd forgotten about Richard and about Nell's dictate to play ignorant. "I . . . I—"

She glanced to Charlotte and Francis for help but they had already followed the guide into the next room.

"It's all right, Sabrina," Richard said, as he passed in front of her to examine a terra-cotta fragment. "You don't have to pretend to be a brainless twit any longer. I was never fooled."

A flush suffused Sabrina's neck and face.

"I only wonder why you ever bothered." Although Richard put the question lightly, his eyes probed hers with disturbing intensity as he glanced up from the piece of statuary.

At a loss, Sabrina was obligated to settle for the truth. "I . . . thought you'd like me better that way."

His eyes widened with shock before narrowing beneath a scowl. He whirled away, obviously angered by her answer.

Oh goodness, now I've done it! Nell must have been

right. Panic gripped Sabrina, paralyzing her. *What should I do? Should I tell him I'm not very clever, after all?*

Blindly she reached out to him, but before she could concoct any sort of explanation, Richard turned around. His gaze flew to her hand extended in silent supplication.

At the back of her mind, Sabrina thought she must surely combust from the fever-hot blush scorching her cheeks. Her hand fell limp at her side.

Richard's scowl relaxed and, for the first time, he appeared uncomfortable, unsure of himself.

"You were wrong," he said, his voice so low she had to strain to hear it. "I do not like you better that way."

"Oh." A rush of relief threatened her balance. She blinked to steady herself. "I . . . I am glad. You don't, then, object to . . . education in a woman?"

Richard recovered somewhat. "No, I do not object." And then, to her surprise, his lips curved slowly into that hypnotic Lucifer smile of his. "In fact, far from objecting, I have an idea. You like to play games, Sabrina. What would you say to a little sport?"

"Sport?"

He nodded and a lock of inky hair looped across his brow. Sabrina thought he looked more like a pirate than ever.

"Yes, a game. A contest."

"What sort?" she asked uneasily.

"A battle of wits and education. The rules are that we must use the antiquities as a basis for our game, posing questions based on the figures. You try to stump me and I try to do the same."

"Oh, but that would not be fair," she objected.

"Not up to the challenge?"

She compressed her lips. "I meant unfair for *you*."

"Don't worry about me." His smile deepened. "But what shall we play for? What will be the prize?"

For the space of a second, Sabrina dreamed she might answer "Simmons House." But that would be dishonest when she knew before the game had even begun that victory would be hers.

"A kiss?" he asked.

Sabrina's heart did that maddening tattoo again. "I—"

"Naturally," he interrupted, "if you should win, you may choose your own spoils of war. For my part, I demand a kiss."

Sabrina might have protested but confidence led her to only nod demurely. "Very well, though I do not yet know what prize I will claim."

"Fair enough. Ladies first." Richard waved around the room. "Whatever subject you choose."

Chock-full of figures, the room appeared to contain more mythological than historical characters, a factor which Sabrina believed was to her advantage. Tapping her finger against her cheek, she looked around consideringly. Her gaze fell upon a statue of a woman wrapped in a swan's embrace.

"This figure here," she said, pointing. "Who does this represent?"

"Come now, Sabrina. You must either think me a lackwit, or you wish for me to win." He leered, his implication plain.

She brushed off his innuendo. "Very well. Who is it then?"

"It is the fair Leda. As the story goes, Jupiter lusted after her, so changed himself into a swan in order to seduce her." Richard angled a black brow, inviting her confirmation.

She *had* made it too easy.

"My turn?" he asked.

"Yes. Go ahead."

"All right, then. Name Leda's offspring."

"Castor and Pollux."

"And?"

"And Helen, of course."

"And?"

Sabrina hesitated. Another? There was Castor, Pollux, Helen and . . .

"Clytemnestra!"

Richard smiled. "Ah, I have found myself a worthy adversary. Shall we move on to the next chamber for our next round?"

As they moved through the ground floor, then upstairs to the second-floor rooms, their questions became increasingly erudite. Sabrina was astonished by Richard's knowledge of mythology and classical history. If she hadn't known better, she might almost have imagined he'd planned to trap her into this game and had studied beforehand. Of course, he couldn't have. He hadn't even known she was coming to London.

They spied Charlotte and Francis during their tour, but the other couple always managed to stay one room ahead of them. It made no difference to Sabrina, although she was curious if Richard might not feel resentful of Francis's attention to Charlotte.

Richard, however, neither said or did anything that even remotely hinted of a simmering jealousy. No craning of his neck to check on the pair in the next room, no frowns or attempts at eavesdropping. He certainly did not act like a man on the verge of issuing a marriage proposal.

"Ah-hah!" Richard eyed a painted vase tucked into a niche. "Proserpine. Or Persephone to the Greeks. Forced to pass half the time in the arms of her dark husband Pluto in order to spend the other half happily with her mother Ceres."

An unbidden parallel sprang to Sabrina's mind. *Just as I will be forced to lie with Richard in order to remain with the boys at Simmons House.*

"Since I know, sweet Sabrina, that you are familiar with your Milton, this should not prove too difficult a question for you." He grinned cockily. "What was the name of the field where Proserpine was gathering flowers when Pluto abducted her?"

"The name of the field?"

"Hmm-mm. Milton names it in *Paradise Lost.*"

"He does? Are you sure?"

"Oh, yes. I am sure."

"Well," she mumbled. "Then I ought to know."

"You ought."

But she did not. She stood there probably a good five minutes while he waited for her response.

"I do not know," she finally confessed.

Richard's satisfied smile defied description.

"Enna," he pronounced. "The fields of Enna."

He leaned toward her. Closer yet. His eyes—those diabolically beautiful eyes—grew as sultry as a hot summer's night.

Alarm and anticipation shot through Sabrina. Dear heavens, he wasn't going to kiss her here and now. Was he?

"Enna?" Charlotte's soft voice intruded. "Is that near Bristol?"

Sabrina jerked her head around to find Francis and Charlotte standing in the doorway. She lurched back a step, her heart pounding, while she made a great show of adjusting her gloves.

Richard answered as smoothly as if he hadn't been but a

hairsbreadth from kissing her. "No, Charlotte. The vale of Enna was the home of Proserpine."

"The Proserpines?" Charlotte raised a puzzled face to Francis.

"I don't think we're acquainted with the family," Francis assured her in a confiding tone. "They don't come to Town."

"Oh."

Sabrina had to bite her lip. She felt giddy and silly. As naughty as Teddy snitching a tart from Hattie's oven. She hadn't the slightest idea what had come over her.

"Well, I, for one, have seen enough marble and stone to last me a lifetime," Francis said, affecting a yawn. "Are we ready to take our leave of this place?"

"Yes, I think we are done," Richard said, taking hold of Sabrina's elbow. "*Here,*" he added for her ears alone.

She shivered. The single word had held a wealth of veiled promise.

"As a matter of fact," Richard said, "if you wouldn't mind escorting Charlotte home, Francis, I'd like to talk to Miss Simmons . . . about the history of Leyton Hall. I'll just hail us a hackney. No need for you to go out of your way any more than you have to."

To Sabrina's amazement, neither Francis nor Charlotte questioned Richard's flimsy excuse for their parting of ways nor gave any indication of its untoward nature.

On the contrary, Francis appeared rather too pleased with the suggestion. "Right-o," he readily agreed. "Well, then, it was smashing to see you again, Miss Simmons. Hope to see you again soon."

"Yes, please do call on me, Miss Simmons," Charlotte offered. "If you plan to stay in Town."

Before Sabrina fully recognized what was happening, she found herself outside, bidding good day to Charlotte and Francis. When next she gathered her breath, she was sitting across from Richard in a closed carriage, listening to him ask, "All right, Sabrina, what was it you wished to discuss? *Privately?*"

Chapter Fifteen

Resentment. Desire. Curiosity.

At the mercy of all three emotions, Richard could not decide if he was more irritated or stimulated or just plain confused. He sat back against the squabs, and the stiff ache in his trousers settled the matter. Desire was definitely winning out over the other two.

He wanted Sabrina. He wanted her badly.

Yet, even while he fantasized about how she would feel naked and writhing beneath him, anger underscored his lust. Dammit, why had she come to London? He had left Shropshire to get away from her, for God's sake. She was hardly supposed to have followed him to Town like some lovesick calf. Why had she?

Here Richard's curiosity gained the upper hand. Although he might well assume she had come about Simmons

House, it seemed to him improbable that Sabrina would travel all the way across England to plead her case. But that was precisely what she had done, hadn't she? All this trouble merely to ask him not to buy her home? Why couldn't she have simply written to him?

For whatever reason, she had gone to great lengths—and distance—to seek him out. Now he would know the reason why.

His gaze settled on her as he shifted to ease the tautness between his legs.

Sabrina folded her hands in her lap. Primly, as she always did, reminding him of the puritanical little Quaker he'd so often compared her to in his mind. Today she smelled of soap and lilac, not the heavy perfume she'd worn in the past. And she'd foregone the cosmetics.

"Yes," she said. "I did, that is, *do* need a private word with you."

Richard indicated the walls of the carriage and the curtained windows. "Is this not private enough?"

She licked her lips. She looked a hell of a lot less like a puritan when she did that, Richard thought. The way she caressed the fullness of her lower lip made him think of a dozen places he would like to see her tongue. All of them on him.

"This will be fine . . . I suppose." Uneasily she glanced to the windows, as if planning an escape route. She then stared down at her linked fingers.

"Richard?" Her gaze raised to his with abrupt determination.

"Hmm-mm?"

"About Simmons House . . ."

Of course.

"I know that you are considering assuming the delinquent mortgage—to purchase it for yourself. I would ask . . . you not to."

No surprises after all, he thought with a hint of regret.

"I would ask," Sabrina rushed on, "that you pay off the mortgage. For Andrew. In Andrew's name."

He stilled. "I beg your pardon?"

Sabrina took a swift breath. "I know that it is a fair amount of money, but not really that much when compared to other . . . expenses. It might be asking too much—I hope it isn't— but I would ask it of you all the same."

Wait a minute. . . .

"Let me understand you," Richard said slowly. "You are asking me to pay off the mortgage, to settle the account . . . for your brother?"

"You would be recompensed."

"I would?"

"Yes." Her chin rose. Shakily. "*I* will repay you."

Suspicion twisted Richard's gut. "How, Sabrina? How do you plan to repay me?"

A sheen glossed over her turquoise eyes, but she did not falter. "I"—another sharp intake of breath —"I will become your mistress."

A numbness immobilized him. It was soon followed by an inexplicable rage. *Damn you, Sabrina!*

She could have no idea what she was asking.

"And what makes you think I'd be interested?" he questioned angrily, his eyes ice-cold as they raked over her.

Her composure wavered. "I had thought—or believed— that perhaps you found me . . . appealing."

The absurd little innocent. If it weren't for the meager amount of honor he had left, she'd be sprawled across that bench with her skirts shoved up to her neck, while he pounded himself into her with a fury.

He clenched his fists to keep from grabbing her and doing just that.

"Even if I did find you 'appealing,' " he bit out, playing her along, "what experience do you have?"

"None. But I can learn."

Richard's eyes slitted. "Teaching yourself Latin is nothing like learning how to pleasure a man, Sabrina."

Her chin raised a fraction of an inch. "You don't think I can do it?"

Hell, he *knew* she could. Right now, just her touch would send him over the edge.

He lifted a corner of the window curtain and pretended to gaze onto the street. Feigning indifference, he said, "Sorry, Miss Simmons, but virgins are not my style."

"I would only be a virgin the first time."

His manhood swelled painfully. He continued to stare out the window.

"Please . . . Richard."

The halting entreaty undid him. His gaze jerked to hers as lust and fury swamped over him. "Hell, Sabrina, why? Is the blasted house worth so much to you?"

But as soon as he said it, Richard realized that more was at stake here than Simmons House. He suddenly saw Sabrina, her hands folded protectively over Teddy's shoulders as if she might shield him from life's every sorrow and sadness. He saw Andrew—gangly, bespectacled and nervous—defending his sister with a devotion that had touched even Richard's hardened heart.

This was about more than a house.

"It is our home," she answered.

Richard cursed beneath his breath.

What was wrong with him? He wanted her. By God, he'd been obsessed with her. Why shouldn't he take her up on her offer? She was right, too, dammit. The mortgage would cost him no more than the expense of setting up a new bit o'muslin. And Sabrina would certainly make for a refreshing change of bed partners. He could actually hold an intelligent conversation with her, unlike any other woman he'd ever had under his protection. It was tempting. Too tempting.

"What are your terms?" he abruptly asked.

Her eyes rounded. Her fingers ceased their twining. "Ah. My terms." She wet her lips again and the sight of her small pink tongue nearly sealed Richard's decision.

"You would agree to pay off the mortgage, but . . . quietly. It cannot be flaunted—my brothers cannot ever, *ever* know." She shot him a look of desperation to which he responded with a bland nod. "As for me, I would continue to reside at Simmons House with the boys and to make myself available to you."

"For how long?"

"As long as you choose."

He snorted. "You don't drive much of a bargain, Sabrina. Aren't you concerned that you might be selling yourself short?"

Even in the dark carriage, he could see her color rise.

Suddenly he could not stand to look at her. "Very well," he said, as he flicked an imaginary thread from his coat sleeve. "I accept your offer."

Her light gasp drew his attention again, but this time it was she who could not hold his gaze. She glanced to her fingers in her lap.

"But first," Richard said, "you must agree to accompany me on a tour."

"A tour?"

"Yes." His anger built anew at what he planned, but he knew of no other way. "Usually a woman in your circumstances knows exactly what she is getting herself into when

she accepts a man's carte blanche. You, Sabrina, do not."
He folded his arms across his chest. "Therefore, before I
can agree to finalize our arrangement, you will join me in a
guided tour." His voice hardened. "Of the world of whore-
dom."

The word hit her like a slap in the face—as he'd intended. She blanched, but held her ground. "Agreed. When
do we go?"

Her facile acceptance irked him. "Tomorrow night," he
answered tersely. "I will pick you up at nine o'clock. Wear
something dark. A cloak with a hood if you have one.
Where are you staying?"

"Camden Town."

He mocked her with a raised brow. "How appropriate."

He banged on the roof of the carriage with his balled fist
and, when the driver called down through the opening,
Richard gave him the address. Sitting back down, he eyed
her uncertainly.

"Why me, Sabrina?"

She ran her palm over her temple, smoothing a gold-
brown curl. Her voice sounded less sure than before. "I did
not want to have to leave Simmons House. If I wanted to
remain in Leychurch, there were not many gentlemen to
choose from."

"So, 'twas a question of geography? I suppose I ought to
feel flattered but, as you said, who else was there? Though
I imagine that the oily cleric might have made you an offer.
He seemed interested enough."

Sabrina looked him straight in the eye. "He could not
have afforded me."

"Ah, pragmatic, as well." Richard laughed softly as he
inclined his head. "Your estimable qualities continue to as-
tound me."

"Thank you," she said, her answering smile every bit as derisive as his own.

Beneath the veil of her lashes, her blue-green gaze stormed like a gale-swept sea, causing Richard to wonder what it would take to let loose that tempest. He always had admired her extraordinary self-control.

The coach pulled to a stop. Richard lifted the curtain once again to find that dusk had fallen. Lamplight illuminated the front window of the Camden Street house.

"Whom are you staying with?" he asked.

"A friend of a friend."

The driver opened the door and Sabrina hastily gathered her skirts to climb out. On impulse, and spurred on by his irrational anger, Richard reached out and grabbed a fistful of her dress, jerking her down beside him. She let out a small cry as she stumbled to the banquette.

Pulling her to him, he covered her mouth with his, plundering with one rough sweep of his tongue. She tasted warm and fragrant. He deepened the kiss, ruthlessly laying his claim, then released her. She drew back, her eyes wide, the back of her hand pressed to her mouth.

She said nothing. She understood.

With that leashed tempest still brewing at the back of her eyes, she calmly stood and stepped down from the carriage. The driver was waiting, looking bored.

Richard watched her climb the few steps to the front door. She withdrew a key from her reticule and inserted it into the lock. She let herself in and closed the door behind her, not once looking back at him.

Nell was fit to be tied. All afternoon she'd been pacing about, awaiting Sabrina's return. One hour had gone by. Then two. Three, four, and five. She had chewed her spectral fingernails to nubs, while staring out the window so long that her eyes had started to cross. Blast it, where *was* the girl?

"I shouldn't 'ave done it," Nell muttered.

She shouldn't have let Sabrina leave today without helping her get ready or wishing her good luck. And she definitely shouldn't have cozened that Lord Merrick into calling at the house yesterday afternoon.

Gor, but Sabrina had been cross. When she'd come stomping into the kitchen with her eyes spitting sparks, Nell had started to wonder whether throwing the earl and Sabrina together was really such a bang-up idea. But then she'd figured, why not have a go at it? A few minutes alone together might just do the trick. And he was the prettiest fella . . .

But she had been wrong. Dead wrong. It couldn't have been more than five minutes before Lord Merrick was jawing away about being in "love" with some bird named Charlotte. Nell sniffed derisively. *Love.*

Flouncing over to the parlor sofa, she threw herself down with a sigh, wishing she knew how Sabrina was gettin' on with Lord Richie. Nell could tell that the girl had been bothered by the earl's story—the one about Lord Richie's mother and the carriage accident. Even Nell had felt sorta rotten to think that all these years, the poor bloke had been blaming himself. Actually it explained a lot, it did.

Turning her gaze heavenward, she nibbled thoughtfully at the side of her thumb. Maybe . . . maybe when she returned to the other side—be it Purgatory or the Pearly Gates—she could somehow get a message to Lord Richie's mother. Let her know there was business to clear up down here. Nell couldn't say if it would do any good, but it might be worth a try. And in the long run, it might help out Sabrina with her troubled viscount.

Chapter Sixteen

The carriage pulled up in front of the house and Sabrina edged back from the window before she could be seen. The last thing she wanted was for Richard to discover her hovering in front of the window, her breath frosting the glass with anxious puffs.

After yesterday—and that terribly mortifying kiss—she was loath to reveal to him even the slightest indication of weakness or apprehension. That kiss, that fleeting moment when his mouth had held dominion over hers, had been . . .

Well, she could not adequately describe it. It had been an experiment, a challenge. It had marked her as his possession and his plaything. But above all, Richard's kiss had been a warning.

But a warning of what?

Pressing herself against the wall, Sabrina closed her

eyes, her palms damp inside her gloves. She knew, instinctively, that tonight would be a test. The battle of wits and words that she and Richard had engaged in from the first had subtly shifted to become a contest of wills. Sabrina knew that tonight she would be sent through Richard's own version of the gauntlet. And that this evening's trial would be nothing as innocuous as a review of her knowledge of history.

"He's here, Nell," she said as she picked up her cloak, black and hooded, from the chair beside her.

The ghost materialized in an instant, a frown creasing her brow as she floated to the window. Wringing her hands and biting at her lips, she looked tired and worn with worry. If one could say that of someone who had already been dead for half-dozen years.

"Are you sure you don't want me to tag along?" Nell asked with a fretful moue.

Sabrina spread the cloak over her shoulders and shook her head. "No, this is only the beginning, Nell. If I cannot handle whatever Richard has in store, then I don't see how I will be able to see the seduction through."

Nell tugged at her earring, a nervous habit Sabrina recognized.

"Well, luv, remember what I taught you about them randy coves. They can be as tenacious as a tick on a dog. If Lord Richie tries anythin' cagey, you tell him flat out that you're not playin' no slap and tickle tonight. Not 'til he gives you proof—and I mean in writin'—that he's paid off the house are you to go anywhere within a mile of his bed, you understand?"

Sabrina pulled the hood over her head. "Do not worry, Nell. I won't let you down."

The tension in Nell's features slackened. Floating close, she laid a transparent arm across Sabrina's shoulders, patting gently. The warmth of the gesture made up for the chill of her supernatural touch.

"Blimey, Sabrina luv, you could never do nothin' to disappoint me. You've got more pluck than anyone I've ever met and it's spankin' proud of you I am. Why, I couldn't be more proud than if you was my own bleedin' dau—uh, sister."

Sabrina smiled. Her bawdy madam ghost was starting to remind her of a protective mother hen.

A knock sounded at the door, tentative and furtive.

Sabrina gave Nell a reassuring look. "Don't worry," she said. "If Cleopatra could conquer the indomitable Caesar, I can best one brooding viscount. Remember what Virgil said: *Audentes fortuna iuvat.*"

" *'Fortune favors the brave,' "* Nell translated.

Sabrina pulled up in surprise. "Why, Nell, you've been reading!"

The ghost lifted a sheepish shoulder. *"I've had time on my hands."*

Another knock sounded, this time louder.

"I'd better go," Sabrina said.

"Good luck, luv. God be with you."

As Sabrina followed the coachman to the waiting carriage, she saw that Richard had again hired a private coach rather than bring his own vehicle. The thought occurred to her that he must prefer anonymity for where they were headed—a realization that did little to comfort her.

The interior of the coach was deep with shadows as she stepped inside. Dressed all in black, Richard at first looked to be nothing more than a creature of the darkness. His long, shiny black hair hung unbound to his shoulders and his unearthly eyes glinted in the coach's gloom. He reminded her more than ever of Dante's fallen angel.

"Sabrina," he greeted, his voice wholly empty of inflection.

She nodded and sat across from him and to the side, leaving as much distance between them as was possible.

"Are you ready for your night's education?" he asked.

"I am."

"Are you certain? If you want to turn around and go back inside . . ." He hesitated. "You don't have to do this, Sabrina."

Do what? Submit to his test or become his mistress? Either way the answer was a firm, "Yes, I do."

"Very well."

Clenched in Richard's right fist was an ivory walking stick. Sabrina had never seen him use a cane before, and wondered if his leg was paining him this evening. He lifted the walking stick and used it to rap upon the carriage roof, signaling the driver.

The coach set off.

Sabrina huddled in her corner, glad that she'd pulled her cloak so far over her face. Silly though it might have been, she felt as if the concealing hood offered some protection from the intensity of Richard's gaze. After all this time, she might have thought she'd have grown accustomed to those soul-stealing midnight eyes. But the way her pulse was hammering . . .

"Where are we going?" she asked.

"Our first stop is the home of an old friend, Simone Jesel."

Sabrina took a stab in the dark. "Your ex-mistress?"

"You have heard of Simone?"

"No. Not really."

Sabrina lowered her gaze to where Richard's fingers were playing across the length of the walking stick like a flautist fingering his instrument. He seemed to be following a pattern. First finger, third, fourth, second. It was almost as if he were tapping out a secret code.

He caught her gaze and his movements stilled.

" 'Tis an unusual cane."

"A useful one," he answered. "The sheath conceals a blade."

Sabrina's trepidation returned in full force. "Do you believe you will have need of it?"

"One cannot be too cautious."

Again, that note in his voice. Warning. Cautioning *her*.

When they stopped in front of a discreet little house on a quiet side street, Sabrina thought they must have detoured. The quaint brick building with the flowering window boxes did not look like the home of a demimondaine.

As Richard led her up in the steps, she debated whether or not to throw off her hood. The act of baring herself, even in such an insignificant manner, was not appealing. She decided to hide behind her cloak for a little while longer.

A maid answered the door, recognition in her face.

"Lord Colbridge. M'moiselle awaits you in the drawing room."

Richard gestured Sabrina forward and she diffidently stepped into the foyer. Simone's home was nothing like Miss Bright's—no cheap lace or pink-painted furniture. It was tasteful and subdued. Very much like the woman who met them at the drawing room door.

"Richard." The petite ebony-haired Simone gave his name the French pronunciation, caressing the syllables with her deep, velvety voice. A voice that seemed too large for such a diminutive person. Beside her, Sabrina felt like an overgrown amazon.

"Simone." Richard saluted her dainty fingers. "Allow me to present Sabrina."

The woman turned to her, her thickly fringed eyes almost

as black as Richard's. "But I cannot see her, *mon cher.* Do you bring her here only to hide her from me?"

Lifting her hands, Sabrina pushed back the hood.

Simone arched a delicate brow. *"Interessant."*

Although not precisely a compliment, Sabrina accepted it as such. She dipped her head and answered in Simone's native tongue. "Thank you. I try to be."

"Ah, you speak French. I like you better already. Come sit down," she invited. "As I told Richard, I can give you only an hour before Michel will want me all to himself." She slanted Richard a sideways glance as if to say, *Remember what you are missing?*

Richard ignored her, checking the pocket watch dangling from his waistcoat. "I will return in an hour then." He bowed and Sabrina realized with a shock that he was going to leave her.

"A toute à l'heure," Simone said.

Sabrina said nothing as Richard departed.

Simone urged her to sit, the woman's every movement as graceful as flowing water. "Please, may I offer you a sherry or something to drink?"

"No. No thank you," Sabrina answered. She unclasped her cape, allowing it to slip down her shoulders and pool at the back of the chair. Simone sent her a surreptitious look, quickly taking in the inexpensive gown and the slim figure beneath it.

"I am not what you expected, am I?" Sabrina asked.

Dark chocolate eyes met hers frankly. *"Non. Pas de tout."* But then she smiled, taking the sting from her words. "But Richard is an unpredictable man, Sabrina. It was foolish of me to anticipate what you might be like."

Even so, Sabrina could well imagine the Frenchwoman's surprise. Based on what she'd seen of Charlotte Wetherby and now Simone Jesel, plain Sabrina Simmons was not Richard Kerry's usual cup of tea.

"What did he tell you?"

Simone lifted a shoulder in a classic Gallic gesture. "He told me that he had offered you carte blanche. He asked if I would speak with you so that you would know what to expect."

Sabrina glanced around the beautifully appointed drawing room.

"Yes," Simone said, divining her thoughts. "Richard paid for all of this. And, when we parted—as a token of his esteem, he said—he gifted me with the house. He is, if anything, generous with his coin."

"But less generous . . . in other areas?"

Simone unconsciously, or consciously, trailed her palm up the side of her thigh.

"He is generous in bed, Sabrina, if that is what you ask. You need have no concerns about your own pleasure. The trouble with his leg affects him not at all. He is very skilled and knows how to satisfy a woman better than most. Richard never left me unfulfilled, and I did the same for him."

Sabrina swallowed. A lump had suddenly formed in her throat as she pictured Richard in this woman's embrace. Simone was lovely and sensual and . . . everything Sabrina was not.

For a second, she questioned whether Richard had brought her here to demonstrate how woefully unfit she was to take Simone's place. Perhaps he thought that once she'd seen the type of woman he kept that she would rescind her proposal and leave him a gentlemanly out.

Yet, as quickly as the thought came upon her, Sabrina dismissed it. Richard was not the sort of man who needed a gentlemanly out. Gallantry was not his forte. He did not need an excuse to refuse her. If he had not been interested, he would have simply said, "No."

But he had said, "Yes."

"How?" Sabrina asked. "How did you fulfill him?"

Simone's eyes narrowed shrewdly. "You have not been with a man before, have you?"

"No."

"Mon Dieu," Simone murmured. "Richard has developed a penchant for *les vierges*." She fluttered her fingers as if that explained it all. "No wonder he brought you to me. Do you want to know what he likes, Sabrina?"

Sabrina held her breath to forestall the blush she felt creeping up her neck. "Yes," she answered with difficulty. "Please."

"Bien." Simone tossed her raven curls. She might have been sharing a favored recipe, she spoke so easily. "He likes to be touched. Very much. Massaged, caressed. His back, his legs—even the bad one. Everywhere. He does not like a lot of chatter during lovemaking. Usually he is tender, but sometimes he likes it fast and rough."

"Rough?" Sabrina's fingers clenched.

"Oh, *non*. Non." Simone made a little *poof*ing sound . . . utterly French. "I forget you know nothing of this. There are as many different ways to make love, Sabrina, as there are cheeses in France. By rough, I do not mean that Richard was ever cruel. He was not.

"Michel, on the other hand . . . Michel enjoys a little pain, but fortunately so do I." Simone suddenly smiled. "Ah, I have shocked you, haven't I? *Tant pis*. You still have much to understand."

Sabrina winced, shamed by her naivety. "Michel. He is your new . . . gentleman?"

"Yes. He is very good to me. He is not as young as Richard nor as unselfish, but I am lucky. Since Michel does not have to pay for the house, my allowance is uncommonly large. I will be well taken care of when I no longer have this." With a sweep of her elegant hands, she indicated her hourglass figure.

Refusing to look down at her own slim frame, Sabrina asked, "What else should I know? About Richard?"

Simone sighed. "Oh, let me think. There are certain rules, of course. Do not ask about his injured leg or about his family. I do not know why, but do not."

Sabrina knew why and she had Francis to thank for it.

"What else, what else?" Simone muttered impatiently to herself. "Oh, yes, our Richard has no faith in women. You might already know this, but he does not trust us even the littlest bit. You must be very careful if you think to have outside liaisons. He will cut you off like that"—she snapped her fingers—"if he believes that you are not faithful to him."

Sabrina thought of the mother who had been prepared to abandon him without even a word.

" 'There is no more trusting in women,' " she quoted softly.

"What? What is that?"

"Homer's *Odyssey*," Sabrina answered, her mind filled with the picture of a dark-haired child sobbing in the middle of a London street.

"*Alors,* another lover of books." Simone rolled her eyes. "Oh yes, one more thing," she said. "You might have to ask Richard if he has changed his custom but, when we were together, he took care of the precautions. I thought it most considerate of him. I did not have to worry about it."

"Precau—" Sabrina began to question before suddenly recalling that particular conversation with Nell. Now *that* had been an edifying, if vastly embarrassing, discussion. One she did not want to have with Simone Jesel.

The Frenchwoman rose and shook out her skirts. "I think our time runs short. Is there anything else you wish to ask me before Richard returns?"

Sabrina looked up, thinking that she shouldn't ask, but knowing that she would. "How long has it been since you have . . . seen Richard?"

A tinkling laugh met her question. "Seen or slept with, Sabrina?"

Sabrina flushed. "Slept with."

Simone looked at her for a moment, then, leaning forward so that her face was very near, she whispered, "I have not had sex with your Richard since last November. Does that make you feel better?"

Five? Six months? Oddly enough, it did make Sabrina feel better, though she wasn't certain as to the reason.

Pulling back, Simone shook her head of ringlets in obvious censure. "Be careful, Sabrina. Be very careful. For when I told you that Richard was generous, I was not speaking of his heart."

Simone's admonishment stayed with Sabrina after Richard returned and they made their farewells. Climbing back into the hackney, she reexamined the Frenchwoman's words with a sense of annoyance.

The implication bothered her. What should it matter to her what Richard Kerry did with his "heart"? Why, she wasn't even sure he had one, much less care how generous he was with it. Why did she need to be careful?

But why, an inner voice taunted, had she been relieved to learn that many months had passed since Richard had last visited Simone's bed? Why indeed? Sabrina did not have an answer.

Under the screen of her hood, she studied him as he took his seat opposite her. His glossy black hair made her fingers itch to sink into it and she was struck with an insane desire to stroke her palms across his broad back. Simone had said he liked to be touched.

Sabrina wrenched her gaze away. Perhaps she *did* need to be careful. Richard's effect on her was growing more potent every day. Nell had told her not to worry—that desire for a man was a normal, healthy thing—but Sabrina did not feel normal or healthy. She felt strange and breathless all the time, her insides forever in knots.

"Did you enjoy your chat?"

She sank further into her cloak. "It was . . . enlightening."

"I wager it was." Richard twirled the cane through his fingers. "Undoubtedly you will find our next stop equally so."

"And where is that?"

"The Harem." His eyes flashed like hell's own brimstone. "After our visit to the fair, I feared that you might have garnered the wrong impression. What we witnessed that day were two sweethearts engaged in a romantic tryst. The act of sex is not always so entertaining."

She remained silent and he went on.

"I think it only fair you appreciate what can happen to women less fortunate than Simone. She has had the good sense to squirrel away a tidy nest egg that will serve her once her desirability wanes. But not all are as astute or as fortunate. Once time diminishes their charms, many women must go from pampered courtesan to brothel whore."

Sabrina's spine went rigid. She had no absolutely no intention of ever being with another man after Richard. But he did not know that.

She deliberately said nothing. Her silence seemed to irritate him.

"Come. Sit here." He jerked his chin to the spot beside him. When she did not immediately rise, his expression became mocking. "Sabrina, a prerequisite to being a good mistress is obedience. Do you disobey me already?"

Her jaw clamped, but she moved to the other side of the banquette. Richard reached over and lowered the hood of her cloak, exposing her face to the coach's meager light.

"Ah. She obeys even as her eyes flame with outrage. Good."

Bending over her, he traced her lower lip with the rough pad of his thumb. She shivered and he suddenly frowned. He thrust a handkerchief into her hand.

"Wipe that substance from your mouth. And your eyes," he instructed. "Do not wear it again."

Sabrina rubbed the cosmetics from her face, emotions bubbling inside her hot and thick.

"Now kiss me."

She froze. How could he ask that of her?

"W-we have not yet reached an agreement."

Richard's gaze bored into her. "If you want an agreement, you will kiss me."

She thought of Cleopatra. Then she placed her mouth on his.

"Is this all you have learned?" he derided, his lips forming the words stiffly against hers.

Was she doing it wrong? She'd only been kissed twice and he'd done all the work. Raising her hands tentatively to his shoulders, she increased the pressure of her lips.

"Hmm-mm," he coaxed. "Better."

It was better. Even she could tell.

Haltingly, she slid her palms lower, gently kneading the muscles of his upper back. His groan took her by surprise, even as the warmth of his breath reminded her of something.

Oh, yes.

Her tongue made a hesitant foray into his mouth. He

tasted—Oh God, he tasted like Richard. She felt her fingers curl into his shoulders, as she found his tongue.

A touch at her calf pulled her lips from his. Richard's hand was under her skirt.

"I . . ."

His eyes dared her to protest. Her voice lodged in her throat. His palm traveled up and over her knee. She was breathing too fast.

"Kiss me," he said.

But she could not move. His fingers were skimming across her inner thigh, reaching higher to that secret place. That secret place pulsing and moist.

"Kiss me," he demanded again, more forcefully.

Sabrina had never been so confused. Furious at the control he was wielding over her, she was at the same time dying inside. Dying from the pleasure his touch was bringing her.

Half in anger, half in need, she jammed one hand into his too-long hair and crushed her mouth to his. She would meet his challenge, damn him.

She could but feel, not hear, the rumble of satisfied laughter that shook his chest.

His hand moved ever higher. . . . Sabrina twisted on the seat, trying to prevent him from reaching his goal, even as his mouth commanded hers. But he would not be deterred. She gasped when his fingers delved through the curls at her apex. He parted and touched her.

The agony-sweet sensation pushed her almost to her feet.

Richard's hand fell away and she collapsed back onto the carriage seat. Wildly she looked at him. What was he doing to her? Turning her into a mass of nerves and wants and needs?

His features were still, completely unreadable. A vein pulsed in his neck.

Sabrina could not think what to say. To be touched so intimately. So casually.

"Pull up your hood."

"Wh—"

Then she realized that the hackney had come to a halt. She swiftly drew her cloak up and over her face. The door opened, flooding the coach with the salty smell of the sea, and another odor, less pleasant. Evidently they were in the vicinity of the London docks.

As she stepped down from the hackney, Sabrina noticed the pistol visibly tucked into the driver's coat. He had taken no pains to conceal it. Richard followed her from the coach and he, too, appeared more alert, wielding his walking stick with inarguable authority.

Involuntarily, she sidled closer.

The night had grown so dark that Sabrina had difficulty in seeing the house that Richard led her to. She could smell it, however. The sharp aroma of spirits mixed with decaying rubbish and other noxious smells that singed Sabrina's nostrils.

"Keep your head down," Richard whispered as the door to the brothel pulled open amid a shaft of golden light. She ducked her head and Richard guided her into the house. Smoke hazed the air.

"We're here for the viewing," Richard said softly to a woman whom Sabrina could only see from the waist down. She wore a midnight-blue gown. It looked as if money exchanged hands, but Sabrina was too reluctant to risk exposure by lifting her head.

Between her thighs her womanhood still throbbed, a compelling reminder of Richard's intimate touch. Shifting slightly, Sabrina edged her legs apart, trying to ease the ache.

The woman turned away and Richard's hand urged her

to follow. Beneath her feet, stains randomly splotched the red-and-gold carpet. The woman stopped before a staircase and mumbled something. Sabrina sensed Richard's nod.

"Upstairs," he said.

At the top of the steps, he opened a door and none too gently pushed her inside. When he shut the door, the room fell into total blackness but for two lamps at the far end of the large chamber. Their light was directed onto a bed.

Sabrina could not fathom how Richard negotiated the darkness, but he steered her into the pitch-black room until her knees came into contact with a piece of furniture. A sofa.

"Sit down," he said, pushing her hood back. "The show is about to begin."

Horrified realization suddenly slammed into Sabrina like the blow of a fist. This was what he'd been referring to! He was going to force her to watch another couple—

She swallowed and sank onto the moldy-smelling sofa. Closing her eyes, she reminded herself that tonight was to be a trial. A trial by fire. She would not weaken.

Richard seated himself beside her, both hands wrapped around the walking stick.

Another door at the opposite end of the room opened with an ominous creaking. Into the sparse light entered a very blonde woman—who distressingly reminded Sabrina of Nell—leading a man by the hand.

The woman wore some type of nightrail or negligee, filmy and shiny. The man, overweight and slumping along as if intoxicated, stumbled after her. By the cut of his hair and his clothing, he looked as if he could have been any London gentleman that might be passed on the street.

They gave no indication they knew that two strangers watched them under the shelter of darkness.

The woman led the man to the bed, quickly removing his

boots, his coat, and his shirt. His skin shone a sickly yellow in the lamplight. As the woman began to remove the man's trousers, Sabrina felt Richard's gaze swing to her, but she did not so much as blink.

She had never in her life known anything so degrading. The fair experience had shamed her to her core. Richard's blatant manipulation of her moments earlier in the hackney had been truly humiliating. But this—this was beyond words.

All she could think was that Richard was trying to make a point. And possibly succeeding.

The man sat naked on the bed. The blonde woman fell to her knees before him, scooting forward, her silky night-gown rustling.

Every muscle in Sabrina's body tensed.

The man reached out and cupped his hand around the back of the woman's head. She placed her hands on his thighs as he guided her to him. . . .

Chapter
Seventeen

Richard hated himself. But he almost hated Sabrina more for making him do this.

She sat beside him, motionless, like one of the statues they had viewed yesterday at Soane's. He could feel her quaking beneath her rigid posture, but she did not back down. She did not shut her eyes or turn her head or wince. Or anything.

She merely sat there with her blasted hands folded in her lap.

He glanced to the bed. The whore had finished her "opening act" and the man was taking her with all the grace of a rutting rhinoceros. Even Richard felt nauseated at the sight.

Then the idiot on the bed started to grunt. A harsh, grating sound that echoed into every corner of the room. Sabrina moved. Slightly.

Finally, Richard thought. He could scarcely credit that she'd held out this long.

But that was it. Just that small shifting of her shoulders. Richard's hands curled into fists.

I don't bloody hell believe it.

The man's cries grew louder, sharper. Sabrina sat there as if she were carved of ice.

"Aaagh," the man wailed. "Aagh!"

Richard could not take it. He broke. Snatching Sabrina by the wrist, he hauled her off the sofa, practically dragging her to the door.

"Richard," she protested in a whisper. "Wh-what are you doing?"

Too angry to speak, he ignored her, roughly yanking her hood over her head. He threw open the door so that it crashed against the wall, then towed her down the stairs, hauling her behind him like a child's pull toy. From the back of the house, the sounds of laughter and clinking glasses punctuated the acrid smoke-filled air.

As Sabrina staggered along, tripping on her skirts, he dragged her out the door and down the steps to the waiting hackney. He virtually shoved her into the carriage, and slammed the door behind them.

"Damn you, Sabrina! Damn you."

She steadied herself on the seat, her hands curving around the leather banquette.

"I was going to take you next to Fleet Street so you could see how a whore working the streets must live! Let me assure you, it's not even half as pleasant as what you've just seen in there." He jerked his chin in the direction of the brothel. "Can you imagine, Sabrina, what it would be like to be shoved up against the wall in a fetid back alley while a gin-soaked bastard takes you for a few coins? Can you?" he demanded, his voice rising.

Slowly Sabrina pushed the hood away from her face. Richard registered her unnatural pallor. And her determination.

He dug the heels of his palms into his temples. "There's no point in going to Fleet Street, is there, Sabrina? It's not going to make any difference to you, is it?"

She shook her head and her dark blond curls brushed against her cape.

"*Nothing* is going to change your mind?"

"No, Richard. Nothing will change my mind."

He fell back against the squabs. He did not know where to go from here.

Sabrina stared at him, her cheeks as pale as morning frost. Richard muttered an oath.

What was he to do? On one hand, he wanted to pull her into his arms and soothe her until the fear melted from her eyes. On the other, he wanted to shake her until her teeth rattled in her sweet, fact-filled head.

"Do you not want me for your mistress, Richard? Is that why you wish for me to change my mind?"

Yes.

No.

He wanted her, yes, he wanted her. But perversely and completely inexplicably, he also wanted her to renege on her proposal.

God, just look at her! A little Quaker temptress who could recite Latin and Greek like a bloody Cambridge instructor. A woman who didn't know the first thing about flirting but who, with a single look, could make him as randy as a damned goat.

Sabrina Simmons simply was not the kind of woman a man made his mistress. But what . . . what did a man do with someone like Sabrina? What was he supposed to do when he wanted her so badly he ached with it and she was offering herself to him on a blasted silver platter?

"I cannot do it."

Sabrina regarded him with a pale calm. "Why not?"

"Because, I cannot. I *will* not."

She lifted her chin, defiance in the tilt of her jaw. "What are you afraid of, Richard?"

"Afraid?" he questioned. "Just what in blazes are you talking about?"

"I think that you are afraid . . . to reveal yourself."

He waved a hand from his chest to his knees, and answered her, boldly and willfully provocative. "I've nothing to be ashamed of."

"You and I both know that I am not referring to your physique."

He could have throttled her. So, she thought she knew him, did she? She thought herself so clever as to challenge *him*?

"Very well, Sabrina. What is it you want?"

Confusion drifted into her gaze. "I . . . told you. The mortgage . . ."

"Yes, yes," he curtly interrupted. "I am agreeing to your proposition. I want to know when? Where?"

"Oh." She appeared surprised by his sudden capitulation. "Not here. Not in London."

"Where then? Leyton Hall?"

Her eyes shifted quickly, consideringly. "Yes. As . . . as soon as possible."

Richard felt tempted to laugh. In spite of the anger and frustration churning acid in his stomach. "Your eagerness flatters me."

Blood rushed to her face. "How soon can you return to Leychurch?"

Her hands smoothed over her skirts in a self-conscious gesture.

As he followed the path of her hands, Richard abruptly recalled his own hand skimming up under her skirt and his fingers burned with the memory of her female dampness.

He cleared his throat. "I don't know." There was Charlotte to consider—the woman he was going to marry. "There are a few personal matters I'll have to take care of before I can join you. I presume," he added dryly, "that you'll want me to settle the mortgage prior to our assignation?"

"Yes. Please."

Her labored courtesy struck him as peculiar under the circumstances.

"Shall we say a fortnight? Two weeks from today you will come to me at Leyton Hall?"

She bit into the lushness of her lower lip. "You cannot get away from London sooner?"

He would have liked to. But he had to settle matters with Charlotte. "No."

She nodded. "I shall leave for Shropshire tomorrow."

For the space of a heartbeat, Richard wondered at her impatience. He knew that it could not be lust that drove her to such apparent enthusiasm. Her eagerness must be due to her desire to conclude their "business" and to see Simmons House secured for her brothers.

"The fourteenth?" He questioned how he would last that long. "You will come to me at Leyton Hall the evening of the fourteenth?"

Her eyes met his, their blue-green depths glinting with an almost metallic sheen. "I will be there," she promised. "That night . . . and as many more as you require."

Richard's loins clenched. He had a feeling that he was

going to *require* much more of Sabrina Simmons than she could ever begin to suspect.

Five days later, Richard stood on the landing in front of the Wetherbys's town house. He would have wished himself anywhere else on the planet. Preferably Leychurch. More precisely, Leyton Hall. Specifically, in bed with Sabrina.

By now, she would have returned to the provincial serenity of Simmons House. Did she sit at home in her drawing room counting down the days to the fourteenth with eagerness or trepidation? He wondered what she must be feeling, for his own emotions were more muddled than he cared to confess.

He wanted Sabrina so badly that he could taste her. Quite literally. Hauntingly, sweet memories of her kisses, her mouth, her tongue, had tormented him every minute since he'd left her. He missed her wit and their playful contest of words. He missed her prim mannerisms and her innocently seductive glances. He missed her.

And yet, a small part of him remained furious at the realization that she was going to go through with this. For the life of him, he could not determine why he should be angered by the fact she was giving him exactly what he desired . . . but he was.

One question that troubled him about their impending rendezvous was the issue of whether or not Sabrina desired him. Perhaps it was but masculine vanity; however, Richard wanted Sabrina to want *him*. He did not like to think of her sacrificing her virginity on the altar of his bed solely for her brothers' inheritance. Her determination was such that, for all he knew, she could despise him and yet still yield her chastity to him while gritting her teeth with silent loathing.

No, he should have made it clear to her that he would not

take her half-willing. He wanted her wholly willing. He wanted all of her in his bed, not just her body.

With a grim tightening of his lips, Richard set aside his thoughts of Sabrina. A man on his way to deliver a marriage proposal ought not to be fantasizing about his soon-to-be mistress, he chided himself.

Grabbing hold of the knocker, he rapped soundly at the Wetherbys's town house door. Instead of the rotund and halitosis-inflicted butler, a young maidservant answered. Richard thrust his hat at her.

"Is Miss Wetherby in?" he asked, striding determinedly into the hall, impatient to be done with his long-postponed task.

"She is, m'lord. I think she's in the music room. The butler's just stepped out, but I do believe Miss Charlotte is at her piano."

"No need to take me up," Richard said. "I'll find her."

Taking the stairs two at a time, Richard made his way to the second story room where Charlotte routinely mangled the works of Steibelt and Beethoven. Though skilled in most feminine avocations, the accomplished Miss Wetherby never had been able to master the piano.

His footsteps were muffled by the plush Aubusson runner as he approached the music room at the far end of the hallway. Noting that the door was ajar, he was poised to enter when Francis's familiar voice carried into the corridor.

"No, darling, I insist. I should never have expected you to take care of this. It is only right that I speak to him man to man."

Darling? Richard checked his stride, his brows coming together over the bridge of his nose.

"But Francis, what if he challenges you? I-I fear that Richard must have a dreadful temper."

"My precious angel, please don't cry."

A brief pause followed in which Richard assumed Francis was consoling his "precious angel." *Precious angel, indeed.* Richard raked a hand through his hair, silently cursing his stupidity. How could he have been so blind? Or had he merely willed himself not to see?

"Come now, Charlotte, please," Francis implored. "Richard is an honorable man. Granted he might be furious with me—he might even demand satisfaction of me—but he won't do anything rash."

Like hell, I won't.

Richard was lifting his hand to shove open the door when Charlotte said, "Francis, I do love you so. I should feel wretched to be the cause of a break between you and Richard. I know how very much you value his friendship."

Richard's hand dropped lifelessly to his side.

"Yes, darling, it would pain me"—Francis's voice broke—"pain me severely to fall out of his good graces. But what kind of man would I be, Charlotte, to let you marry him without a fight?"

Richard shook his head. And what kind of man would *he* be to give Francis a fight? Granted, he was a little put out. He had always assumed that Charlotte was his for the asking. But to be honest, he had no genuine feelings for the girl—she meant nothing to him, other than as a vehicle to his uncle's inheritance. What good would it do to burst into the room and play the role of the wronged suitor?

In fact . . .

Richard hastily stepped back from the door.

In fact, he realized that he was relieved. He'd never been able to reconcile himself to wedding Charlotte, but had been pushed along by the Wetherbys's expectations and his own urgency to marry. Why, instead of calling him out, he should get down on his knees and thank Merrick, the old dog!

Of course, Francis's pirating of his intended did place him in a bit of a bind. He'd have to line up some desperate little debutante pretty quickly if he hoped to secure his uncle's fortune before his birthday. But hell, he could worry about that later. Right now, he needed to figure out what to do about the cooing lovebirds.

He turned around and retraced his steps to the top of the staircase.

"The music room, you say?" he called out as if to an imaginary servant. He then clomped back down the hall, his uneven gait announcing him as clearly as a calling card.

Outside the music room, he hesitated as Charlotte's agitated whisper was answered by Francis's murmured reassurance. He pushed open the door and entered.

Sitting at the piano, Charlotte was clutching one of Francis's overpriced handkerchiefs in her fist. The pink stain of tears rimmed her eyes and her lips betrayed her with their trembling.

"Richard," she breathed before her gaze scuttled across the room to Francis.

The earl, who had judiciously moved over to the window, stepped forward with undisguised purpose. Richard cut him off before he could speak.

"Francis, old fellow, good to see you." He clapped him—perhaps too heartily—on the back. "What *have* you been up to?"

Francis flushed a guilty red. "I . . ."

Leaning forward, Richard whispered, "Glad to find you here. It'll make it easier for me. Charlotte won't dare make a scene with you standing by."

"Wh-what?"

Richard sent a faint smile over his shoulder to Charlotte

then added *sotto voce,* "You were right, Francis. I can't go through with it. I've got to break it off."

"You're . . . you're throwing Charlotte over?"

Richard nodded tersely, though he wanted to laugh at the comical blend of shock and delight playing across Francis's features. "Stand by me, won't you?"

"Don't you think you should speak to her privately?" Francis whispered.

"Oh hell, I suppose you're right. But don't go far, all right?"

Francis jerked his head in an assenting motion.

"Richard? Francis?" Anxiety made Charlotte's voice thready.

They both turned and Francis, after a conspiratorial nod, walked over to the piano bench.

"I, um, I've got to make a quick check on my horses," he told her. "A new pair of grays I picked up at Tatt's and they're a handful for my tiger to manage."

Charlotte's lips trembled more fervently.

"It's all right," he saw Francis mouth to her. "It's all right."

Richard pretended to check his pocket watch, thinking it a pity that Charlotte could not share a measure of Sabrina's commendable self-possession. But then again, he had to remind himself, Sabrina Simmons was unlike any other female he'd ever known.

When at last he looked up after taking a full minute to put away his watch, he saw that Charlotte had evidently received the message. Her eyes had brightened and she no longer gazed upon him as if he were a princess-devouring dragon.

"I'll just check on those grays and, um, be right back," Francis mumbled.

Everyone nodded in unanimous understanding.

As soon as Francis left, Richard wasted no time in making his point. Already he was growing weary of the farce.

"Charlotte," he said bluntly. "I've been thinking it over and have decided that I am not good enough for you."

She bestowed on him a watery relieved smile. "Oh, Richard—"

He interrupted her with a curt slash of his hand. "I know that we had an unspoken understanding, but I hope you will find it within yourself to forgive me. I would not make a proper husband for you, Charlotte, and I daresay you can do better."

"Richard . . . I don't know what to say."

"You needn't say anything. I apologize for leading you along and I wish you the best." There. Done.

Now he just wanted to get the hell out of there. He wanted to jump on his horse and race over to his solicitor's to find out when the Simmons House transaction would be complete.

Fortunately, Francis must have been eavesdropping in the hallway for he appeared in the doorway before Richard could draw another breath.

Francis waited on the threshold until Richard asked, "Are the grays all right?" Although all three of them knew that Francis hadn't had enough time to reach the staircase, much less visit the stables.

"Splendid," Francis replied.

"Well, then. I hate to hie off like this, but I've business to take care of. I'm leaving for Shropshire in a few days, so I'll have to catch up with you both upon my return. Until then."

With a brief bow, he headed for the door. Francis halted him with a hand on his shoulder. "Thank you, Richard," he said quietly.

For a second, Richard was going to pretend he didn't

know what Francis was talking about but the understanding in his friend's eyes stayed the lie before he could give it.

Reaching up, Richard clapped his hand over Francis's. "No, old man. It is I who should thank you."

A hint of a smile curved Francis's lips. "Give Sabrina my regards, will you?"

Richard stilled, realization flooring him like a well-thrown left hook.

"You always did see too damned much, Francis."

Chapter
Eighteen

"B-but I don't want you to go. You just g got here."

Teddy's button nose began to turn bright red as he struggled manfully to hold back the tears glistening in his eyes.

Nell wanted to kick herself square in the bum. She should have put it to the little fella in a more roundabout way. But she'd never been much good with words.

"Ooh now, it's not like I'm really goin' away. I'll still be keepin' an eye on you, urchin. 'Tis only that we won't be able to talk like we do now."

"Everybody always goes away," Teddy whimpered. "Mama and Papa and you. It's not fair."

Nell sat down next to Teddy on the garden bench. The flame-orange sun shone like a torch this afternoon, causing Nell to shield her eyes with her hand as she looked heavenward. Tomorrow morning she would not be here to see the sun rise. For today was her last on earth.

"It's not as if anyone wants *to leave you, Teddy,"* Nell endeavored to explain. *"I'm sure yer Mama and Papa didn't want to leave you. 'Tis only that when yer time comes, it comes."* She hoisted a helpless shoulder. *"That's just the way it is, luv."*

Wiping his nose with his coat sleeve, Teddy asked, "Where did they go, Nell? Have you"—he sniffed noisily—"have you seen my Mama and Papa?"

"Well, I don't actually recall seein' 'em pass through, but I'd bet me earbobs they're havin' themselves a jolly good time on the other side of the Pearly Gates. Why, I figure just the fact they brought up two fine youngsters like yerself and Andy would earn 'em a halo or two."

Teddy pushed out his lips in obvious deliberation as he dug a hole with the toe of his shoe. "It was really Rina who raised us," he pointed out.

Of course it was. Nell had figured that out practically from the start. But she still had to convince Teddy that his parents were in good hands.

"And who do you suppose raised your sister?" she argued. *"Raisin' a girl like Sabrina is reason alone to get into heaven."*

Teddy lifted his face to her, his strawberry-colored freckles wrinkling together. "Is that where you're going, Nell? To heaven?"

She caught her breath—so to speak. *"If everythin' goes the way it's supposed to tonight, I will. I hope."*

With a gloomy frown, Teddy pulled the head off a flowering bachelor button. "It's all his fault, isn't it? Your leaving and this whole bloody mess."

"Mind your tongue now, luv. You know Sabrina don't like you usin' words like that."

"But it is, isn't it?" Teddy shredded the blue flower between his skinny dirt-encrusted fingers. "If that rotten old viscount hadn't come looking to buy Simmons House, we would have been just fine."

Clearly, Teddy didn't know how bad off the family's coffers were. But then Sabrina would never have wanted to worry the little mite.

"Don't do much good to throw stones, Teddy. One lesson you gotta learn in this here world is to roll with the punches life throws at you. God knows, Sabrina's had to do just that."

"Does she like him?"

Nell smothered a smile. *"The viscount, you mean? Hmm, I'd say she likes him right 'nough."*

Sighing, Teddy tossed the flower's fragments onto the ground and cupped his chin in his hand. When he looked up at her, his eyes bluer than the spring sky, Nell felt something move in her long-quiet chest.

"I'll miss you, Nell," he said sadly. "But I sure hope you get your angel wings."

It turned out to be the hardest day of Nell's death. Saying good-bye to Teddy had been difficult enough, but when Andrew had blushingly shoved a piece of paper at her, entitled "Ode to Nell," she'd nigh on to lost her ghostly composure.

Nobody had ever compared her to a moonbeam before.

Although her heart felt as if it had come to life again merely to ache, she'd tried her best to let Andy down easy. She assured him that someday he'd find a *live* woman worthy of his affections, a girl with enough smarts to appreciate a first-rate catch like him. He'd stammered and flushed and sworn that he'd be true to her until the end of time.

And her, silly old thing that she was, had almost wanted to believe him.

"Andy, there is somethin' I'm goin' to ask you to do for me, luv," she'd said, once she'd rid herself of that funny lump in her throat.

"Anything, Nell. Anything."

She drew her shawl around her more tightly, feeling as if the chill of Purgatory was creeping up on her as the day progressed.

"I want you to help Sabrina. I know you're already doin' all you can, but you need to understand that she's goin' to be . . . well, she's goin' to be under an awful load, Andy. Don't go askin' her too many questions, just do as she says, all right? It's always been her that people have depended on, and she might just be needin' a shoulder of her own to lean on from time to time."

Andy's fervent nod jarred the spectacles right from his nose. Setting them back in place, he vowed, his voice slipping two octaves, "I'll do as you say, Nell. I give you my word."

And so it was that an unusually sober Nell watched dusk descend like a shroud over the hills surrounding Simmons House. Her mission was almost at an end. Tonight, Sabrina would take the final step in reaching her goal—becoming the Viscount Colbridge's kept woman.

Disquieted, Nell turned away from the library window, tugging pensively at her earring. Although it was no more than a vague impression, she had the unsettling feeling that somehow she'd missed something. That there was a task she had not completed or a lesson she had not learned.

Like one of those bugs Andrew liked to collect, the feeling flitted about, annoying and persistent, and she couldn't quite seem to pin it down.

Nell glanced to the ormolu clock on the mantel. Six

hours remained until she was called away, only two until Sabrina left for Leyton Hall.

All day she'd been avoiding talking to Sabrina, worried that she might say the wrong thing. In truth, the girl had held herself together fairly well during these past two weeks of waiting. But with each passing day, Nell had seen Sabrina's anxiety move closer to the surface like a pot getting ready to break into a boil. Tonight, that wicked Lord Richie would probably stoke those fires until Sabrina had no choice but to erupt.

Nell looked at the clock again. She couldn't put it off any longer. She had to say good-bye.

She drifted upstairs to Sabrina's bedroom, calling out, *"Yoo-hoo,"* as she approached. Sabrina always hated it when she popped in on her unannounced.

"Come in." The calmly controlled voice didn't fool Nell for a minute.

She floated through the door to find Sabrina sitting in front of the window leafing through the pages of a book. Although it was too dark to read without a light, Sabrina sat in the expanding shadows flipping the book's pages slowly one by one.

"I wondered where you'd been hiding yourself," Sabrina said. "Did you say good-bye to the boys?"

Nell nodded, averting her gaze.

"You have certainly provided them some interesting memories to carry with them," Sabrina said softly. "Andrew in particular."

Nell wriggled her nose to dispel the slight burn of something that closely resembled tears. But that was ridiculous, she thought, since everyone knew that ghosts couldn't cry. Could they?

"He's a proper gentleman, that Andrew. You should be fierce proud of him."

"I am."

Nell cleared her throat. *"I figured I ought to make my farewells now 'fore you get in a flurry to take yer bath and get dressed and such."*

Sabrina turned and gazed out the window. A full moon had just crested the horizon, peeping over the vista like a large golden eye.

"Yes, this is it, Nell. The night we have worked toward. I am only sorry we had to cut it so close."

"It don't really matter none. By midnight, it'll all be decided."

In the faint light, Sabrina's features tensed. "I . . . hope so."

That unsettled feeling nagged at Nell again. *"Are you goin' to be all right, luv?"*

"Yes. Of course." The answer came too quickly, but Nell did not press her. She didn't want to see Sabrina finally reach a boil.

"Um, Sabrina." Nell tugged at her earring. *" 'Fore I go sashayin' off to heaven I'd like to be sure that there aren't any hard feelin's 'bout what I did in London. With the earl, I mean."*

Sabrina whirled around. "Good gracious, Nell, we talked about that. Believe me, I understand that you were simply trying to do what you thought best. How ungrateful I would be to be angry with you after everything you have done to help me."

"Well, I'm not so sure I helped you all that much," Nell murmured contritely. *"At times, I downright mucked it up."*

As Sabrina crossed the room, Nell had to fight the urge to remind the girl that frowning caused wrinkles.

"Nell, you cannot begin to understand how very much your friendship has meant to me this past month. Never have I had someone whom I could depend on, an ally I could count on when I doubted myself. You were always there for me. Without censure, without judgment. Truly, you have been a heaven-sent gift."

Nell blinked. Well, hell, her nose was burning again.

Extending her palms, Sabrina, for the very first time, invited Nell's touch. Nell placed her hands in hers. Both their gazes fixed to the contrast of material and immaterial. Flesh and vapor. Real and surreal.

Overwhelmed, Nell withdrew her hands and forced a brilliant smile. *"Gor, what am I thinkin'? Yappin' away at ye when you should be gettin' ready for Lord Richie."* She shook her head and her bonnet swayed. *"Well, good luck, Sabrina luv. I'll think of you often."*

"And I you, Nell. I will 'think on thee, dear friend.' And 'all losses will be restor'd and sorrows end.' "

"Willy Shakespeare, right?"

Sabrina laughed softly. "Right."

Nell started to back away, then added, *"Remember, Sabrina, you'll have to get Lord Richie into bed before midnight."*

"I know, Nell. I remember."

Neither of them wanted to conjecture aloud what might be the outcome if Sabrina failed.

Especially not Nell.

Chapter
Nineteen

The Leyton Hall carriage arrived precisely at eight o'clock, as Richard's note had indicated.

The boys had already been sent to bed, bribed with Hattie's sugar cookies, and Nell, after complaining of a "burning nose," had disappeared over an hour earlier.

So it was a very much alone and solemn Sabrina who closed the door to Simmons House and walked out into the night to the waiting carriage.

As she climbed into the closed coach, she turned for one last look at her home. Her home where her brothers slept peacefully, unaware of the dishonorable path she was about to set upon. She could but pray that they would always remain so unaware.

Her gaze wandered over the manor's shadowed facade, abruptly fixing on a faint glow in the library window. A feathered and beribboned bonnet bobbed in front of the glass. Although the image was indistinct in the dimness, Sabrina saw Nell lift her hand in a fluttering salute. Sabrina waved back.

Farewell, my friend. My madam ghost.

The carriage set off with a loud snap of the reins.

Placing her hand over her middle, Sabrina closed her eyes and swallowed. Richard's note had indicated they would sup together, though Sabrina doubted she would be able to choke down a bite.

Despite the serene face she'd presented these past days, she had been severely troubled, haunted by the suspicion that Richard did not honestly want her for his mistress. She had tried to set aside her worries, but they had persisted in taunting her, undermining her confidence and weakening her resolve.

In light of all that had happened, how could she forget? How could she dismiss the fact that Richard had done everything he could to try to persuade her to recant her offer?

She winced every time she recalled that humiliating night spent at the waterfront brothel. Why, the backs of her hands still bore the marks of her nails where they had carved painful crescents into her skin. And then, when she had refused to back down, Richard's reaction had confused her even more. He'd been furious, damning her with his words and his soul-searing eyes.

Yet he claimed that he wanted her. Even though, to her mind, he had done all in his power to drive her away.

Did he desire her or did he not? Had she succeeded in making him want her or had he only taken pity on her after she had, in essence, thrown herself at him? Sabrina shook her head. She simply did not know.

Unfortunately her confusion was many-layered, not only

as it pertained to Richard's feelings, but also to her own. Certainly, she approached this evening with apprehension. What woman would not? But it wasn't the prospect of lying with Richard that frightened her—it was the possibility that he might refuse her.

Sabrina raised her hands to her cheeks, their heat burning through the thin silk gloves. That she should anticipate— eagerly—their intimacy shocked her right to her very core. Somewhere along the way, perhaps during their visit to Soane's, the idea of making love to Richard had ceased to be intimidating and had become positively . . . tempting.

Then, in the carriage, when he had touched her . . . She shivered with the memory. Good Lord, when he had touched her so intimately, so *amazingly,* instinct had caused her body to respond to what her mind had not yet acknowledged. Richard was a man she had come to desire. A man she had come to care about.

He was not the demonic ogre she had at first painted him in her thoughts. Like her, he had known suffering and loss. Like her, he harbored a great love for literature and history. But, unlike her, Richard did not fear his passions.

Although the truth was difficult to admit, Sabrina could not lie to herself: Richard had touched her, more deeply than with any physical possession. He had liberated a part of her that she had always been too frightened to accept. Always she had secretly feared the explosiveness, the emotional vulnerability, that had ruled their father and nearly ruined their family. The intensity that Teddy so easily manifested, Sabrina had buried inside herself—controlling it, tamping it down with the logic of Hume and Wollstonecraft.

After all, she *had* to be the dependable one. Never had she had the freedom to give rein to bouts of passion or moments of impetuosity. Hadn't their father's rashness already cost them too much? And tonight Sabrina would pay that price. With her virginity. With her dignity.

And yet, could she say she regretted what she was about to do?

She glanced to her hands still linked across her stomach, and wondered how Richard had done it. How had he opened the way to that very small part of her that was darkness and passion and wildness? Even if it did not comprise a large part of the woman who was Sabrina Simmons, it was undeniably there. And strangely enough, she was glad to finally call it her own.

The carriage rocked to a shuddering halt.

Sabrina did not meet the coachman's eyes as he helped her down. She had begun counting, realizing that less than four hours remained in which to lose her innocence. She felt as if she were in a private race to Richard's bedchamber.

Richard opened the door. Her already unsteady stomach flipped ten different directions. He was breathtaking.

The dark curtain of his hair had been left unbound, so rich a black that it almost looked silvery-blue against the sharp white of his cravat. His eyes were hooded, his lips curved in a faint smile. She could not say if it was welcome or derision that curled those lips.

"Good evening," she said, her voice low to hide any tell tale quavering.

"Good evening, Sabrina." He looked past her and signaled the coachman with a nod. The harness jingled and hooves clomped away as Richard ushered her inside. "Please. Come in."

He indicated the empty hallway with a sweep of his hand. "I decided to give the servants the night off. To ensure our privacy." Pulling shut the door, he added, "And you needn't worry about the driver either. I brought him up from London and he knows better than to risk his post by gossiping. I have done what I could to guard your reputation."

"Thank you. I appreciate your . . . discretion." The words were stiff, as were her shoulders when Richard reached from behind to remove her wrap.

His hands hesitated at the tops of her arms. "It's only your cloak, Sabrina."

She nodded curtly, chagrined that her anxiety was so plain to see.

Richard finished removing her cloak, then draped it over the crook of his arm. He stood close enough that Sabrina imagined she could feel his body heat reaching out to her. But that was all that reached out to her. He did not touch her as he gestured her forward down the black-and-white marble corridor.

"I laid out our supper in the parlor," Richard explained. "The dining room is somewhat dreary, I fear."

Dreary? Sabrina thought. The dining room would have to be positively funereal if the gloomy parlor was preferred. Faded rust-colored upholstery and smoke-stained wallpaper colored the room in cheerless shades of brown-orange. Although a fire and a large floral arrangement on the mantel did help to ease the drabness, the room still felt cold and uninviting.

In front of the fire, a table had been set with crystal goblets and silver, covered dishes.

"Are you hungry?" Richard asked.

"No." Standing in front of the hearth, Sabrina spun around so quickly that she made herself dizzy. She'd been staring at the table only because she hadn't the courage to meet Richard's gaze.

Now, however, she was trapped.

His eyes caught and held hers. Dark. Penetrating. Relentless. At the back of her mind, Sabrina wondered how she'd ever thought them soulless. Richard's eyes were like reflecting pools in a sun-starved cavern, midnight mirrors rippling with emotion. And questions.

She jerked her gaze aside. She did not want to answer any questions tonight.

"Shall we begin with some claret?" Richard asked.

He did not wait for an answer but walked over to the small table and poured from a decanter. Covertly, she studied him, watching the play of muscles beneath his form-fitting jacket. He moved with indolence and grace. Everything about him suggested control, power and . . . danger.

She accepted the glass, again refusing to meet his eyes, and sank onto the mud-colored sofa. Her legs felt wobbly and weak. She must be more tired than she realized.

Sipping at her wine, she stared trance-like into the garnet liquid. The tension was palpable, almost visible. In a bizarre turn of thought, she found herself wondering whether the tension *could* be seen if you looked hard enough—like the supernatural glow that surrounded Nell.

She glanced at Richard. He was watching her, his usual mockery less pronounced this evening. Or perhaps it only affected her less now that she knew it was nothing more than emotional armor.

"Drink up," he ordered softly. "It will help."

Obediently, she drained the goblet and Richard refilled both their glasses. He handed her the wine, then sat down next to her so that his thigh rubbed against hers.

"Are you comfortable?" he asked.

Cradling the goblet in both hands, Sabrina searched for a suitable response. Should she be honest and tell him that his leg was searing hers like a red-hot branding iron? She settled on a simple, "Yes."

Again the tension began to draw out. The fire sizzled.

The air hummed. The quiet was so pressing that Sabrina fancied she could hear the daffodils wilting on the mantel, their stems creaking as they bent closer to the earth.

What ought she do? Nell had instructed in her the different openings, but suddenly none of them felt right. A skimming of her fingers across his knee? A flirtatious dip of her shoulder?

Sitting so close as they were, the mere act of breathing seemed outrageously intimate. The gentle rasp of his trousers against her skirts was like a pumice stone across her nerve endings. His remembered scent, masculine and rich, made her head spin and her insides churn. Or was it the second glass of wine she'd just finished?

"Sabrina."

He compelled her to look at him and she felt the empty goblet pulled from her slack fingers. Although he said not a word, the question in his gaze was as clear as if he'd voiced it: *This is your last chance, Sabrina. Are you sure?*

She tilted her chin. . . . The faintest of affirmations.

His gloveless fingers, hot and firm, wrapped around hers. He drew her to her feet. Legs that had been flimsy before now felt numb beneath her. She could feel them moving, following Richard as he led her upstairs, but she felt as if she were gliding along, floating as Nell did, not actually touching the ground.

A surreal quality settled over her. On the one hand, Sabrina felt more alive than she'd ever felt in her life. Tingling and breathless with anticipation. Yet, at the same time, she saw herself as slightly distanced from the scene, as if she were viewing herself from outside her body, watching Richard guide her into his bedroom and close the door behind them.

Her breath came a little quicker.

She noted a series of inconsequentialities. The intricate

pattern of the wood parquet floor. The fact that two candle-stands had already been lit on the table and mantel. The odd coincidence of the bed's silk counterpane matching the periwinkle blue of her dress.

The room was very warm. She automatically began to pull off her gloves, then paused with one glove half-off. How annoying, this self-conscious awkwardness. Defiantly, she jerked both gloves from her fingers, although she could not bring herself to remove anything more.

Richard had knelt down before the hearth to stoke the fire. He stood and, with his back to her, shrugged out of his jacket. The shirt's fine lawn hugged his shoulders with an intimacy Sabrina envied. He tugged his cravat loose.

Her mouth went dry. A stab of desire cut through her with shameful acuteness. She wanted Richard. She wanted him to make love to her.

"Would you like me to snuff the candles?" he asked without looking directly at her.

She didn't care, but she nodded. She forced herself to walk over to the bed while Richard moved around the room to douse the candles. As each candle was snuffed, the fire-light's glow seemed to focus on the center of the oversized four-poster. Sabrina wondered if the lighting were by chance or by design.

Richard sat down on the edge of the bed and yanked off his left boot. Sabrina's fingers curled. What was she supposed to do? Offer to help? Begin to undress herself?

Richard's calm matter-of-factness underscored her gaucheness. He knew she was inexperienced, so why wasn't he telling her what he wanted her to do? She felt clumsy, inept, standing there with her arms hanging limply at her sides while he wrestled with his Hessians.

The right boot fell to the floor with a thump.

He looked up at her, his inky hair swinging along one side of his face.

"Come here, Sabrina."

The tersely voiced command came as a relief. She swallowed and took two steps forward. Richard placed his hands at the side of her hips and drew her between his legs. His face was level to her stomach. With his head slightly bent, and his thumbs cupped along the front of her hipbones, he held her. He just held her as the seconds ticked by, and then the minutes.

Sabrina found it increasingly difficult to breathe.

She gazed down at the top of his head, thinking how white his scalp looked against his blue-black hair, how defenseless the exposed nape of his neck. And subtly—without quite understanding how—she felt the power between them shift. His pose made him look so accessible. So . . . vulnerable.

As if of its own accord, her hand raised. She couldn't say what made her do it other than the fact she wanted to more than anything else she'd ever done. Slowly, so slowly, she lowered her hand to the top of his head. At first, her hand just fluttered across his hair. Then, growing bold, she wove her fingers through the silky thickness, spilling the strands across her palm.

He sighed a soft sound.

Encouraged, she lifted her hand and did it again, her fingernails gently scraping over his scalp. His thumbs dug deeper into her hips and he leaned forward to rest his forehead against her abdomen.

It felt wonderful. So wickedly wonderful.

Sabrina could not believe her daring, yet she reveled in it. She spread the fingers of both hands across his shoulders to span the breadth of his back. His skin burned beneath the thin white cotton and Sabrina suddenly became aware of her own flushed state, her cheeks hot and tingling.

In that moment, she scarcely knew herself. She tried to tell herself that this was required of her, her role as soon-to-be mistress. But that was a lie. She wanted to caress him. She wanted to know Richard more intimately than any woman ever had.

She felt giddy in the knowledge of her own desire, light-headed and overheated.

Guided by instinct—instead of Nell's tutoring—she started to tug at Richard's shirt, pulling it from his trousers to bare his back. Along the crest of his spine, muscles rippled golden brown in the wash of firelight.

She started to lean forward to feather a caress over his back when suddenly Richard raised his head. Meeting his hot-eyed gaze, Sabrina started. Dear God, what was she doing? How could she be so forward?

She pulled back but he grabbed hold of her hands and, before she knew what he was doing, he fell back onto the bed, toppling her over onto him.

She gasped.

With a deft movement, Richard rolled her onto her side, locking one leg around the back of hers. The power had shifted again and now she was the defenseless one, her fists trapped against his iron-hard chest. He loomed over her like a diabolical force, his eyes burning brimstone. Burning with promises. He fulfilled one of those promises as he leaned forward and took possession of her mouth.

Sabrina had been waiting for this. She opened to his teeth and tongue with a small, glad whimper. His splayed hand stroked along the length of her back to cup her buttocks in a firm squeeze. Her abdomen clenched and she arched into him as he drew her more closely against him. A ridge of hardness settled against her thighs.

He kissed her and kissed her, taking her mouth in a thousand different ways. His hand continued to massage her buttocks and she realized that her skirts had been pushed up so that she was bare to him.

As he tongued the curve of her ear, whispering soft, beautiful words of nonsense, he worked at the buttons of her gown. Her chemise and dress were slipped from her shoulders and she gasped to see her breasts swell beneath his gaze.

"You are lovely, Sabrina. So lovely."

She closed her eyes as he lowered his head, sensation shooting through her when his tongue flicked over the tip of her breast. He teased her, lapping and nipping, until finally he drew her into his mouth and suckled. Sabrina had never known such ecstasy—the deep pull of his mouth and the silky caress of his hair as it brushed across her skin.

He brought her to a fever-pitch then turned his attention to her other straining nipple. Sabrina squirmed and writhed, reaching toward something unfamiliar and dark. She felt Richard's hands tug at her clothing and suddenly she wore nothing more than her stockings and slippers. She lay beneath him open and exposed, panting with her need, her breasts rosy and tingling.

Gently, but insistently, he pushed her thighs apart and his fingers found her. She cried out and he caught her cry on his tongue. She was wet. She was drowning.

His fingers pushed against her and found a spot that made her lower body convulse and jump against his hand. Richard was merciless. He stroked and probed as her hips rocked beneath his ministrations.

"Richard," she cried out in desperation, twining her arms around his neck.

"Yes, my darling," he whispered. "Come to me, Sabrina."

And like the rhythm of waves upon the shore, his fingers washed over her, lapping in and out like the tide. Sabrina felt herself drowning, going under beneath a wondrously dark wave of desire. She clung to him even as he pulled her down to the depths of passion, as she was sucked under. The feeling pulled at her, pulling, pulling . . .

Then it came. It crashed over her with stunning force, driving the air from her lungs.

"Richard!" Salty tears stung her eyes. It was unbearable. It was perfect.

She still clung to him, her hands gliding over him feverishly while he pulled out of his clothing. He soothed her with his whispers, but she would not release him, holding to him as if he were her lifeline.

There was an urgency in her she did not understand. An urgency to send Richard crashing into that same torrential whirlpool of feeling she'd just experienced. Her palm grazed over his side, drifting over his hip. His indrawn breath led her to greater boldness. Her fingers wrapped around him, a heated shaft pulsing in that familiar wave-like rhythm.

"Oh God, Sabrina." His eyes closed in an expression of pleasure-pain.

She tested the length of him and he groaned. Her fist moved over him again and she leaned up to dip her tongue between his lips.

She could feel his stomach muscles jerk with reaction and suddenly she was flat on her back, curtained by the thick fall of his hair. He pushed up on his elbows, his knee pressing apart her legs, his breath coming hard.

Need flowed through her, throbbing in her breasts, in her abdomen, between her legs. Anticipation made her squirm.

Richard lifted his head and froze above her. The muscles in his arms shook as he searched her gaze.

Then she saw it. She saw it in his eyes.
Indecision.

Richard gazed into Sabrina's face, absorbing its every nuance and shade. The way her eyes turned up at the corners. The faint dusting of freckles over her nose. The tiny indentation at the base of her too-sharp chin.

He wanted her so much in that moment, it terrified him. Never had he desired a woman with such intensity. Never.

But . . . he wasn't going to take what she offered. Even though he was about to spill his seed all over the damned bed, he could not go through with it.

Thrusting away from her, he rolled onto his back, feeling his heart threaten to burst from his chest. His body ached with unslaked passion, his lungs burned.

Beside him, he could hear Sabrina's breath fast and halting. He dared not look at her. At her firm rose-tipped breasts, her sleek ivory thighs.

He had hoped—God, how he had hoped—that she would be the one unable to see this thing through. But no. He had to accept the truth: Sabrina was willing to whore herself to him for Simmons House.

Disappointment swelled in him, strangely hurtful. That was all that he meant to her. He was nothing more than a means to saving her home.

Sabrina stirred and he had to squeeze shut his eyes to keep from reaching for her. He wanted her, but he damn well would not have her like this.

It was wrong. He could not say how, but he knew it was wrong. If he were to make love to Sabrina this night, he would be lessening himself. He would be making tawdry, diminishing, the feelings he had for her. Feelings that he was just now beginning to understand.

He had sensed that something was amiss these past two

weeks. He had agonized over his decision to take Sabrina as his mistress even as he met with his solicitor, paid off the mortgage, and made plans to meet her here. But all the while, uncertainty and doubt had preyed on him like vultures on carrion, tearing him apart.

"Richard?"

He flinched at the hesitancy in her voice. Damn it, what could he say? How could he explain what he was feeling when it still wasn't clear to him?

"Richard, is something wrong?"

He shoved off the bed with a muttered curse and strode across the room to his nightrobe. Yanking the tie so snugly around his waist that it bit into him, he finally turned to look at her.

Hunched over in a protective ball, Sabrina knelt in the center of the bed with her folded arms covering her breasts. The firelight behind her cast a rosy glow over her skin. Her dark blonde hair streamed over her shoulders, and her turquoise eyes were huge with confusion.

"Did I . . . did I do something you didn't . . . like?"

He threw back his head and stared at the ceiling. God, he hurt.

"Richard, I'm sorry. Please. Tell me what you want and I—"

"I know," Richard interrupted bitterly. "All I have to do is ask and you'll do it."

If possible, her eyes grew even larger. "I don't underst—"

"Just get dressed, Sabrina." He pivoted away from her, picking up a pocketwatch to keep his hands busy.

A long silence preceded the muted creaking of the bed.

Chapter Twenty

It was half past eleven when Nell snuck upstairs to say one last goodbye to the boys.

Above Simmons House, the moon had risen full and round like a large circular portal beckoning her back to the realm of the nonliving. Already Nell could feel the pull from the other side. Her skills had been weakening in the last few hours; floating through walls wasn't as easy as it should have been and her levitation was shaky.

Her ghosthood was slipping away.

Although a small sadness came over her as the clock ticked ever closer to midnight, Nell refused to feel too sorry for herself. After all, why should she? She'd lived more these past thirty days as a disembodied spirit than she had her whole thirty-four years alive. Thanks to Sabrina and the lads, she'd learned what it was to be part of a family, to give and to sacrifice. To put someone else's needs before your own. To care.

Really, it was flat-out curious when she stopped to think about it. Here she'd been sent to tutor Sabrina but she felt as if she was the one who had done all the learning. *Now ain't that a puzzler?* All along, she'd assumed that her mission had been to teach the girl about life. . . . Or had it been the other way around?

Was she the one who'd had the lesson to learn? Perhaps it was her own bloody fault she'd not yet made it to heaven—maybe if she'd only believed in herself and her ability to love, she would have had those angel wings a long, long time ago.

Still pondering, Nell floated through the door into the boys's room, where she was greeted by a faint snuffling snore. The snore came from Andrew's bed. Drifting across the room, she reached into her pocket where she had tucked away his poem—the one that had described her as a "moonbeam." What, she wondered, would happen to the piece of paper when she was summoned back to her immaterial world? Would it disappear, leaving her with nothing but memories? Would she had even those?

A crooked smile tipped one corner of her mouth as her gaze fell on the sleeping Andrew. With his lips pressed together, and a tiny frown between his blonde brows, he was the very picture of solemnity.

Of course she would not forget. How could she? Each of the Simmonses had carved out a place in her heart—a place so secure that neither death nor what came after death could change its permanence.

"Take care of yerself, Andy darlin'. You've got a bright future ahead of you, luv."

She smoothed the coverlet, and blew him a kiss. His face appeared to relax as he burrowed into his pillow.

Turning away, Nell started to glide over to Teddy's side of the room when suddenly she pulled up short. Panic sliced through her like the remembered pain of a knife.

"Blimey . . ."

Teddy wasn't in his bed.

And then she felt it. With frightening clarity, Nell's supernatural instincts told her that Teddy was in danger. Very serious danger.

"Oh, Teddy, what 'ave you gone and done?"

She tried to focus, tried to still her panic. Twisting her hands together and closing her eyes, she fought to locate Teddy with her spectral abilities. Where was he? What had happened?

But her skills were fading, growing weaker with every minute. She fought harder. Then, after a few moments of frenzied concentration, a vague image slowly began to come through. Leyton Hall. Teddy was at Leyton Hall.

"Damn," Nell whispered.

She did not hesitate. As fast as she could, she sped across the valley, traveling through time and space like a puff of wind. She refused to think what she might find at Leyton Hall, instead pushing herself to her limits, struggling against the limb-numbing iciness that was opening up inside her. Midnight pulled at her, draining, exhausting.

It was impossible to say if the trip had taken her minutes or seconds but, when she arrived at Leyton Hall, Nell thought she must be dying all over again the way her lifeless heart seemed to stop in her chest.

Teddy—her sweet, ginger-freckled scamp Teddy—was dangling from a tree limb that hung over Leyton Hall's roof, three floors above the ground. In a nightshirt and jacket, he clung to the branch, his arms wrapped around the slippery-smooth bark, hanging on for dear life.

"Teddy!"

"Nell?"

The mix of terror and hope in his quavering voice curdled Nell's insides like rotten milk. She hovered close, noting how the moonlight bleached his thin face to a deathly white. His cheek was pressed up against the branch, his eyes glittering with fearful tears.

"Nell, I-I think I'm going to fall."

"No! Don't you say that, Teddy!"

She looked around frantically.

The enormous ash overhung the manor, its branches spreading low above the west end of the house. Teddy had to have climbed the tree . . . but why?

"Hang on, Teddy. I'm goin' to get help."

"No, Nell! Don't leave me! Can't you get me down?"

She bit into her lips, hard enough to have made them bleed if they hadn't been bloodless.

"I can't, luv."

With her weakened powers, she was having trouble just keeping herself afloat. It would be impossible for her to lift a material object of Teddy's size.

Sabrina.

In the time it took to blink, Nell accepted that she might be sentencing herself to an eternity in the emptiness of Purgatory for what she was about to do.

"Hang on, Teddy luv. I'll be right back."

She had failed.

In a pained daze, Sabrina reached for her gown that lay crumpled in a heap at the base of the bed. Her movements were wooden, puppet-like.

Her greatest, most secret fear had been realized: Richard had rejected her. She had been unable to make him desire her enough. She had failed. Failed her brothers and Nell. Failed herself.

With trembling fingers, she labored to fasten her dress, not taking the time to search for her shift. She wanted to get out of that bedroom and away from Leyton Hall as fast as she could. Humiliation weighted her chest and made her fingers clumsy.

"*Sabrina!*"

The hysterical cry exploded in her ear, rocking her back on her heels.

"Nell?" she whispered as the ghost materialized like a vapor from a morning mist. Sabrina had never seen her so indistinct; she could barely make her out in the dark shadows.

"*Sabrina, I don't care what you're doin, but you gotta come quick. Teddy's hangin' from a tree above the roof!*"

"What?"

"I asked that you get dressed," Richard said stiffly as he turned toward her.

Sabrina ignored him and looked back to Nell.

"*Don't ask me to explain,*" Nell pleaded, wringing her hands. "*Just come quick. I don't know how long the little fella can hang on.*"

"Oh, my God."

Sabrina's stomach dropped to her toes. Snatching up her skirts, she jumped from the bed, breaking into a run before her feet even hit the floor.

"Where the hell are you going?"

Richard's confused-angry query stopped her halfway to the door.

For the love of— How could she explain? She sent a harried glance to Nell but the ghost had already vanished.

"Teddy, my brother—he's about to fall from your roof or onto it or . . . I don't know!"

Richard looked at her as if she were crazed and she knew she sounded it. "What in the hell is he doing up there?"

Sabrina couldn't think. Her mind was spinning as swiftly as her stomach churned. "I don't know!" she repeated desperately, throwing her hands into the air. "I only know he needs help."

Her urgency must have communicated itself to Richard for he refrained from further questions as he raced after her into the hallway. "This way," he said, indicating left. He'd had the sense to grab a candle stand. "The servants' stairs."

Lifting her skirts, Sabrina sprinted down the dark hall. But Richard ran faster. Up the stairs they raced, Sabrina chasing after Richard's bare heels, the candle flickering yet miraculously remaining lit. A drop of hot wax flew onto Sabrina's cheek. She flinched and flicked it away but did not slow down.

Her heart was pounding at what seemed an impossible rate when Richard shoved open the door to the roof and they burst into the chilly night.

"Where?" Richard demanded.

Sabrina glanced around the bare flat roof. "I—"

"Here, Sabrina!" Nell called.

Barely visible, the ghost was only a faint amorphous glow, like a wavering shaft of moonlight. Teddy was easier to detect, his white-blonde hair bright among the shadowy depths of the tree branches.

"Teddy!"

"Rina?" The wobbly, tear-filled voice nearly rent Sabrina in two.

"I'm here, Teddy. Hang on. I'll get you down."

But she had no idea how. The branch he clung to hung at least twenty feet above the rooftop. Far too high for Teddy to jump even if she could be sure he'd land on the roof and not fall to the ground. He had to be a good forty feet up in the tree.

But to race downstairs and then try to climb up to him would take an eternity. Too long.

"I'm so cold, Rina. I can't feel my fingers anymore."

"You can do it, Teddy," Richard called to him. "Just one more minute and we'll have you down safe and sound, all right, old man?"

Sabrina's gaze swerved hopefully to Richard. He sounded so confident. As if he had a plan.

"Here." He handed her the now-extinguished candle stand. Then, tightening the sash to his nightrobe, he backed up three or four steps.

"Wh-what are you going to . . ."

The words died on her lips as Richard suddenly charged across the roof in an awkward limping run, then leaped across the yawning chasm.

He slammed into the tree trunk with a bone-crunching *smack* that raised both bile and a scream in Sabrina's throat.

She crumpled to her knees.

Somehow Richard had borne the impact without losing his hold of the tree. He gripped the trunk with his legs while his right hand reached above him to the closest limb. He caught hold of the branch and Sabrina breathed again.

"All right, Teddy. Here I come," Richard called.

Teddy made a whimpering sound that Nell echoed.

"He's slipping!" Nell's voice seemed to come from a great distance.

"Teddy, Richard is almost there!" Sabrina yelled, scrambling to her feet.

Her anxious gaze tore back and forth between the small figure suspended far above and the larger one climbing swiftly through the branches. As he ascended, Richard's nightrobe swung open, exposing his nakedness.

Sabrina shivered and wrapped her arms about her waist.

The night had grown uncommonly cold; a freezing wind seemed to have whipped up out of nowhere.

Richard reached the branch from which Teddy hung and, as he crawled out onto the limb, he seemed to pass right through the faint glimmer that must have been Nell.

"I've got him!" Richard called triumphantly.

"Oh, thank God," Sabrina whispered.

And that moment, as if in answer, a bell tolled from the far end of the valley. The Leychurch church bells.

"Midnight," Sabrina breathed. A distant crack of thunder heralded a sudden and icy gust of wind.

Sabrina glanced up to where Richard now cradled Teddy in his arms in the crook of a tree limb. The glow was gone. Nell was gone.

"Sabrina?" Relief shook Richard's voice.

"Yes?" she called back, her own voice almost unrecognizable.

"I'm going to carry Teddy down. It's going to take us a few minutes. Why don't you go inside and stoke the fire and gather blankets? He could use something hot to drink, as well. He's rather chilled."

Although loath to let her brother out of her sight, Sabrina needed to do something useful. "All right. But please be careful."

As soon as she'd said it, she realized it had been a silly thing to say. He'd just risked his life, for heaven's sake. And saved Teddy's.

Fumbling her way down the first flight of stairs, Sabrina felt reaction start to set in. The darkness, the quiet, the musty emptiness. She had to pause on the staircase and lean against the wall for support. Against her frozen hands, even the cool stone felt warm.

Unable to yet sift through her emotions, she could only allow them to sift through her as they would. The loss of

Nell, Teddy's near brush with death, Richard's spurning of her . . .

No, it was too much right now. Too much for her to take in. Sabrina drew in a lung-filling breath. There. She felt a bit better.

Hurrying down the next flight of stairs, she tried to put her thoughts into some semblance of order. Stoke the fire, Richard had said. Find blankets. Though she would have rather entered a viper's pit than return to Richard's bedroom, she made herself do it. Teddy needed blankets.

Her cheeks burning, she marched into Richard's room, forcing down memories less than an hour old. She yanked a blanket from beneath the silk counterpane and, as she did, her shift floated out from between the sheets.

That single, innocent garment mocked her—a testament to her failure.

Flattening her lips together, Sabrina kicked it under the bed. She then rushed out of the chamber before barely suppressed emotions overtook her again.

Richard had said he'd dismissed the servants, and the only other fire already laid was in the parlor. Sabrina stumbled through the darkness, opening two wrong doors before she located the correct room. She quickly set about lighting candles and coaxing the fire's embers into a toasty blaze.

The uneaten dinner still sat under silver covers before the hearth, and the food odors permeating the parlor brought a vague queasiness to Sabrina's stomach. The intimately laid table did not sit well with her either, for she didn't want Teddy to see it and to start asking questions.

Spying a writing-table tucked into a corner of the room, Sabrina grabbed up the plates and carried them over. As she set the plates onto the bureau, her elbow connected with a loosely stacked mound of papers. They scattered willy-nilly across the floor.

"Oh, fie."

Stooping down to collect them, she noted that the top document was from a London solicitor. She scanned the first line. *This communique is to confirm that, per Your Lordship's request, all liens against the property known as Simmons House outside Leychurch of Shropshire have been paid in full* . . . Sabrina bit into the side of her cheek.

So Richard had upheld his end of the bargain. He just hadn't found her . . . agreeable enough to fulfill her part.

As she shuffled the documents into a pile, her gaze fixed on Richard's distinctive handwriting. She recognized the bold, messy scrawl from the note he'd sent her only a few days earlier. Her eye caught a fraction of a phrase penned atop the page: "Her laughable, lamentable attempts at flirtation." Sabrina went as still as a mouse.

She had just pulled the paper from the pile when footsteps rang out in the hall.

"Sabrina?"

Guiltily she stuffed the paper into her pocket and tossed the other documents atop the writing table just as Richard pushed open the door to the parlor, Teddy in his arms.

"Teddy," Sabrina cried. Rushing across the room, she scooped her brother out of Richard's embrace.

"Oh, you—" was all she could manage as she hugged him tightly against her.

"By Jove, Rina, you're going to crack my ribs," Teddy squawked. But despite his protestations, he didn't try to get down, rather snuggling his face into the crook of her neck.

" 'Twould be no more than you deserve, you scamp," she whispered jerkily.

Richard cleared his throat. "Perhaps I should see about some hot tea."

Though she'd been avoiding looking at Richard, Sabrina

could not hide behind Teddy forever. She glanced up and winced.

Understandably, Richard *looked* like a man who had leaped headfirst into a tree. From the top of his cheekbone to the middle of his chin ran a wide, oozing scrape. His left shin shone red with blood and his nightrobe was torn to mid-thigh.

"Are you all—"

Teddy interrupted her. "I don't want any tea," he said, suddenly whiny, holding to her neck. "I just want to go home."

Sabrina's gaze met Richard's. She prayed he could not see her relief. The piece of paper she'd stolen was burning a hole in her pocket—a hole very much like the one Richard's rejection had shot through her heart. After all she'd endured this evening, she was not above using Teddy as an excuse for a hasty exit.

"Perhaps we should . . ."

"Of course," Richard agreed, so quickly that he sounded insincere and forced. "I'll call for the carriage."

He left the room and Sabrina felt as if she should have called him back. She should have said something. But she was too raw inside.

Holding Teddy close, she edged closer to the fire. When Richard returned a few minutes later, she noticed that he'd thrown on trousers and a shirt.

"The carriage is waiting out front." He indicated Teddy. "Shall I take him?"

"No." Sabrina shook her head. "He's fallen asleep. I can carry him."

She stepped toward the door, but Richard did not move.

"Sabrina."

She paused, turning only enough to indicate she'd heard him. No moment could have been more awkward. . . . Or so she thought until she made the mistake of lifting her gaze. Their eyes met and Sabrina relived it again. Her humiliation, her failure.

Before Richard could speak—and it looked as if he were about to—Sabrina dropped her gaze.

"Richard," she said in a breathless rush. "I cannot thank you ever enough for what you did tonight. The words are inadequate, I know, but thank you. Thank you so much. I'll never forget . . . what you did for Teddy. For us."

She turned and did not look back.

Chapter
Twenty-One

By the light of a single candle, Sabrina sat reading beside Teddy's bed. Although she had already read the page twice, some inexplicable need compelled her to read it yet again.

As she postured and posed, her piteous endeavors to gain my attention were painful to observe.

Now, at least, she understood Richard's reasons for spurning her. She was "pitiful." The word sliced through her like the point of a blade. How could he be so cruel? But then again, she reminded herself, Richard had always possessed a lethal flair for language; why should she be surprised that he expressed himself so . . . eloquently?

Her chin sank slowly into her chest, and she squeezed her eyes shut to ease the sting of unshed tears.

Dear Lord, how he must have laughed at her. What lively entertainment she had provided him these past weeks. To think that while he had been toying with her, chronicling her blunders and gaffes with careful and callous precision, she—God help her—had been falling in love with him.

That, of course, was why she hurt so very much. To be made a joke of by a stranger . . . 'Twould not be pleasant, but she could survive ridicule from a distance. However, to realize that she had given her heart to a man who believed her "pathetic" . . .

And she did love Richard. Despite logic and Mary Wollstonecraft and her own fears, Sabrina Simmons had succumbed to the perils of love. "A mighty pain to love it is," Cowley had written, and she felt the truth of those words to the depths of her soul. This love of lovers was a perilous and frightening thing. It was an emotion that stripped you bare, making you as vulnerable as . . .

Sabrina's gaze fell tenderly on Teddy's sleeping form. *As vulnerable as a child.*

For some reason she had failed to see it coming. Perhaps she'd been so focused on seducing Richard that she'd neglected to see how deeply he was affecting her. Her fingers clenched around the paper in her lap. Most obviously, making her fall in love with him had *not* been his intention.

Nonetheless, when Richard leaped from Leyton Hall's rooftop and hurtled through the air three stories above the earth, Sabrina had known. In that instant, she had known that she loved him, though it had naught to do with his unexpected heroism, and everything to do with his brilliance and wit, his anguish and need to trust. From the beginning, she had responded to Richard, not understanding why—connecting instinctively with his passion and pain, somehow sensing that he was the one to bring her alive.

She glanced to the essay, and her shoulders tensed. She wondered if Ennui's treatise was already scheduled to be published or if she might hold a missing page to the only copy. Not that it signified one way or the other. Even if the article were published, very few people, if any, would be able to recognize her as Ennui's "provincial pigeon."

But she would know.

She shook her head in disgust, scanning the page again.

Little wonder that Richard had turned from her tonight. His contempt for her was plain, though he'd hid it well till now. Had he loathed her as he kissed her? What had been his thoughts in those final moments before he'd lost the courage to make love to her?

Her humiliation could not have been more complete.

Teddy groaned feebly and Sabrina reached over and ran a soothing finger across his brow.

My dear Nell, where are you? Sabrina wished she knew where midnight had taken her madam ghost.

For in essence it had been Nell who had been responsible for saving Teddy's life. When she'd burst into Richard's bedchamber, the ghost could not have known that Sabrina had already failed in her seduction. She could not have known that Sabrina's mission was already lost. Nell, in the ultimate sacrifice, had thrown away her chance at heaven to save Teddy. She had selflessly gambled it all way, knowing she might have to return to the deadly nothingness of Purgatory.

And Sabrina had failed her. As she'd failed everyone.

Squeezing shut her eyes, Sabrina forced the guilt to the back of her mind. She could not allow herself to wallow in self-pity the whole night long. Decisions awaited, the first of which was where she should go from here.

Clearly, they could not remain at Simmons House, even if she could face Richard again in this lifetime. By all rights, Simmons House belonged to him now. Perhaps not legally—the solicitor's letter had stated that title was held in Andrew's name—but for all practical and ethical purposes, the house was his. She had not fulfilled their bargain.

Pain reached into her chest and squeezed her heart. Only one course remained. Her very last option—the one she'd been praying she would not have to take.

Sabrina glanced to the other side of the room, to the window above Andrew's bed. Dawn would be breaking in two or three hours. She'd best hurry. She hadn't much time to pack.

Alone in the quiet of Leyton Hall, Richard did not sleep that night. Cursing himself in five different languages, he paced for hours up and down the empty halls until finally his abused and bruised knee collapsed beneath him. He sat where he fell, questioning if he weren't the greatest fool since Adam.

"A fine time for your conscience to come alive, Colbridge," he muttered darkly, feeling the floor's coldness seep through his clothes directly into his bones.

"Of course Sabrina wasn't meant to be a kept woman. I knew that." But why then hadn't he done something about it? As soon as he'd realized that Charlotte belonged with Francis, it ought to have occurred to him: He needed to marry. Charlotte was no longer available. Offer for Sabrina.

He could not believe that he hadn't arrived at the idea sooner. It was the solution to both their problems. If only he'd had the wits to think of it before tonight.

Damn. I'm a bloody idiot.

Even at this moment, he had only to close his eyes to remember. The texture of Sabrina's skin. The shy invitation in those incredibly expressive eyes. The way her touch had brought his blood to an impassioned boil.

Then, like a cursed specter, his conscience had risen between them. His conscience and his disappointment.

Cautiously, Richard flexed his leg. Above all else, he'd wanted Sabrina to come to him of her own volition, to come to his bed because she wanted him, not the blasted house. But the unholy agreement they'd made in London had hopelessly muddied the waters.

Besides, he knew that Sabrina's options were few. Before he'd left Town, his solicitor had fully apprised him of the Simmons's financial situation. He'd known that they weren't flush, but the severity of their predicament had caught him by surprise. What had he expected her to do? Lose her family's home?

Where his conscience was concerned . . . Sabrina was simply too educated, too strong, too clever, too *everything* to be any man's possession. She was not the sort of woman to be taken lightly. She deserved more than his carte blanche.

He would tell her so.

Many unanswered questions had been left hanging last night, and dammit, he wanted them resolved. Today. This very morning, in fact. He'd hand her the title and documents to Simmons House, and ask her to marry him. They could be wed within the fortnight.

Decision brought relief. Richard pushed himself to his feet, flinching only slightly as his knee protested. The sun would be rising soon. Common sense demanded that he clean himself up before the servants returned. Not that he cared what they thought of him, but he still didn't care to be found in his bloodied state hunkered down in the corridor.

He grimaced as his injured leg took his weight, the skin on his face pulling taut. He must look like hell. He could feel the wound on his cheek drying and trying to close. His trouser leg was stained rusty and the hair at his forehead felt stiff with matted blood.

He limped to his room and, an hour later, after a sponge-bath and meticulous attention to his dress, Richard hobbled downstairs to the parlor. The returning servants chattered at the back of the house, pots clanging, doors banging, as sunlight filtered into the early morning. The aroma of frying ham predicted that breakfast would soon be served.

An unusual lightness buoyed Richard's step in spite of his limp. The decision to marry Sabrina was a good one. He could trust himself with her, something he'd never done with any other woman. In a way he had yet to understand, Sabrina brought out the best in him when he'd grown accustomed to revealing only the worst.

The parlor was warm when he entered, the ashes still rosy with heat. He'd have his breakfast, then ride over to Simmons House straightaway and hand Sabrina the signed deed. He'd give it to her as an early wedding gift. He assumed that the family would rise early with two young boys in the house, and he was anxious to see Sabrina. To settle the matter of the betrothal as soon as possible.

As Richard began to sift through the papers on the writing desk, a hazy sense of disquiet pricked at the nape of his neck. The solicitor's documents had been easy enough to locate, but something felt wrong. The papers' disarray . . .

The essay. Ennui's essay. Hell, he'd nearly forgotten about it.

Swiftly, he rifled through the pile, his fingers clumsy in their speed. He found the first page. The third and the fourth. Where was the second? His pulse accelerated and his mind's eye recreated the picture of Sabrina standing only a few feet away from the desk last night. The dishes had been moved from the table. . . . Dear God, she couldn't have—

What had been her expression? He pressed his fingers into his temples, trying to recall. But so much had happened. He hadn't even the opportunity to explain about the aborted lovemaking. Too much had been left unsaid.

He searched through the papers one more time. Perhaps he'd overlooked it in his haste. But no. It was not there. His heart beat fast, racing uncomfortably beneath his bruised ribs. Maybe he'd only misplaced the second page—left it at his London town house.

He could not bear the uncertainty. Sprinting out the parlor door, he came close to colliding with a young maidservant.

"Oh, pardon me, milord. Breakfast is—"

"I'm not hungry," Richard answered, rushing past her.

In the stables, he had to bite his tongue to prevent himself from bellowing at the groom. *Hurry.* The word—repeated over and over in his head—*hurry, hurry*—while his memory called forth bits and pieces of the profane treatise he'd written.

Painted like a Charing Cross whore . . . the wench succeeded only in turning my stomach.

God, he thought, could there be another man alive as vile as he?

The groom had barely tightened the last strap and Richard was throwing himself into the saddle. He raced across the valley like a madman, pushing his mount mercilessly. The wind stung his eyes like pellets of sand, the ruthless pace pounded at his sore ribs like the battery of fists. But the pain was no more than he deserved. Even if Sabrina had found the essay, punishment was due him simply for penning such venomous filth.

He drew up to Simmons House and the first thought that seized him was that it was too quiet.

It's early yet, he reminded himself. *It can not yet be eight o'clock.* But the familiar ostler did not appear from the stables to take his mount, and as Richard looped his horse's reins through the hitching post, the fine hairs on his neck bristled.

He hammered at the front door. He waited for the space of three breaths, then struck the door again with all his might.

His final blow was still echoing through the house when the door swung open to reveal the pigeon-like maid. This morning she was eyeing him like a hungry hawk.

"I need to speak with Miss Simmons," he said impatiently, gazing past her into the foyer.

The maid squinted at him. "She ain't here."

Alarm hit him square in the gut. Where could Sabrina be at this hour? Had Teddy taken ill?

"Where is she? When is she due back?"

The maid placed one fist onto an ample hip. "She ain't coming back," she said belligerently.

"Ain't coming— What in blazes are you talking about?"

Angrily pushing past her, Richard spun around the foyer as if he expected Sabrina to come walking in at any moment. He whirled back to the maid, his fury building. "Where did she go?"

The woman sighed. "She had Peter drive her and the boys to the posting inn near two hours ago."

Two hours?

"Where was she headed?"

"She didn't say."

"Is that what she instructed you to tell me?" Richard took two menacing steps toward the maidservant. "See here, I don't care what Sabrina told you to say," he growled. "I have to know where she's headed."

When the pigeon woman didn't cower beneath his glare, he tried a different tack. "I'll make it worth your while." He started to dig into his pocket before he realized he wasn't carrying any coins. "Name your price."

The woman raked him with a look that was at once pitying and scathing. "Even if Sabrina had told me where she was going, you couldn't buy me, Lord Colbridge. Not Hattie Sydes."

Desperation tightened like a noose around Richard's throat. "Please, Hattie. Did she give you any idea, any clues, as to where she planned to go?"

Hattie shook her mobcapped head. "No. She only said that she had to go. She said that you owned Simmons House now, so she and the boys had to leave. And she told me to give you this."

Richard gazed down at the folded piece of parchment in Hattie's weathered fingers. It might as well have been his death warrant the way his heart was shriveling in his chest.

He took the paper and opened it, praying that Sabrina had left a message. A word.

Nothing.

Nothing but his own malignant writings mocking him more powerfully than he'd mocked her. He stared blankly at the page. Who was it that had written, "To be cautious in the weapon you choose lest it be turned around and used against you"?

Sabrina would have known.

Richard folded the paper and placed it in his coat pocket, feeling as if he'd been hurdled back through time.

He was thirteen again, watching the only person in the world he loved walk away from him without a second glance. But this time it was different, he suddenly realized. His mother had left him for her own selfish reasons; he had driven Sabrina away.

He shook off his paralysis. Two hours, Hattie had said. There was little chance that Sabrina would still be at the posting station, but it was as good a place as any to start his search. How difficult could it be to track down a young woman traveling with two young boys?

Chapter
Twenty-Two

"Impossible."

The word set Richard's teeth on edge. He glowered threateningly at the investigator before turning his ire in the direction of his man of affairs, Baker.

"You recommended this man to me as the best," Richard spat. "I'm not paying this kind of money to be told something I want is 'impossible.' "

"Lord Colbridge, I understand that this investigation is of utmost importance to you," Baker answered soothingly in a voice that sounded as if it were intended only for crying babies and madmen. "But Bartlett here is just one man. The scope of search you're requesting would require a small army."

"Then get one, dammit!"

The solicitor shot a look at the investigator. *He's gone*

off, the look said. "Bartlett, wait outside, won't you? I believe that Lord Colbridge would like to speak with me in confidence."

"Like hell," Richard muttered.

The burly investigator nodded and left the solicitor's office.

Richard planted his fists on Baker's desk and leaned forward, his unbound hair swinging across his cheek. "Don't you dare tell me I'm asking for too much," he said tightly. "All I want is to have her found."

"And we will find her, I assure you, my lord."

"When? It's been over three weeks and her trail grows colder every blasted day!"

"As I said, Bartlett is but one man, milord—"

"Then hire more!"

Baker's gaze shifted as he cleared his throat. "There is the issue of expense."

Richard tilted back on his heels, deliberately calming himself. "Where do I stand?"

The solicitor made a show of examining a balance sheet, though Richard suspected the man knew to the farthing the status of his account. "Ah. Yes. I see no reason to be concerned as yet, although you have dipped below your normal reserves."

Baker peered at him from under lowered brows. "I, um, feel it my professional duty to remind you, my lord, that your thirtieth birthday falls in but four short days. If you recall, the inheritance your uncle bequeathed—"

"I don't give a damn about the inheritance."

Baker's face took on a purplish hue. "M-my lord, this is no small sum we're discuss—"

"I said," Richard repeated more forcefully, "I don't care about the inheritance. All I care about is locating Miss Simmons."

The solicitor glanced nervously back to the accounting sheet. "My lord, without that income, I fear your circumstances are not nearly as favorable. You'd previously given every indication that you planned to meet your uncle's terms, that you'd marry."

"I've changed my plans."

Baker tugged at his cravat. "I see. Well, then, we might need to reevaluate your finances."

"Sell Leyton Hall."

"I beg your pardon?"

"Sell it. I don't need it."

"But, my lord, if you are going to sell off property, would it not make more sense to consider the neighboring Simmons House? After all . . ."

"No." Richard curled his toes in his boots. "Simmons House is not mine to sell."

"Oh, I think we could get around—"

"No!"

Baker went from purple to white. "Very well," he mumbled, scratching a note onto the sheet. "Leyton Hall."

Richard stalked to the window and glanced out onto the busy London street. Hundreds of nameless men and women scrambled along like ants disturbed from their nest. Was Sabrina somewhere out there? Hiding from him?

"There must be something more we can do," Richard said, speaking more to himself than to the solicitor.

"I know you've resisted it, my lord, but we could still try placing a notice in the papers."

Richard shook his head. After going to such great pains to elude him, Sabrina wasn't going to come forward simply because she'd seen some announcement in the *Times*. If anything, she might go deeper into hiding if she realized how diligently he searched for her.

He rested his forehead against the windowpane, his

breath fogging the glass. If only he could speak with Sabrina for a few minutes. If only he had an opportunity to explain.

He could explain. He could explain everything. It would mean baring his soul to all of England, but what the hell did that matter now?

He remembered the night that Sabrina had challenged him, daring him to reveal himself to her. Well, he would do it. He'd reveal himself to the whole damned country if he had to. For at this point, he would have walked buck naked into Almack's if it meant finally finding Sabrina.

Love left a man no room for false pride. And Richard Kerry was very much in love with Sabrina Simmons.

He hadn't been able to admit it to himself, to accept the truth, until he had lost her. He guessed that he had probably already been in love with her at Soane's. Of course, he couldn't be sure when it had happened, he only knew that when he'd arrived at that Leychurch posting inn to discover her gone. . . . Then, he'd known.

That was why he hadn't been able to make love to her. He loved her too much to make her his mistress—if only, he thought, he had understood his reasons at the time.

He'd be taking a huge risk exposing his feelings to her. She might despise him. Who was to say if Sabrina cared for him at all? But whenever Richard pictured her expression from that night, her vulnerability as she crouched naked on his bed . . .

He did think she had feelings for him. He just couldn't say if they went as deeply as love.

Pivoting on his heel, Richard fixed his man of affairs with a steadfast gaze.

"Yes. A notice in the papers," he said. "Every paper, do you hear me? The *Times,* the *Herald,* the *Globe,* the *Chron-*

icle, the *Post.* I want the announcement run in all the morning and evening papers this Sunday."

Baker lifted his pen. "And how do you want it to read?"

Richard dismissed the solicitor's query with an impatient wave of his hand. "I'll write it up tonight and deliver it to you tomorrow."

He would have preferred to rush home and write it this minute but he was obligated to attend an engagement dinner for Charlotte and Francis. Might look like sour grapes if he didn't show.

"You, my lord?" The solicitor's tone expressed doubt that Richard could scribble his own name.

"Yes. Me," Richard retorted. Baker would soon learn— as would all of society—that he was more adept with a pen that anyone had ever realized.

"Please, Rina. Take us with you."

Sabrina bit into her lip and tilted her head back, using pain and gravity to hold back the tears she refused to let fall. Judging by the wetness expanding on her dress it appeared Teddy was not having as much success. With his arms wrapped around her waist and his head buried in her stomach, he held to her fast, his frail shoulders shaking with sobs.

Sabrina dropped to her knees, hugging Teddy as if she'd never let him go.

"I told you, poppet, the minute I have enough money saved, I'll come straightaway to fetch you and Andy. The very same day, I promise you. We'll find a sweet little house with a garden, and bake tarts as often as you like"— her voice cracked as Teddy released another sob. "But lodgings are expensive, and I . . . I don't have enough money."

She glanced at Andrew, who was studying the tips of his shoes.

"But why can't you stay with us here at Auntie's?" Teddy sobbed. His face was pressed into her shoulder and Sabrina felt a hot tear fall on the side of her neck.

She swallowed hard. "Because I have to find employment, love. Aunt Ellen cannot support the three of us. And it's not fair of us to ask her to try."

When first they'd arrived in Chippenham, great-aunt Ellen had not exactly thrown open her arms in a celebration of welcome. Like the rest of Sabrina's mother's family, Aunt Ellen had long been estranged from her niece, Sabrina's mother. Correspondence between the families had been infrequent at best these past years, so that Sabrina could not blame the old woman for the tepid reception.

Only after Sabrina had pleaded, arguing that the orphans had not another living relation in all of England, had their great aunt agreed to take them in. Unfortunately, after a week or two, Sabrina had soon realized that the sleepy village of Chippenham had no work for a young woman of limited talents.

After begging Aunt Ellen to keep the boys for a few months, Sabrina had decided to go to Bath in search of a job. She had handed over the lion's share of her meager savings to their aunt to ensure that the boys would not be a financial burden. What monies she was left with to take to Bath might last her a week—if she were lucky.

"Andy."

He looked up, blinking rapidly behind his spectacles.

"Andy, you'll be all right, won't you?" Aunt Ellen might be strict, but she'd make sure the boys ate well and that they applied themselves to their studies. . . .

Andrew's Adam's apple bobbed as he nodded. "We'll just miss you, that's all."

Sabrina forced a stiff smile, gently rubbing Teddy's back. "I have to go now."

Teddy's little fingers dug tighter into her waist.

"I cannot miss the coach, sweeting. It's time for me to go."

Andrew stepped forward and laid a comforting hand on his younger brother's shoulder. With a loud sniffle, Teddy released her. His eyes were swollen and red. Sabrina wondered when they would light again with a mischievous twinkle.

"I'll write you as soon as I get into Bath," she said, determinedly cheerful. "And behave yourselves for Aunt Ellen."

She hugged them both one more time before she turned and began the long walk to the posting inn. She prayed that fortune would smile on her, and smile on her soon.

Two days later, a despondent Sabrina was still waiting for fortune's smile. After taking a room in a shabby boarding house on the outskirts of Bath, she'd spent her first afternoon in town, walking the streets, searching for employment. Her second day had passed as dismally as the first, with the single exception that Sabrina had foregone dinner in an effort to conserve her dwindling funds.

Today, a Sunday, the local businesses were not taking applicants.

A day of rest, Sabrina thought to herself. But she was too agitated to enjoy it. After spending the morning writing letters to the boys, while her stomach growled unhappily, she made herself take a walk along the River Avon.

The town of Bath was quiet as Sabrina trudged under the warm summer sun. A stone dug into the sole of her foot where her boots had grown thin and she winced, tears springing to her eyes. She'd never been one to indulge in bouts of self-pity, but today Sabrina was feeling unusually vulnerable and frightened. And very, very sad.

Already she missed Andrew and Teddy. She had steeled herself against the pain of parting—knowing that she must find a way to provide for the boys—but as pragmatic as the decision had been, it still hurt. Everything hurt. Leaving the boys and losing Nell. And, of course, Richard . . .

Sabrina quickly dropped her gaze to her folded hands, trying to think of anything else but the man who had held her thoughts prisoner these past weeks. She focused on the clouds of dust her boots kicked up from the path. She listened to the river gurgling its cheerful song.

But, like the man himself, memories of Richard would not be ignored. His ebony hair swaying around his shoulders. The deep timbre of his voice as he quoted the classics. His eyes that were either portals to heaven or to hell.

She'd given up trying to forget him for it had proven a futile exercise. He was always there. Always in her thoughts.

'Twas a lesson, she realized, in how little she understood romantic love. She might have believed that her love for Richard would have withered and died that fateful night, a victim of his deadly scorn. Certainly she would have suffered less if it had. But love was more tenacious an emotion than Sabrina had ever expected.

And today of all days, Sabrina could not dispel Richard's image, for it was his thirtieth birthday. She remembered how Lord Merrick had said that on this day Richard stood to inherit the bulk of his uncle's fortune—provided, that is, he had wed. Had he? Had Richard already married Charlotte Wetherby?

Over the past weeks, Sabrina had been careful to avoid the newspapers, fearing that she might happen across either Ennui's article or Richard's wedding announcement. But simply because she had not read it did not mean it had not come to pass. For all that she knew, the article might well have been published. And most probably, Richard and Charlotte were now husband and wife.

Sabrina pressed her lips together, willing the heartache to stop. She knew that eventually memories of Richard would not pain her so very much. It was merely a question of time.

And she had the rest of her life to forget Richard Kerry. The rest of her life . . .

Kicking a pebble out of her path, Sabrina let loose a sigh. *Life, yes, but what of death?* What of the rest of Nell's death? Many times since leaving Shropshire, Sabrina had wondered whether the ghost would be given another opportunity to ascend to heaven. Dear God, she hoped so. If anyone deserved that chance, Nell did.

If only, Sabrina thought. *If only I could have done more to help Nell fulfill her mission.* But evidently making a seductress of Sabrina Simmons had been too much to ask of even the famed Madame deNuit.

Perhaps 'twas thoughts of Nell, or perhaps only coincidence, but when Sabrina next looked up, she was headed in the direction of St. Michael's Church. It appeared as if Sunday services had already concluded, for the doors to the church stood open. Sabrina hesitated.

She'd never been much for churchgoing; Leychurch's vicar had rather put her off the clergy. Yet something about this particular chapel did look inviting. The gardens were in bloom and a thick canopy of trees offered a shady resting spot. And maybe . . . maybe here Sabrina could feel closer to Nell. She wouldn't go into the church, she told herself, but a moment's rest on the garden bench might soothe her troubled spirit.

She passed unnoticed through the gates, then sat herself on a stone bench beneath a mulberry tree. She'd only begun to relax in the cool of the shade when she observed a small, silver-haired woman leaving the chapel. The elderly lady took Sabrina's notice because, as she stepped from the church, the woman appeared disoriented. She was looking this way and that, squinting fiercely as if her vision were poor.

Suddenly, she turned toward Sabrina, straightened up, and waved. Sabrina glanced around, then realized that the tiny woman was hobbling toward her.

"Sabrina?" the old lady said.

Sabrina blinked. "Have we met?"

"You are Sabrina, aren't you?" the lady persisted, leaning forward. Wrinkles gathered at her silvered temples.

"I-I . . . yes, my name is Sabrina."

The woman gasped and clasped a frail hand over her heart. "Oh, my stars. She said I'd find you here."

"I beg your pardon?"

"A miracle," the woman murmured, her eyelids fluttering. She tottered as if she might swoon.

"Here, please. Sit down." Sabrina helped her onto the bench, while searching the garden for the old lady's companion. Surely the woman had not come alone.

"Are you unwell?" Sabrina asked. "Shall I hail you a hackney?"

"No, no." The woman appeared to be recovering herself. "I just . . . I just had the most incredible experience." She opened her eyes and bestowed on Sabrina a beatific smile. "My name is Mrs. Canham, Sabrina dear. And you will not believe what has happened to me."

Sabrina wondered if the poor old thing might not be a bit dotty. She did have rather a dazed air about her.

"I cannot imagine what to make of it," Mrs. Canham continued, her expression becoming animated as she sat forward, regaining her strength. "I daresay 'twas the oddest experience of my life."

In spite of herself, Sabrina felt her curiosity piqued.

"And how truly amazing that I should find you here," Mrs. Canham said, wonder in her pale blue eyes.

"Amazing?"

The woman nodded. "In there." She pointed at St. Michael's. "In there, the most extraordinary person spoke to me. Truly extraordinary. I've never seen her before in Bath and I daresay I would have remembered if I had. She had a quality about her. Simply amazing."

Sabrina folded her hands in her lap, swiftly glancing around once more for a maid or companion. At her age, Mrs. Canham must often become confused like this.

"More remarkable still," the old woman said, "this woman spoke to me of you."

"Of me?"

"Indeed. She told me I would find a young woman named Sabrina out here in the garden. It was all so remarkable and this stranger was so exceptional-looking. I know that my vision isn't what it used to be but I tell you, this woman positively glowed!"

Sabrina started. It couldn't be. . . .

"What did she say to you?"

Mrs. Canham leaned forward to peer into Sabrina's face, her breath hot and scented with peppermint. "She told me to make certain you read the newspaper tomorrow."

Sabrina experienced a flash of disappointment. There seemed nothing too mystical about that. "The newspaper?"

"Precisely. She asked that I find you and see to it that you read the paper."

"I see."

Mrs. Canham shook her gray head. "Something about

this woman—I cannot begin to describe it—impressed upon me the importance of doing as she requested."

"Did she give you her name?"

"No. And silly old woman that I am, I didn't think to ask."

"Did anyone else see her?"

"I don't believe so."

Sabrina licked at her lips. "Do you think you could describe her for me?"

Mrs. Canham's expression puckered despondently. "I wish I could but I'm as blind as a bat. All I can claim for certain is that her hair was very fair and she did possess this luminous quality that quite took my breath away."

"Did . . . did you notice anything about her speech?"

"Why, yes!" Mrs. Canham brightened. "She spoke with a cockney accent which one never hears in St. Michael's."

Goosebumps skittered up Sabrina's arms. Could it really be Nell? Visiting this woman after Sunday services?

"So," Mrs. Canham went on, "I do feel it incumbent upon me to meet this woman's request. As I said, it seemed so vitally important to her."

"Of course, I—" Sabrina was interrupted by a loud, rumbling growl from her empty stomach. She felt her cheeks warm as the elderly lady's brows rose. Evidently Mrs. Canham had no reason to worry about her hearing, even if her eyesight was failing.

"Where are you staying, dear?" she abruptly asked.

Sabrina's cheeks grew hotter. "I, um, only recently arrived in Bath, you see, in search of employment—"

"Perfect," Mrs. Canham said decisively. "For I am in need of a . . . What can you do, child?"

"But you don't even know me!"

Mrs. Canham flattened her palm across her chest. "My dear Sabrina, what higher recommendation could you possibly come with? Do you not think it likely that the luminous woman I met in the church was an . . ."

"An angel?" Sabrina finished in a whisper. Why, she hadn't considered that. If the glowing woman had been Nell and she had been in the church . . .

Mrs. Canham nodded. "Come on, child. Let us find my abigail and get you settled. I will not rest easy until I've made certain you've read every newspaper to be had tomorrow."

"Oh, Mrs. Canham, you are too kind. I am sure that I will find employment somewhere—"

"You already have." The old woman struggled to her feet and squinted across the churchyard. "I don't suppose you know anything about books, do you, dear? My library is a frightful mess."

Sabrina blinked then glanced to the chapel. Had fortune at last smiled on her—or had it been Nell?

Chapter
Twenty-Three

Richard was in his study, poring over a list of names his solicitor had procured from a Birmingham ticket booking office. From all indications, Sabrina must have used an alias in her travels—he hoped he might recognize it. A classical name, perhaps? A literary reference?

With a sigh, he sat back in his chair, rubbing his tired eyes with the heels of his palms. No luck. Nothing. After passing the better part of the afternoon and evening reviewing passenger lists, he'd still come up empty. A hell of a discouraging way to spend one's thirtieth birthday, he thought with a wry grimace.

Richard would have even forgotten the date's significance if the ever reliable Francis had not come by to wish him happy.

Good old Merrick. He'll probably be the only person calling at Cavendish Square for quite some time.

That morning, Richard's letter had appeared in all the London papers and, as predicted, the *ton* was in an uproar.

Richard shrugged to himself. He had known the letter was bound to provoke Society's outrage; that it would make him *persona non grata* from Richmond to Essex. He had known and expected this, yet the knowledge had not stopped him from publishing the article.

As far as he was concerned, his world had condensed to but one goal, one issue: finding Sabrina. Gladly would he suffer the slings and arrows of London society—all of which he reasonably deserved—if the announcement succeeded in bringing Sabrina back to him.

He would have to but wait and see if it would.

The sharp rap at his study door surprised him. 'Twas well after midnight.

"Yes?"

"Mr. Bartlett is here to see you, my lord."

"Yes, yes. Send him in."

Bartlett rushed into the room, his ruddy face ruddier than ever. "I think we've found her!"

Richard's heart skipped a beat. "Where?"

"Chippenham. She and the boys are staying with an Aunt Ellen. Ellen Clerk."

Richard pushed to his feet, fighting a dizzying sense of relief. "I'll leave immediately."

Sabrina did not sleep well. It was not that her bed was uncomfortable or that she felt strange in Mrs. Canham's home; nor was it the exhilaration of knowing that at last she had a position and a means to support her brothers. What kept her up that Sunday night was the full moon.

Once Sabrina had seen the golden sphere filling the window of her chamber, she'd been unable to sleep, convinced that Nell would appear to her. She'd lain awake in her bed waiting while the night slowly advanced. Around two o'-clock in the morning, frustrated, she had crept downstairs to Mrs. Canham's library. She had, after all, first met Nell in a library. It seemed a logical meeting place.

But hours later, in a showy display of oranges and pinks—very much the colors the ghostly madam had favored—the sun rose without Nell having put in an appearance.

Battling a sharp sense of loss, Sabrina was forced to conclude that she'd made too much of Mrs. Canham's story. The widow's vision *was* extremely poor, and the glow the old woman had spoken of could merely have been sun shining at the stranger's back. As for the odd request that she read the newspaper . . . Sabrina lifted a shoulder. Who could say what that might signify?

Sabrina applied herself to her new duties with conscientious diligence that morning. She stacked and sorted and stacked some more. She catalogued books, moving them from shelf to shelf until dust covered her apron and her brow grew damp with exertion. And yet, though surrounded by her dearest literary friends, she could not find peace.

For the first time she could remember, Sabrina was unable to find answers in her beloved tomes.

After a long and strenuous morning at her labors, Sabrina was interrupted by Mrs. Canham bursting into the library.

"Sabrina!" her employer called eagerly, squinting as she approached. "I have the periodicals for you, dear. You did promise to read them, remember."

Sabrina nodded. She could not feign much enthusiasm for reading over London's latest gossip, especially now that her hopes about the glowing woman had dimmed.

"Yes, of course, Mrs. Canham. I'll read them after—"

"Oh, won't you take a look at them now? I've been in such a state, so wondrously curious. I tell you, Sabrina, I have not been able to get the woman from St. Michael's out of my mind. She had the most remarkable effect upon me. I won't rest easy until you comply with her request."

Sabrina's shoulders sagged. Tired, hungry, and coated with dust, she could not see what difference an hour would make. And she'd so had her heart set on a nice hot cup of tea. But Mrs. Canham was fair to shaking in her excitement and the widow had been very good to her, giving her a job when no one else would.

"Very well."

The widow clapped her hands together. "I'll have them brought right in to you."

Sabrina had just settled onto the divan when the maid trudged in, her arms piled high with periodicals. Sabrina wondered how Mrs. Canham had been able to find so many editions. Did not every newspaper report the same news?

Shaking out the first sheet, Sabrina was poised to delve into *The Morning Post* when she was distracted by a familiar scent tickling at her nose. Lifting her face, she delicately sniffed the air. Was it . . . Her eyes widened.

Frangipani?

She shot to her feet and spun around. Nothing. No glow, no glimmer. She tested the air again, but the elusive fragrance had drifted away.

"Nell?" she hesitantly called out. No answer came.

Sabrina sank back onto the divan. What on earth had gotten into her? Evidently Mrs. Canham's tale had set her imagination afire and she was in dire need of a cold watery bucket of reality. Certainly, if Nell were able to come to her, she would, wouldn't she? Or was the ghost angry, embittered by Sabrina's failure to release her from the misery of Purgatory?

Sabrina frowned. She would feel so much better if she only knew for certain what Nell's fate had been. Mrs. Canham's story had led her to believe that Nell might have been promoted to an angelic post after all. But there was no way for Sabrina to be sure. She could only hope.

With another shake of the paper, she fixed her gaze on the *Post*'s headline.

And there it remained fixed.

Heat washed into her, immediately followed by cold. The paper crackled loudly beneath her trembling fingers.

In huge stomach-wrenching print, *The Post*'s headline proclaimed: "Ennui Unmasked! Viscount Confesses All!"

Good God, had he done it? Had Richard sent in the essay he'd written about her? Her eyes locked on the boldly printed header as if it were in code, as if the letters themselves might leap from the page to offer an explanation.

Then the pain flooded her. The pain of memories and lost love. She closed her eyes and suffered the emotions, stunned by their intensity.

After a long dazed moment, she opened her eyes. Slowly—cautiously—she lifted another newspaper from the pile. *The Morning Chronicle*. It read: "Ennui's Final Treatise: Confessions of a Lovelorn Cynic."

One word leaped from the page. *Lovelorn.*

Almost against her will, Sabrina's fearful gaze was drawn to the article below.

> *I, Richard Kerry, am the essayist known as Ennui. While it gives me no pleasure to admit this, undoubtedly many of you reading this confession will take great pleasure in learning of my identity. So be it. Over the past years—with a*

shockingly cruel disregard for human sensibilities—I have held many of you up to the vilest ridicule and scorn; 'tis only just that I suffer a similar fate. I shall reap what I have sown. This I accept. I would but ask that my friends and associates not be guiltless recipients of the censure due me, since no one knew that it was I behind Ennui's evil. I am the one deserving of your contempt.

Although my words are woefully inadequate, I hereby humbly extend my apologies to all those who have been victims of my poison pen.

Notwithstanding the foregoing, I should make clear that I do not expose the hateful Ennui in order to ease my conscience with society at large. On the contrary, I write this final treatise for a woman. One woman. She shall remain anonymous, since I would not wish, unless she wills it, for her good name to be associated with that of a man who is irredeemably beyond the pale.

You see, in what could only be described as an exquisite caprice of the Fates, the woman who holds my heart in her hands despises me. With sound reason, you say? Indeed. For in a masterful stroke of irony, my venomous pen was turned against me; she found a letter Ennui had written about her. Alas, the lady could not know that the profane essay had been penned long before I lost my heart to her intelligence, her warmth, and her strength. She could not know that Ennui had ceased to exist weeks earlier, a casualty of the miraculous curative powers of love. My love for her.

> *Although tens of thousands of you will read*
> *this confession and perhaps laugh at the awk-*
> *ward baring of my soul, it matters not. There is*
> *but one woman I speak to. I beg your forgiveness,*
> *sweet water nymph. I offer you my unworthy*
> *heart and my worthless name.*

Something wet splashed onto the newsprint and Sabrina realized that she was weeping. She wiped the tears from her face, but they persisted in welling up again.

Richard loved her. It was there in black and white for the entire world to see.

"I cannot believe it," she whispered, shaking her head and smiling. And crying.

To think that Richard Kerry, of all men, would cast aside his pride and expose himself like this. Not merely confessing his role as Ennui, but laying open his most personal feelings in a public forum . . .

Sabrina felt overwhelmed. She read the last sentence again. "His worthless name."

He wanted to marry her. To give her his name, not his carte blanche. But to marry her . . . that would mean he hadn't already wed Charlotte Wetherby—

She gasped, pressing her fingers against her lips. His birthday. If Richard hadn't married Charlotte, then he had forfeited his uncle's inheritance. Because of her? Could he honestly love her so very much?

As understanding dawned, Sabrina climbed unsteadily to her feet, supporting herself on the arm of the sofa.

Not only had Richard sacrificed his pride for her but he had also relinquished his uncle's fortune. Dear heavens, and what had she given up for him? What sacrifice had she made in the name of love?

Suddenly Sabrina turned for the door. She knew what she had to do. She had to go to London.

Traveling through the long night, Sabrina arrived in a storm-lashed London shortly after dawn Tuesday morning.

The trip from Bath had been grueling because of the bad weather, and an exhausted Sabrina would have liked the chance to bathe and to change her gown before going to see Richard. But she could not afford that luxury. The very last of her monies had been spent on coach fare, and she had to walk the final blocks to Cavendish Square in a thunderous downpour.

As she tramped along the flooded streets, Sabrina shuddered to think what she must look like. Her skirts were spattered knee-high with mud and her hair was hanging down her back in wet, stringy clumps. The gale-like winds had ripped up one side of her umbrella, and the rain unerringly found the gap. Though drenched to the bone and shivering with cold—knowing she must look like a veritable gargoyle—Sabrina could not be less than elated.

Only a few more minutes and the nightmare of the past month would be over. Only a few more minutes and she would be in Richard's arms.

Never in her life had she done anything so impulsive as to hie off to London like this. She could have simply written to Richard from Bath and told him where to find her. 'Twould have been the most practical course to take. But Sabrina had spent too much of her life being practical, using logic to hide from her passions. She had wanted to prove to Richard, in her own small way, that she, too, would take risks for their love.

Twenty-Two Cavendish Square. She quickened her pace.

Thunder exploded around her and she flinched as lightning lit up the sky. The rain came down more heavily and

Sabrina virtually ran the remaining yards to Richard's front door.

She had to bang the iron knocker four or five times to be heard over the claps of thunder.

At last, a light appeared in the front window and the door opened.

Remembering the stiff-spined butler from her previous visit, Sabrina almost laughed out loud. If the stuffy servant had been unwilling to admit her before, heaven only knew what he must be thinking now. She doubted he would even recognize her.

"You may go around to the back," he said, already trying to shut the door on her.

"No, wait." The man must think her a mendicant seeking a free meal. "I am here to see Lord Colbridge."

The butler regarded her as if he were looking right through her. "His lordship's not in."

"Oh." Her giddiness evaporated. "Do you know . . . when to expect him?"

The butler started to shut the door again. "He's left London."

"He's left—" *Slam.*

The door closed.

Sabrina stood there staring at the knocker. Suddenly she was much colder than she had been only a moment earlier.

How could Richard not be home? Wasn't he expecting her, or at least hoping she'd come?

She glanced uncertainly at the door again. The butler hadn't even asked her name. Would he have let her in had he remembered her? But then again, she realized, she could hardly ask to wait for Richard if he'd left town and no one knew when he might return.

Thunder cracked as Sabrina slowly walked down the town house steps. Her first impetuous act, and already she

regretted it. What was she to do? She hadn't any money.
Not even enough to return to Mrs. Canham's house, where
she'd left her trunk. And naturally, there were the boys to
consider. She simply couldn't loll around London, waiting
forever for Richard to show up. She didn't know anyone—

Well, she knew Charlotte and Francis, but not so well
that she could impose on their hospitality. Even in desperate straits like these, Sabrina didn't think she could go to
them. After Richard's revelation, she might be given the
cut direct.

Logically speaking, there was only one person left who
might help her. Paula of Paula's Palace of Pleasure. The
kindhearted madam would never turn her away, Sabrina
felt sure. Maybe the woman would even be good enough to
loan her money for coach fare back to Mrs. Canham's. Sa
brina could leave a letter for Richard, telling him where he
could find her in Bath . . .

Sabrina paused halfway down the street, doubt bursting
upon her like a flash of lightning. She couldn't . . . she
couldn't have been mistaken, could she have? Richard's
letter must have been directed to her. Mustn't it? After all,
he had referred to his "sweet water nymph". . . . Surely, he
had meant her

Surely.

Wrapping her arms around her waist, Sabrina resumed
walking. But with every step, her anxiety grew. If only she
had brought the article with her and could read it again. He
must have written it for her. She had to believe that.

Nonetheless, once the doubt had invaded her thoughts, it
would not be banished.

She could have been wrong, the voice of misgivings
taunted. Perhaps Richard referred to all his ladyloves as
sweet water nymphs. Perhaps it was a favorite phrase of
his.

Sabrina shivered and glanced to the sky, raindrops splashing onto her cheeks and nose. Above her, the ominous clouds blanketed the world in a dark, gloomy gray. She had never felt more alone in her life.

She did not recognize the distant rumbling as carriage wheels until suddenly the vehicle came hurtling around the corner. She scurried to step back, but her skirts were wet and clingy and she could not move fast enough. The carriage flew by, right through the largest puddle, and sprayed Sabrina from head to toe with dirty, wet muck.

It was the last straw. The final ignominy.

Sabrina looked down at herself and took a deep breath. The breath caught on a sob. Before she knew it, she was standing in the rain on a London street corner, crying as if she'd never stop.

She cried for her brothers. She cried for Nell. She cried for Richard and for herself.

She was sobbing so hard that when a pair of warm arms embraced her, it took Sabrina a full second to understand what was happening. She stiffened and instinctively shoved her hands against the chest in front of her. A broad chest . . . a familiar one.

She jerked her chin up. Black eyes met hers.

"Richard."

"Sabrina."

Chapter
Twenty-Four

"Sabrina."

Her name was like a prayer. One he'd repeated over and over these endless weeks of waiting and searching. How could it be, he asked himself. How could it be that after so long, she was here, in his arms?

His gaze possessively roamed every inch of her face, noting the new freckles dotting her nose, the sharper edge to her cheekbones. Swollen and pink-rimmed, her turquoise eyes stared up at him, lashes spiky with tears and rain. Mud splotched one side of her jaw. Richard had never thought her more beautiful.

He opened his mouth to speak, but found himself at a loss, not knowing where to begin. For what seemed like an eternity, his single goal had been locating her. Now that he had, he could not think how to start.

"I'm sorry."

Dear God, how meaningless, how inadequate those words.

"Sabrina, I am so . . . sorry." His voice cracked, breaking beneath its emotional burden. "I will never forgive myself. Never. What I did, what I said—"

She raised her hand, ice-cold, and laid it against his cheek. Dumbfounded by the gesture, he silenced. The rain had eased to a swirling mist.

"Richard, I know," she said softly. "I saw the article."

Hope fluttered in his chest. Dare he believe she forgave him? Even more important, dare he hope that she cared for him? Loved him?

"You didn't marry Charlotte?" she asked in the brandy-husky voice that had haunted his nights.

"No, Sabrina. No."

Her brows inched together, sober and thoughtful. "And that was because . . . ?"

"Because I couldn't." His arms tightened around her. "Because I love you, Sabrina. I love *you*. Didn't you say you read the article?"

Her lips curved faintly, almost mischievously. "I did read it, but I wanted to hear you say the words."

Relief drove the air from his lungs. "And you came back to London," he said, his hand covering hers on his cheek. "And that was because . . . ?"

"Because I love you, too, Richard Kerry. With all my heart."

Richard lowered his forehead to hers and released a shaky sigh. "I don't deserve you, Sabrina." His voice still sounded raw and uneven. "I don't deserve this happiness after all the pain I have caused."

Her eyes softened, shimmering like the silvery puddles pooling around them.

"Yes, Richard, you do. Everyone deserves happiness, my love." Leaning forward, she brushed her mouth against his in a whisper of a kiss.

Her lips, so cold, still managed to elevate Richard's temperature a few degrees.

He nodded in the direction of the town house. "Let's go inside and get you warmed up."

Draped in Richard's satin night robe, Sabrina sat tucked in the corner of the sofa, sipping at a hot cup of tea. Her toes peeked out from under the hem of the robe, wriggling in the most inviting way. Her hair, burnished gold by the glow of the fire, had been left loose to dry, waving about her slim shoulders. She looked warm and content and desirable. Utterly desirable.

Richard stretched out his legs in a vain effort to ease the discomfort in his trousers. He'd had a hell of a time not stealing into the bedroom while Sabrina bathed. After a few minutes of fighting his conscience, he had ultimately decided to wait for her in the drawing room.

Now he found it near impossible to take his eyes from her. After so many days of fruitless searching, he could not believe that he'd finally found her. God, it had been close. If he'd been but a few minutes later, he might have missed her, driven right past her as she walked down the street.

So desperately did he yearn to take her in his arms, to make love to her until she wept with the pleasure of it. Once and for all, he wanted to make Sabrina his and his alone. But after everything that had gone before, the heartache and the doubt, Richard was determined to do nothing that might scare her away.

"Comfortable?" he asked from a safe distance, the chair opposite the sofa.

"Very." Her beguiling smile made his stomach clench.

"Though I'm still not sure I've forgiven you for the dousing you gave me."

"I do feel badly about that," he confessed through a lop-sided grin. "But I had given the coachman instructions to return to London with all possible speed. He took me quite literally."

"He did at that. I'm sure my cloak is hopelessly ruined." Her blissful expression said she cared not one whit about the inconsequential garment.

"I'll buy you another one," Richard offered. "One in every color of the rainbow."

Sabrina's eyes suddenly clouded, drawing the sunshine from the room.

"Oh, Richard, I don't know if I am supposed to be privy to this, but I know all about you losing your inheritance. How could you? How could you give it up?"

"No choice, my love. I'd driven off the only woman I wanted to marry, so until I found her—" He blithely shrugged.

"I still wish you hadn't been forced to give up the fortune for me."

"For the love of God, Sabrina, don't you yet realize that I would gladly give away every penny I owned if it meant making you my wife?"

"Then the offer stands?"

"If you'll have me."

Sabrina lowered her gaze, staring intently into her teacup. "I merely hope that the day does not arrive when you come to regret your decision, Richard dear. Poverty might not suit you as well as it does me," she added, making a weak stab at humor.

Richard chuckled. Though brilliant and well read, Sabrina was, in many ways, yet refreshingly naive.

"Look around you, Sabrina." He waved his hand over the

lavish gilt-and-ivory room. "I assure you we are in no way bound for the almshouse. Granted, we won't be the wealthiest lord and lady in town, but I promise you we will want for nothing. The sale of Leyton Hall alone will keep food on the table for the rest of our days."

"What? You sold your uncle's house?"

"I never truly cared for it, to tell you the truth."

"But Richard. The inheritance, Leyton Hall—"

"None of it means anything, Sabrina. All that matters is that I have found you."

Her answering smile gradually faded into a thoughtful frown. "Why *did* you decide to come back to London? I thought you had said you were on your way to Chippenham."

Richard's gaze flickered, and he shifted in his chair. Sabrina would probably think him the worst kind of fool. . . .

"I had a dream."

"A dream?" she echoed.

"Yes, well . . . I know it's going to sound as if I'm demented, but as we were racing to Chippenham, I must have dozed off— or at least, I think I dozed off." Truthfully, Richard wasn't at all convinced he'd been asleep at the time, but how else to explain it?

"At any rate, I dreamed of . . . my mother."

Sabrina sat up straighter. "Do you often?"

"No," he answered starkly, looking toward the fire. "That's the damnedest part of it. I haven't dreamed of her even once these past seventeen years."

"What . . . what was the dream?"

Richard hesitated, uncertain. "She told me to turn around and return home. She said I would find you here." A short, embarrassed laugh escaped him, and he hurried to add, "I know it's ludicrous, but somehow it seemed exceptionally real. The entire trip back to London, I was thinking I must be deranged to come back when I knew that you were supposed to be in Chippenham."

"But she was right," Sabrina answered quietly. "I was here."

He nodded, still vaguely unsettled by the experience. He would like to have believed it had been intuition, manifesting itself as a dream. That explanation struck him as much easier to accept than any other.

"Did your mother say anything else?"

He shook his head. No, she hadn't said anything more, but Richard had been left with the impression that she had. During the dream, though his mother's vision had not spoken of the accident, after awaking, Richard had felt a strange sense of resolution. As if after all the long years, the hurt and resentment had, at last, been put to rest. At last, Richard forgave his mother. And forgave himself.

"Was there anything else remarkable about your dream? Did you . . . see anyone else?"

"No. Although—" He paused, remembering. "Although I would have sworn I detected some sort of fragrance when I awoke. I cannot say what it was—"

"Frangipani?"

Richard cocked his head. "Why, yes. I think it might have been frangipani."

Sabrina's hand rose to her lips and it looked to Richard as if she were hiding her laughter.

"You must think me hopefully addled," he commented ruefully. "Are you still willing to marry me even if I am subject to mad delusions?"

In answer, Sabrina patted the sofa next to her. Richard did not hesitate in accepting, for he'd been waiting for such an invitation half the night it seemed.

As soon as he sat down, Sabrina scooted close and looped her arms around his neck. "Richard, I do not think you're the slightest bit mad, and I want to be your wife more surely than I have ever wanted anything."

"Are you certain? You know I'm not going to be welcome around Town for a while."

"That suits me just fine, Lord Colbridge, since I'll be much happier at home at Simmons House."

"And what of the boys?"

Sabrina pulled back slightly. "What of them? I don't think you need worry about Teddy murdering you any longer. Not since you saved his life."

"Hmm, that's all to the good I suppose, but I'd also like to believe they'll accept me as family—along with abandoning plans to shorten my life. You don't worry that they'll object to their sister marrying a social exile?"

Sabrina laughed, the sultry, rich sound sizzling along his nerve endings. "Oh, Richard, darling, I've been a social exile my entire life. I don't think the boys will notice one more in the house."

A pang of guilt tweaked Richard's conscience. "And you won't be ashamed? Ashamed to be seen with me after all this Ennui business?"

Sabrina placed her finger against his lips.

"I could never be ashamed of you, Richard. Never. Besides, you can still remedy your mistakes, you know. You can make amends with those people you've hurt. Frankly, I think issuing the confession was uncommonly brave of you. You did not have to do it. No one would probably ever have known that you were Ennui."

"I would have known," he whispered against her finger. "And so would you."

Her gaze fixed to his mouth, her expression suddenly very sober. "I am sorry, Richard, but I have just realized that I have lied to you. I was not speaking truthfully when I said I wanted to marry you more than anything else in this world."

Instantly, Richard's neck muscles went taut, his pulse accelerating. Sabrina had changed her mind, she had not forgiven him after all, never would she be able to—

"What I should have said was that more than anything"—her finger lightly massaged his lower lip. "More than anything I want to finish what I began."

She looked up into his eyes and smiled a shy siren's smile that allayed his fears somewhat, but did little to slow his racing heart.

"I do believe, Richard Kerry, that I still have a seduction to finish."

Then, threading her hand through his shoulder-length hair, Sabrina tenderly, invitingly, scraped her nails across the highly sensitive flesh at Richard's nape. He closed his eyes on a relieved sigh, feeling Sabrina's finger quivering against his lips.

Unable to resist the lure of its softness, Richard sucked her finger into his mouth, swirling his tongue around the delicate tip.

"Oh," Sabrina gasped.

With a wicked grin, Richard gently bit down, holding her prisoner.

The maidenly flush upon Sabrina's cheeks, paired with her passion-dilated pupils, enticed him as nothing else had ever done. She was everything that a woman should be, his Sabrina. She was witty, intelligent, generous. Impossibly seductive. And most importantly, his.

Her hand had stilled in his hair, her eyes wide with wonder as he slowly began to make love to the tip of her finger. He nibbled and licked at leisure, flicking his tongue into the sensitive area beneath her nail, before drawing the length of her finger fully into his mouth.

He watched her watch him, her lips slightly apart, her breath rapid and shallow. His night robe, many sizes too large for her, had fallen open to reveal the shadowed cleft between her breasts.

Richard pictured his tongue traveling to the silken expanse of Sabrina's neck, the pink lushness of her nipple, the perfumed secrets of her womanhood. His shaft set to throbbing with a needful ache. No longer could he hold his fantasies at bay. He needed to touch. To taste. With one hand, he spread open the gaping night robe to reveal the soft milky riches of Sabrina's curves. His breath caught. She was ever so much lovelier than even he'd remembered. With his other hand, he cupped Sabrina's cheek, drawing her close, her face a study of awakening desire.

Richard barely covered her lips with his own, trying to proceed cautiously as he thought a considerate lover should. But Sabrina, it seemed, wanted naught to do with consideration. Her tongue met his with surprising eagerness, and an explosion of need suddenly rocked him, shooting through his stomach and into his groin.

"Sabrina," he groaned into her mouth, urging her to slow down.

But Sabrina could not understand Richard's unvoiced plea, hearing only her name whispered hoarsely—hungrily—by the man she loved. She heard only his desire for her, his need. And she reveled in it, unwittingly rousing him further with her impatient caresses and restless movements.

Richard's kisses found the arch of her brow, the hollow of her throat, the slope of her shoulder. When his lips finally fastened upon her turgid nipple, Sabrina felt as if she were being filled from head to toe with a tingly, hot liquid that was melting her insides. The sensation was unbearable, its promise so sweet.

"Sabrina," Richard rasped again, and she looked down to see that the night robe had fallen fully open. Richard had taken notice, as well, for his smoldering gaze was devouring her nakedness.

"Perhaps, we should go—"

"No," she answered breathlessly, clutching at him as he tried to pull away. "This is perfect, Richard. It's perfect. Right here." And to prove her point, Sabrina slid the sole of her foot along the back of his calf in a provocative caress that nearly unmanned him.

A groan rumbled deep in his chest, and he struggled for control of his fevered body. His conscience told him that it was not right to take her for the first time like this; not, for God's sake, in a hasty heated tumble on his drawing room sofa. But somehow Richard intuitively sensed that this was precisely what they both needed and wanted. In the wake of the suffering and anguish they'd endured these past weeks, they needed this. A closure, a completion. A healing.

He saw the truth of it in Sabrina's eyes. The need was now.

Richard eased away to slip out of his trousers and as soon as he'd done so, Sabrina drew him back to her. Though ready to burst, the need to plunge inside her overwhelming, Richard held back, fanning his fingers through the curls at Sabrina's thighs. Back and forth. Back and forth over her dewy flesh. He grazed the bud of her and she jerked against his hand with a ragged, high-pitched cry.

The need was *now*.

Whispering words of love and other soothing sounds, Richard entered her. It was as if they were coming together not for the first time, but for the thousandth, with an intimacy and a knowledge that could only have come from true love shared. Together they moved as if they'd known each other's rhythms forever, touched and stroked with the expertise of lifetime lovers.

The promise was there in the soft cries and whimpers, in

the powerful thrusts and possessive caresses. The tension built, the rhythm grew more frenzied. Sabrina's head thrashed from left to right, her hair like silken strands whipping across Richard's chest.

In the moment when he could not bear it any longer, when love threatened to spill from him in a fiery spurt, Sabrina cried out, arching her back and shuddering wildly. Tears trickled onto her cheeks and her body clenched around him in racking spasms. Richard filled her.

The promise was kept.

Epilogue

Two weeks later, Leychurch's orphaned bluestocking wed the infamous Viscount Colbridge in St. Michael's Chapel in Bath.

Only a handful of guests witnessed the ceremony though they made for an eclectic group: Charlotte Wetherby and Paula Bright, Francis Merrick and the widow Canham, Andrew and Teddy and Teddy's new kitten.

As Richard slid the simple gold band on to Sabrina's finger, promising to love and cherish her forever, Sabrina knew that only one thing could make her happiness more complete. Nell.

If only my madam ghost could have been here to see this.

The uncertainty of Nell's fate still plagued Sabrina, especially now that her life had taken its fairy-tale turn. Countless times over the last weeks, Sabrina had wished for just one last chance to talk with Nell. To confess that they'd both been wrong about love—that it really did exist and it was even more wonderful and beautiful than all history's poets had described.

Yet despite the unaccountable glowing woman and the mysterious frangipani scenting the air, Nell had not appeared. And so one small part of Sabrina's heart lay heavy, even on this day, the happiest of her life.

The vicar issued the final prayer, Teddy, let out a celebratory *whoop,* and then it was time to return to Mrs. Canham's for the wedding breakfast. With her hand in Richard's, Sabrina walked back down the aisle, sending a silent prayer of thanks skyward. Even if the ghost could not be here, maybe the powers-that-be would see to it that Nell received the message.

Filing past the guests in the pews, Sabrina and Richard had almost reached the church doors when Sabrina abruptly pulled up short.

"What is it, love?" Richard asked.

Sabrina inhaled a deep, deep breath.

Nell!

Frantically, she glanced about, her gaze falling on a figurine of an angel standing atop a marble column. Something about the way the statue caught the light—

Suddenly the angel's stone face appeared to come alive. A beauty mark, a gap-toothed smile . . . Nell's bright eyes flashed saucily, then she gave Sabrina a broad wink, pointing to the halo above her head.

Sabrina's eyes shone.

"Congratulations," she whispered.

"What is it?" Richard asked again, this time with concern.

Instantly, Nell vanished and the angel was nothing more than stone.

Sabrina turned to her husband and smiled up into his eyes, her heart singing with joy.

"Nothing, darling. Nothing. I was just giving my regards to an old friend."

And now for a preview of the next
Haunting Hearts romance

Heavenly Bliss

Coming in July 1997 from Jove Books

"Stop!"

Jill Carey knew the moment she saw the derelict of an ancient house, perched on a gentle rise above the road, that this was it, the refuge she had seen in her dreams, the home that had called out to her! She pictured fragrant jasmines climbing the stout, square columns that marched across the front, clumps of mountain laurel brightening the sloping yard that was now a maze of unkempt brambles.

"You don't want Bliss House." As he pulled his car into the overgrown driveway, Jill sensed terror in the portly realtor's rumbling voice.

"Yes, I do. This is just what I've been looking for. It will be perfect after I renovate it. Is this place in the historical registry? How old is it?" Jill could hardly contain her excitement about the old house, outside the little town of

Gray Hollow high in the Smokies, yet not too far from either Greensboro or Charlotte. Wanting to see more, she opened the door and started to get out.

None too gently George Wilson, the realtor, grabbed her arm. "You don't want this place," he repeated, his voice shaky. "It's been haunted for nigh onto a hundred years. Been on the market, off and on, since long before I started selling real estate around here."

Jill laughed. She had always heard mountain folk were superstitious. And now she was seeing it firsthand. Haunted houses and ghosts. What a joke! If she could live with the mess she had made of her own life, she could certainly make room for these figments of George Wilson's active imagination!

"I'm not afraid of a few spirits, George. Come on, I want to see the inside." She extricated her arm from the realtor's grasp, slid out of the car, and headed briskly up a weed-filled path to the porch.

When George caught up with her, he was huffing and red-faced. "I can't let you go in there by yourself," he grumbled, catching Jill's arm and placing himself in front of her. "Watch out for those rotten porch boards." He reminded her of a very reluctant knight of old she had once seen in a movie, the way he stood there, as if scared to death but determined to shield her from her own perilous folly.

They made their way across the sagging porch, and George fit an ancient, rusty key into the lock of the front door. When he opened it, the creak of long-immobile hinges made Jill jump. Still, the house called out to her, like a living thing too long deprived of the warmth of human care.

"Might be able to salvage some old heart pine," George muttered as he made his way across wide board planks that hadn't seen a broom, much less wax and nourishing oils, for years. "Guess you could build a mighty nice place here after you tear this one down."

Jill could practically feel the old house shudder. "Tear it down? That would be a crime! I'll have it restored! See this detail? It looks as if it was all carved by hand." She knelt and traced a dust-filled crevice in a baseboard, revealing a design of delicate, interwoven leaves and vines. When George made his way down a wide, empty hallway, she stood and followed, taking in the charming ambience the deserted rooms still exuded as the realtor opened doors and stood back for her to look.

"Miss Jill, you don't want to live here," he said again, opening another creaking door and practically leaping back, as if he thought he was in mortal danger. "Here's the very room where they got what was comin' to them. Nobody ever fixed it, just boarded it up and left it to the ghosts." In a shaky voice, hands trembling, George related the tale of ill-fated lovers who had died in the still-charred ruins of what must have once been a cozy bedroom. "You know, they say th' bed burned first," he concluded, closing off the room with a trembling hand and making his way as fast as he could to the gaping front door.

The story—and the sight of the gutted room, where repairs had been limited to the outer walls—shook Jill for a minute. But she had made up her mind. This was where she would mend her life and her battered heart. She wasn't going to rest until Bliss House belonged to her.

The Ghosts

Later, after the sun faded behind a mountaintop west of Bliss House, its ghostly occupants settled in the ruined parlor—as was their habit of a late-summer evening.

"Dry your tears, my dear," said the ghost of Cyrus Bliss. He wished he could do more than whisper in the wind to the spirit of Laura Randall, his love in life and now his companion in death. Silently he cursed that harebrained excuse for a snake-oil peddler who had been halfheartedly trying to sell this place for close to thirty years—and the others who had preceded him, trying with little enthusiasm to unload the place he guessed must have become an albatross around the necks of his heirs.

He had felt Laura's spirit grow sad every time the realtors brought some prospective buyer to the decaying pile of wood and mortar that had been her pride and joy in life. And they all did a damn fine job of scaring anybody away who might have bought Bliss House, what with their tales of bad luck and ghosts.

Cyrus reached out, as if he could comfort Laura with a touch, and he felt her spirit settle beside him in the dark of the moonless night. *"Will she buy it?"* Laura asked, her voice high and reedy, like the sound of tinkling bells.

Cyrus felt her fear. They had been given one hundred years. Nearly a century had passed. Still, his and Laura's scandal lived, fueled by the legends of the hill people and fired by hatred and shame passed down through generations of Blisses and Randalls.

He would have thought, after his family had moved away from Gray Hollow, that the talk would die down. But it never had. And now he and Laura had just three months left to right mistakes that had brought them to this, a limbo where they floated, not living yet not dead. To end the curse on Bliss House or meet the fiery pits of hell.

"Cyrus?"

"Yes, my dear?"

"She reminded me of your Prudence."

Cyrus shrugged his ghostly shoulders. Years had

dimmed his memories, he supposed, for he had seen little in the woman that he could compare with his daughter, the only one of his or Laura's children who had stood by them when they had defied convention and flaunted their ill-fated love for all to see. *"Really?"* he asked as he tried to picture Prudence in his mind.

"Imagine the lady with lighter hair, long like Prudence's instead of cut so short, my love. And with skin untouched by the sun. Heaven knows what the world outside has come to, when ladies ruin their soft white skin by baking in the sun like darkies—and try to look like men with their pants and cropped off hair."

"Hmmm." Actually Cyrus liked the way the woman's scandalous denim pants hugged her trim, taut thighs and buttocks. Her hair wasn't bad, either, with wispy curls that drew his attention to high cheekbones and big, dark eyes that reflected none of the modesty required of young unmarried women in his day. Still, he couldn't imagine running his fingers through a tousled mop of curls no longer than his own.

"Didn't you see the resemblance?" Laura asked, her tone anxious now.

"Perhaps."

"She looked wanton, though. Prudence was always the perfect lady." Laura drifted over to the weathered mantel where a faded daguerreotype still rested in its tarnished silver frame. *"But there was something about her . . ."*

"The woman is not of my family. Remember the legend, Laura. We will know when a Bliss or a Randall returns to Bliss House."

"Always the legend," Laura murmured, her tone conveying a bitterness rare in the woman who had risked everything to share his love, and who had died for it, only to remain trapped here with him for a hundred years. *"She has*

known love and pain, Cyrus. I believe she is the one we have waited for. Do you think she will buy the house?"

"Time will tell." Cyrus would not raise Laura's hopes too high, but he could not bring himself to dash them by mentioning what he knew Laura had already seen. The woman who came today had been alone—and she was neither a Randall nor a Bliss. But he had seen one encouraging sign—the woman's finger, where he might have seen a wedding band, was bare.

To break the spell that bound them to Bliss House, he and Laura must entice another pair of lovers, one of whom had to have descended from either Laura or himself, to settle here in Bliss House. And these lovers had to be free to say the vows fate had denied Cyrus and Laura so many years ago.

But Cyrus had felt the young woman's excitement as she knelt and raved over hand-carved baseboards long obscured by dust and grime, and when she followed the reluctant realtor through dingy rooms that made his Laura fret and cry for the way they used to be. He had a hunch this woman would be the one to buy Bliss House. Perhaps fate would bring a modern-day Bliss or Randall here as well. If it did, he and Laura would do their best to see that romance bloomed between that as-yet-unknown man and the new owner of his ill-fated home.

Gathering Laura's fragile spirit gently to himself, Cyrus allowed them a bit of hope.